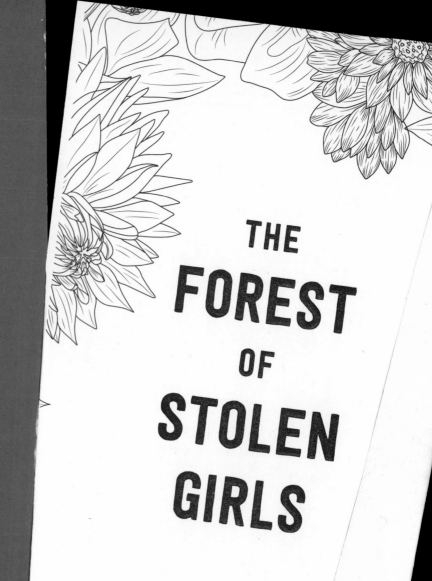

THE
FOREST
OF
STOLEN
GIRLS

THE
FOREST
OF
STOLEN
GIRLS

JUNE HUR

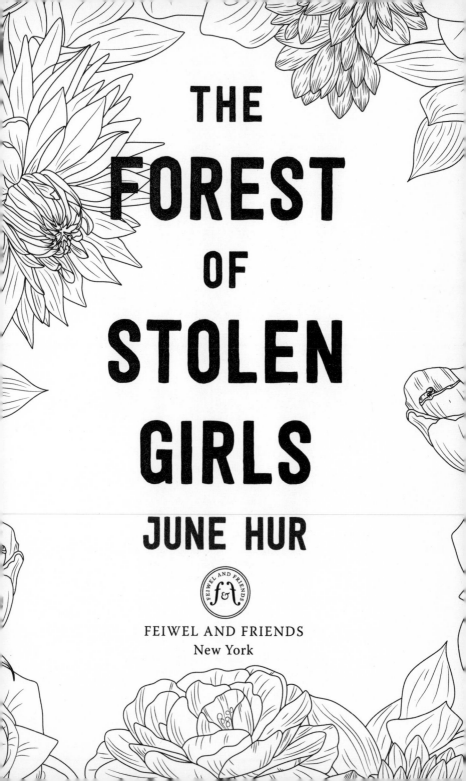

FEIWEL AND FRIENDS
New York

A Feiwel and Friends Book
An imprint of Macmillan Publishing Group, LLC
120 Broadway, New York, NY 10271

fiercereads.com
Copyright © 2021 by June Hur. All rights reserved.

Our books may be purchased in bulk for promotional, educational, or business use.
Please contact your local bookseller or the Macmillan Corporate and Premium
Sales Department at (800) 221-7945 ext. 5442 or by email at
MacmillanSpecialMarkets@macmillan.com.

Library of Congress Cataloging-in-Publication Data is available.
First edition, 2021
Book design by Michelle Gengaro-Kokmen
Printed in the United States of America by LSC Communications, Harrisonburg, Virginia

Feiwel and Friends logo designed by Filomena Tuosto
ISBN 978-1-250-22958-8 (hardcover)
1   3   5   7   9   10   8   6   4   2

To my siblings:

Sharon, *you* are my supersis.

Charles, thank you for being you.

Throughout my twenty years of detective work, I have never failed to solve a case.

Except for one: the Forest Incident.

In general, the most difficult thing to comprehend under heaven is a man's mind, and the most difficult task is to uncover hidden truths. As this incident occurred so many years ago, the case is therefore difficult to grasp and nearly impossible to trace.

What I have gathered so far is this: Victim Seohyun was found at the bottom of a cliff and was said to have died by suicide. But before an inquest could be conducted, the body was buried by orders of the county magistrate. With no way to conduct an examination of the corpse, it was difficult to ascertain the facts behind the incident. Testimonies are the only materials to resort to, yet testimonies have greatly altered over the years, and so lies could easily become the truth.

There were two possible eyewitnesses: the siblings Min Hwani and Min Maewol. My daughters.

They both were found almost frozen to death near the scene of the crime. Hwani unfortunately woke up with no recollection of the incident. Maewol claims that before she lost consciousness, she saw a man stalking through the forest.

A man in a white mask.

—From the journal of Detective Min Jewoo

THE
FOREST
OF
STOLEN
GIRLS

one

THE SCREEN OF MIST WAS thick around the red pine-wood vessel, as though secrets hid beyond of a land I was not permitted to see. But I knew by memory the windy place a thousand li south of the port. A place with jagged coasts and grassland dotted with black lava rock huts, and with mountains layered upon misty layers. Somewhere on Jeju, this island of wind and stone, between the ancient Gotjawal forest and the cloud-topped peaks of Mount Halla, my father had disappeared.

My eyelids itched with exhaustion as I leaned against the edge of the boat. Mokpo port grew smaller in the distance. The bamboo sails high above billowed in the wind, laced with sea spray, which left everything damp—my robe, the deck, the posts, the shivering passengers huddled around a game, a square board with roughly cut wooden pieces.

These passengers were likely returning home to Jeju, not heading there to look for the missing, as I was.

I glanced over my shoulder and looked past the strands of my dancing hair, caught in a blast of wind, and searched for Mokpo port again. This time I couldn't see anything other than the mist and the swelling black waters. Gripping the vessel's edge, I took in a deep breath, trying to ease the panic fluttering in my chest. It was 1426, the year of the crown princess selection—the period when young ladies like myself would be dreaming of entering the palace. Yet here I was, cast away at sea, headed toward a penal island of political convicts.

Forget about the investigation, fear whispered in my mind. *Whatever is on that island, it might kill you.*

I shook my head and reached into the cotton sack filled with everything I'd brought with me. My hand moved past the wrapped-up dried persimmons, past the necklace with a wooden whistle, to Father's five-stitched black notebook, which I withdrew. The cover flew open in the wind and pages fluttered, burnt and curled by fire. The last half of the notebook was so badly incinerated that only stubs of black edges remained. A stranger by the female name of Boksun had sent this to me, and I had so many questions about her: Who was she? Why had she sent the journal? How did she know my father?

The deck creaked. I cast a sidelong glance to my right and noticed a gentleman pausing in his steps to gaze out at the sea. One of his hands was braced on the edge of the ship, while the other rested on the hilt of the sword tied to his sash belt. It was as though he were on the lookout for Wokou pirates from the East. By his long, sleeveless overcoat made of stormy purple silk, worn over a long-sleeved lavender robe, I could tell that he was a nobleman.

"Good morning, sir," I said, my voice quiet. It failed to reach him over the crashing waves.

I dug my nails into my palm. I was not Min Hwani today. I was not a young lady with her hair plaited down her back and tied with a red daenggi ribbon, marking me as a vulnerable and unmarried woman.

"Good morning, sir," I called out to him, my voice louder and lower than usual.

He turned his head at last, and beneath the shadow cast by the brim of his tall black hat was the face of a middle-aged man with a square jaw framed by a wispy beard. His hooded eyelids weighed over his solemn gaze and whispered of hidden secrets.

"Yes?" The question rolled out from deep within his chest.

"Do you know how long it will take to reach Jeju?"

"No longer than half a day, unless the weather grows worse." He stared a moment at me, then returned to gazing ahead.

"And how far would the travel be from the port to Nowon Village?" I asked.

A single brow arched. "Nowon?"

"Yeh."

"Perhaps a three hours' walk," he replied. "I would not know, as I have never traveled by foot. But why are you going there?"

"I'm looking for someone."

He shifted on his feet to fully face me, his hand still resting on the edge of the boat. "Who are you?" he asked, his question poised as an order.

My muscles tightened. I was the child of Detective Min, but I could not tell him that, for he might have already heard of my father—if not from his famous police work, then for his inexplicable disappearance. And everyone who'd heard of him would have also heard that Detective Min had only a daughter (he did, in fact, have two daughters, but not many knew of my estranged sister). And young ladies like myself did not belong so far from home.

I ran a hand over my disguise—a man's robe of sapphire silk, long enough to hide my figure and secured by a sash belt. I'd thought I would have more time to spin myself an elaborate cover story to explain my disguise, so I had nothing but a blank page.

Clearing my throat, I said slowly, to buy myself some time, "Do you wish to know who I am, or are you asking for my name?"

"Both."

"My name is . . . Gyu." I took the name from the most recent book I had been reading. "And I . . . I am a nobody."

He continued to stare at me, a stare that was flat and unamused. "Those that call themselves a 'nobody' are always people of significance. Or a person hiding a secret."

"Truly, I am no one of much significance," I said evenly. "I'm a student who recently failed the civil service exam."

The words flowed out even before crossing my mind. I was a skilled liar, like my mother. Her blood coursed through me, even though I hardly remembered her, as she had passed away too soon. "I have nothing but time, sir, and so I decided to visit Jeju."

"Is that all you are here for?" His hooded gaze surveyed me, looking unconvinced. Why did he care so much? "You said you were looking for someone."

I leaned on the edge of the ship and gazed out, trying to appear calm and confident. But I could already feel cold beads of sweat on my brow, drenching me further under the pressure of this stranger's gaze. Prickly whispers intruded my mind—*he is laughing at your disguise; he sees that you are a girl, a helpless, foolish girl*—

Using my sleeve, I wiped my forehead. "M-m—" My voice was tightening; I cleared my throat. "My uncle, who is originally from Jeju, went missing."

The deep pouches beneath his eyes twitched. "A boy who looks barely seventeen should be studying, not solving another man's disappearance."

Actually, I was eighteen—almost nineteen. "Since I was young, my relatives knew me for my ability to solve petty crimes, and even once a murder." This was technically true; I had solved the murder of my friend's pet hawk. "The family was desperate for more information, more than a mere two lines of explanation from the police. They asked me to learn more about Detective Min."

"Detective Min . . . Detective Min . . . Where have I heard of this name . . . ?" He tilted his gaze to the sky, and for a long moment, both of us remained silent. Then he let out a knowing *ah*, a word of recognition that stiffened my spine. "The case from a year or two ago. The police have done their work and have found nothing."

"The police had to worry about the turmoil occurring on the mainland; they had no time to really search Jeju," I explained. "Whereas I . . . I have nothing but time and the promise of a reward should I find something. Anything."

"It was too long ago for any evidence to remain. Memories fade, become faulty. Physical evidence washes away in the rain and mud. You won't find anything."

"Detectives do not simply disappear, sir."

"But a detective who relies on a walking stick?" He offered me a smooth, polite smile. "I am told he is—*was*—unable to walk far without it."

I returned his smile, my lips straining across my teeth. "Indeed, he did have trouble walking, but, mind you, sir, it was no ordinary cane. It was a jukjangdo, a cane that sheathes a sword—quite deadly when wielded by Detective Min. Or so

I am told. He is also considered to be the greatest detective in all of Joseon."

A breath escaped the man, sounding almost like a laugh. "The greatest?"

"In all his twenty years of detective work, he has solved more than two hundred crimes and has never failed to solve a case."

I waited for his response, but all I heard were the hollow waves crashing against the hull.

"So you are going to Nowon Village. I will do you a favor and warn you: When you arrive there, do not heed those rumors spread by peasants," he said. "The moment you go around asking about this missing detective, the people of Nowon will tell you about their missing daughters instead. But trust me, young man, Nowon is the safest village in Jeju."

For a moment I forgot my immediate dislike of him. "Missing girls?"

I remembered Commander Ki's words, that Father had gone to Jeju to investigate the disappearance of several girls. Perhaps they were the same ones this gentleman was referring to. I lowered my gaze, trying to regain my composure; I watched a cloud of stringy jellyfish swim just beneath the water's surface.

"I can tell you one thing in common about those missing girls." The gentleman smoothed his thumb over the engraved design at the hilt of his sword. "They were pretty."

"What do you mean—"

"Magistrate Hong!"

I looked across the vessel to see a servant—he looked like one, in his plain white jeogori coat and knee-high trousers—making his way toward us. "Did you summon me, Magistrate?" he asked.

I tried not to gape at the gentleman before me. He was a *magistrate.* I watched as he slipped out a scroll from his robe and placed it into the servant's hand. "Find the fastest courier the moment the ship docks."

"Yeh." The servant bowed and withdrew.

The magistrate slid his attention back to me, and he must have noticed my wide-eyed look but chose not to acknowledge it. "I won't stop you from searching for Detective Min, and I won't make your job harder," he said. "But I must do mine. And right now, I am tired of all the speculation ruining the reputation of my district."

It took me a few moments for his words to register.

"Detective Min investigated into the missing thirteen girls," he continued. "And do you know what I told him? The same as I've told you: The missing girls were pretty. Perhaps they were tired of their poverty, tired of their life in a small village, so they ran away. I do not think any of them were or are in trouble." He shook his head. "I've heard of Detective Min's renowned sleuthing reputation, and so I was quite stunned that he seemed ignorant of such a common fact: Girls disappear every day. Jeju women, especially, disappear all the time once they are older. They think they are free to act without restrictions and so venture out into the world. They disappear to live with their sweethearts, to hide their pregnancies, to sell themselves, to become gisaengs. The reasons are endless."

I swallowed hard and pulled my robe closer around me as I watched Magistrate Hong stride away with long, measured steps. The decision I'd made—a lone girl leaving home and traveling to a village where girls were going missing—suddenly seemed quite foolish. No, more than foolish. *Dangerous.*

Now I understood why Father had made me dress like a boy whenever we traveled. Once, while riding through the forest, I had asked Father why I was in a boy's clothing. He had silently pointed to a moth camouflaged against the tree bark.

"A moth pretends to be what it is not," he'd whispered to me, then only a child of seven winters, "to escape from things that would hurt them."

Perhaps Commander Ki had been right when he'd told me not to go looking for Father. "A young lady like you belongs safe at home," he'd said. "Leave the work to us and *trust me.* We will find him."

I had trusted him. I had believed him. I had waited twelve full moons for answers and would have waited another year had he not closed the case, declaring Father dead.

"We found the left sleeve of your father's outer robe in Gotjawal forest," Commander Ki had said, his gaze lowered, too ashamed to meet my resentment-filled eyes. "It was a bear attack, a brutal one. We searched everywhere for his body, or any sign of him. But—" He'd shaken his head. "It's been an entire year, Hwani-yah. He is gone."

What had Commander Ki expected of me when he'd told me this? Had he thought I'd fold my hands neatly together and accept Father's death, when no one had answered a single question of mine?

How does the greatest detective in Joseon go missing? Where is the body? How can he be dead when there is no grave to visit?

Young ladies were not supposed to leave home to investigate the missing or dead. But no one needed to know who I was.

I'd be a young scholar while traveling overseas, but later in the day? I could be anyone I wanted, anyone who would make it easier to find Father.

I stretched out my hands before me. My hands were pasty—my skin had forgotten the warmth of sunlight since I'd turned seven, the age when women were physically separated from men and the rest of the world. But my mind had always lived beyond the walls, taken there through the five-stitched books in Father's study. I knew I'd be able to hold a conversation with any man about Confucian classics and history.

My father is a scholar who dwells in Mokpo, I recited to myself, weaving a tale with the threads taken from the books

I'd read, *an impoverished gentleman who makes a living by tutoring aristocrats in the province. As I am his youngest son, he does not expect much from me, but my hope is to write an essay that will astonish him and his high-standing acquaintances . . .*

The passengers on the vessel likely thought I'd lost my mind, for I continued to pace the deck for the remainder of the trip, reciting over and over in my head the new history I'd written for myself. A history in which I didn't have to wait on others to find the truth for me.

Past the vast stretch of water, through the string of fog weaving the sky, I saw the sharp cliffs and the shadow of Mount Halla. The ancient mountain that had witnessed history clash and shift before its watchful gaze.

In the olden times, Jeju had fallen under Mongol rule, along with our entire kingdom. Mongol darughachi were governors, and part of the island was used as grazing area for the cavalry stationed there. Then more than a hundred years later, our kingdom had fallen under the power of Ming China, forced to bow before their throne as a vassal state. But the inhabitants of Jeju had bowed lowest, plundered of all their goods. Their horses taken by Ming emperors and their abalone, mandarin oranges, and medical herbs taken by our king.

I knew the bleak history of Jeju as well as I did the blood pulsing through me, for this island was home, the place of my birth. I'd never thought of returning, not since Father had whisked our family away—all except for one of us. My little sister, Maewol, had stayed behind, a sister I rarely corresponded with, not out of hostility but simply because we shared nothing in common. She didn't even know that I was returning. I wasn't *supposed* to return; I had promised Father I would never step foot on Jeju again. That I would never again enter the woods.

Waves crashed against the ship. The deck swayed, and I held on tight to Father's journal as I looked ahead. The fog parted, opening to the bustling port of Jeju and, beyond it, the black lava huts dotting the sweep of grassland. As I watched it all grow nearer, the immensity of my decision sank around me. I was breaking all my promises. The promise not to return to Jeju or its woodlands. The promise not to get involved in Father's case.

Taking in a few quick breaths, I tried to ease the flutter of dread. *Father is still alive*, I reminded myself. *He is alive, I know it.*

I could feel this truth bone-deep, even though Aunt Min said I was being delusional to think so, and even though Commander Ki said feelings did not always point to the truth. No one needed to believe me; I'd always done everything on my own after Mother's death. And perhaps—just perhaps—my little sister would be willing to assist me. We had been separated by five years, bound by nothing but a few threads of memories, but now we finally had something in common: My father was her father as well, and he was missing.

I lowered my gaze to the burnt journal, and the conviction solidified in my chest. Father was out there. Somewhere on the mountain, deep in the sprawling forests, or along the jagged coast—somewhere on Jeju—Father was waiting for us. My sister, I hoped, thought so as well.

two

THE ISLAND WAS SO VAST, and I felt so small as I made my way southward, away from the bustling port and deeper into the overwhelming wilderness. The same sharp pang of panic I'd felt when I had first learned of Father's disappearance again struck me in the chest. The only human being in this entire kingdom who loved me had disappeared like the morning mist.

"Where did you go, Father?" I whispered, wishing the wind could take my words to wherever he was. "And *why*? Why did you leave me?"

This question had haunted me for an entire year, ever since I'd discovered the note in Father's chamber, scrawled clearly across hanji paper:

Will I go? Must I go?
Can man undo his errors? Undo his sin?

The forest watches me,
Hostile and still, with remembering eyes.

All I knew was what Commander Ki had told me—that Father had come to Jeju to investigate the case of thirteen missing girls. But the commander's answer had only left me with more questions: Why would Father care about a case that was outside his jurisdiction? Why did he suddenly rush off without telling anyone? What did the strange, fearful words in his note mean?

Jeju was no small island, and finding answers would not be easy. But first, I had to worry about finding my way to Nowon Village. I followed a misty road filled with the salty scent of the sea, a path that wove its way through coastline villages and traced along stone-walled fields. The road continued on, stretching around oreum hills and through slippery valleys.

Now and then, I stopped to ask for directions from passing travelers, and for a long trek afterward, I didn't encounter another soul. The last traveler I'd met had told me to look out for a hill that had a stack of rocks, marks of where villagers had performed ancestral worship rituals. But even after walking until my grumbling stomach indicated that it was noon, I still couldn't find the village.

I was lost. Very lost.

You can't even find your way to your hometown, my aunt would have hissed if she could see me now. *What makes you think you can find your father?*

I stood frozen, unable to take another step. Agitation rushed through me like cold liquid, along with the numbing thought that I had made a terrible mistake, that I shouldn't have come to Jeju. I glanced around me, but I couldn't even figure out how to get back to the port. "Damnation."

Then, to the east, movement caught my eyes. A band of wild ponies with rain-soaked manes trotted over the hill, coming into view.

I blinked, suddenly remembering my sister. Even when we were young, when we ventured out, Father always told Maewol to take care of me, for while I could recite a thousand Confucian verses, I could never manage to find my way home.

But Maewol? Like the wild ponies of Jeju, the Maewol I remembered was a vicious and tough little beast who liked to kick and bite and was capable of braving the harshest conditions to find her way back home.

"Let's keep walking," I told myself. "Someone is bound to pass by."

I pushed myself onward, past the undulating hills, the ripe green zelkova and nettle trees, the low stone walls that appeared wherever I went. Walls made of large, stacked rocks with pebbles filling the cracks. And as I continued on, I kept myself distracted by wondering what I'd say to my sister when I finally met her again, what we'd talk about.

All I could imagine was silence. I had no idea what to say to Maewol, or what she'd say to me. She was, after all, more a stranger to me than family. Still, I had done my best to be her elder sister. I'd tried to write to Maewol every month, even though there was little to write about, but over time, finding a servant to travel all the way to Jeju to deliver a letter had grown strenuous. So I'd written to her whenever I could, usually once every five or six months, asking about her health and happiness. She would take so long to reply though that I'd forget what I had written about in the first place.

I paused in my journey, squinting into the distance. *Finally*. I saw an old woman sitting outside her hut, peeling garlic with her wrinkled fingers. I hurried my steps until I was near enough to call out, "Ajimang! Could you tell me if I'm going the right way?"

She narrowed her eyes at me, and the moment she opened her mouth, her thick Jeju dialect rolled out. "Eodi gamsuggwa?"

Those from the mainland always struggled to understand this dialect, but I had grown up hearing and speaking it. "I'm heading to Nowon Village. Will this path take me there?"

She clucked her tongue. "Why would you want to go there?"

"I have matters to attend to," I answered.

Phlegm rattled in her chest as she coughed into her ragged sleeve. "You've come too far," she said in her scratchy voice. "You ought to have turned a long way back—at least a thousand steps back."

I cursed under my breath and turned to retrace my steps,

but paused, sensing she wanted to say more. Though her head was lowered, her hands were no longer stripping the garlic into naked yellow cloves but merely picking at the roots of the bulb.

"What is wrong with this village?" I asked.

"Nowon, the most peaceful village, they say it is," she rasped. "But enter and you might not ever leave it."

Apprehension knotted in me as I looked southward at the fog-swept clouds and the craggy landscape. The first thing I'd noticed upon arriving in Jeju was that people acted oddly at the mention of Nowon Village. The previous travelers, too, had either turned pale or had frowned at the name.

"It seems many fear that village," I remarked.

"It has been one year since the thirteenth girl went missing," the woman explained. "Thirteen girls missing in the past four years. All girls from the same village—Nowon. But there was an elderly witness claiming to have seen the thirteenth girl last night, dashing through the woods near Seonhul Village."

I shot her a glance. "How do you know?"

"Her relatives came all the way here searching for her. Hyunok, they called her. Only fourteen years old. Their speculation is that she was kept somewhere secret for a year but managed to escape. So after what the witness reported, the family waited at home, expecting their girl to return. She did not. They searched the area where Hyunok was last seen, but—nothing. Perhaps she got lost." She pursed her wrinkled lips and dusted the papery white garlic skin off her skirt.

Standing, she pressed a hand against her aching back and grumbled, "*Aigoo, aigoo.*" She propped the bowl against her arm and side, then limped toward the crooked wooden door.

"Don't let it be said that this old lady didn't warn you."

Mist rolled down from the hills, pooling over the fields swaying with silver grass, and the mist climbed up the black stone wall that surrounded Nowon Village, a mid-slope community closer to the mountain than it was to the sea. I walked around until I found the entrance, which opened onto a settlement crowded with rock huts and roofs made of thatch, sturdy against the constant blast of wind and rain. I walked through narrow stone-walled paths that ran between streets and huts, wondering if the direction I was going would lead me to where my sister was living.

I took timid steps in one direction, turned, and tried another path. I thought I would stop getting lost once I reached Nowon. After all, I had lived in this village for the first thirteen years of my life and had secretly traveled these paths to visit Shaman Nokyung, the woman who had taken Maewol in as her assistant.

But I had been young then, only ever following Mother, seeing nothing but her hands firmly wrapped around mine or staring up at the sky and the birds in the air—never at the way we were going. Now the village warped before my eyes. The path appeared stretched and twisted, as though it had been lifted off the earth and rearranged. Then it struck me: For all my life, I had always followed someone. First my mother and then, when she'd died, my father. I'd never needed to get anywhere alone.

I paused at the center of the village, where paths stretched out in all directions like rivulets. I closed my eyes and allowed my mind to sink into the memory of the jeomjip, the fortune-teller's hut. Images flickered, of rolling hills, of a lone hut surrounded by a vast plain, of the jagged edges of Mount Halla . . .

My legs hurried forward before I even knew where I was going. I cut through Nowon, and, after a vigorous walk toward the shadow of Mount Halla, the northern village gate was a mere streak in the gray distance. Isolation yawned around me. A peregrine falcon soared overhead. Windswept pine trees and sharp rocks sparsely protruded from the earth.

Two hours later, I saw what looked like a shadow of a hut through the moving smokelike mist.

The last time I'd visited Shaman Nokyung was when I had followed Father there five years ago, watching him lead Maewol to the hut while holding her small hand, only to transfer her clingy hand into the shaman's grasp.

"I will visit often," he had assured Maewol, and he had visited frequently, as promised. He'd made sure that his youngest never felt abandoned, and we had found a sliver of comfort in the knowledge that Shaman Nokyung was like an aunt to Maewol.

They'd grown close ever since Maewol had suffered from the shin-byung, an illness of unknown origin suffered by those called to become a shaman—a calling that was often deadly if resisted. Maewol's days of suffering night chills, fevers, and vomiting had ceased completely the day Father had left her at the jeomjip to accept her fate. As for myself, the shaman was a mere ajimang, and I doubted she cared much for me either.

I slowed my pace, side aching, my lungs filled with too much cold fog by the time I arrived. The thatch-roofed jeom-jip was held up by crooked wooden beams, and its walls were made of lava rock like the other homes on Jeju, except the hut was smaller than I'd remembered. The main house had only four hanji-screened wooden double doors: the largest quarter where the shaman entertained her customers, and the other three quarters for sleeping and storage, including where my sister had chosen to live in as the shaman's assistant. Across the yard was a small shed, and from it I could hear the sound of horse hooves pawing the ground.

My gaze turned back to the main house, where the first door was slightly ajar, allowing me a glimpse of a woman sitting before a low-legged table. Her head was bowed over a strip of paper as her calligraphy brush, dripping with red ink, moved across it. A charm paper, perhaps.

"Ajimang," I called out, crossing the yard. "Ajimang!"

She looked up, revealing a slit of her face through the crack. What I saw was not an ajimang of sixty winters, but a young lady with a face glowing with pink youthfulness and brows shaped like a delicate willow leaf.

Her stare intensified as she slid open the door and stepped out. "Who are you?"

As I stepped forward I could see that her youthfulness was an illusion. A thick layer of white powder hid her aging lines, rouge stained her lips and cheeks, and her hair, severely drawn back and twisted into a coil, stretched out the wrinkles along her temples.

Standing under her unwavering, charcoal-lined dark eyes, I said, "Don't you remember me?"

"I've never met you—" She paused, narrowing her eyes, and reexamined my face. Her brows lifted. "It can't be . . ." A slow shake of her head, and then she whispered, "You look almost just like your father."

"I've come to find him."

At first a look of sadness illuminated her eyes, but then a shadow shifted across her expression. "You came alone?"

"Aunt Min knows I'm here," I lied. I'd spent the night before at my aunt's residence, staring up at the ceiling, imagining how I would unbolt the inner gate of the woman's quarter to escape to Jeju. "She said she'd give me a few weeks to visit Jeju. For closure."

Silence beat between us. Then she buried her hands into her wide sleeves. "Come inside," she said under her breath. Her long robe of snowy white fluttered in the wind as she turned, and the door creaked like old bones as she opened it.

I followed her in, my gaze at once sweeping the hut for signs of my sister. But all I saw was a room swamped in curling incense, cramped with bulging-eyed statues, and cluttered with instruments the shaman used for her rituals. As I stood at the center and looked around, the shaman's voice crept up behind me.

"She will be here soon."

The longer I stood observing the place, the sharper it became, the memory of the uneasiness I'd felt the day we'd left Maewol behind with Shaman Nokyung. Father must have felt the uneasiness too, like he had committed something unforgivable, for I remembered seeing his downcast eyes and the gloom knotting his brows. It wasn't my fault—or Father's fault—that Maewol's shamanic calling had anchored her in Jeju when the waves of life had swept the rest of our family to the mainland. Still, Maewol had been only a child then. Only ten years old.

And yet . . .

Father had been offered a position in the police bureau that no man would have turned down. A chief inspector of the sixth rank. *I need to protect our family,* I remember Father telling us, *and if I am to do so, I need to be more than a low-ranking police officer working for corrupt officials. I need more power.*

I wanted to believe Father had made the right decision, that he always made the right decision.

"Your father visited me when he arrived in Jeju a year

ago." The shaman's voice returned me to the present. She was sitting cross-legged on a floor mat, her skirt puffed around her. "Do you know why he came here?"

I too sat down and smoothed out the wrinkles in my robe, using the moment to reorient myself. "To investigate the case of the missing thirteen girls. Commander Ki informed me of this."

"And did Commander Ki inform you about the white mask?"

A frown tugged at my brows. "What white mask?"

"A witness claimed to have seen a man in a white mask taking one of the girls."

I sat even straighter, my shoulders and back tense with memory. *A man in a white mask* . . . "The Forest Incident," I whispered.

She nodded. "Your father realized there might be a connection between the case of the missing thirteen and the Forest Incident that you and your sister were involved in."

I dared myself to remember back to the incident, but when I did, as usual I saw nothing—no trees, no people, no voices. Just a blank space. It was as though a sharp pair of scissors had snipped out an important passage from a book.

Agasshi, I hear you and your sister were in the forest that day, but did you see *the dead girl?*

I remembered our servant girl asking me that, and I recalled the confusion I'd felt then—not knowing what she'd meant, convinced she'd mistaken me for someone else, only to later learn from Mother that a terrible event had indeed occurred. That my sister and I had truly been in the forest where a dead girl was also found. An incident I could not remember, but my sister did. She was the one who'd claimed that she had seen a man in a white mask running through the forest with a gleaming sword.

My frown deepened as I connected the pieces. "So Father came to Jeju . . . to investigate the case of the missing thirteen . . . because he believed it was connected to the Forest Incident?" I'd never understood why Father would have traveled all the way to Jeju to solve a case unrelated to his jurisdiction—until now. "How very much like Father," I whispered. "Of course he'd want to solve this case. It was the one he could never figure out."

"No. That was not the reason he wanted to solve the case. He came to Jeju for your sister."

"What?" The word left my lips, a burst of disbelief, before I could stop it.

"He was worried Maewol might be in danger. She is, after all, a witness from the Forest Incident. And with girls going missing, who was to say she might not be next? He wanted to solve the case once and for all, and he promised her that this time, he really would bring your family together."

Why hadn't Father told me this? He'd never even spoken of Maewol back at home. The only time he mentioned her was to ask if I'd remembered to write to her.

There was a burning sensation in the pit of my chest, as though I'd swallowed steaming hot tea, an ache that sharpened into thought: It was unfair. I had done everything right, I had never disobeyed Father, yet he had left me behind for the daughter who had always been trouble.

"I see," I said, my voice flat.

"Every year your father visited Jeju Island, he promised to bring your family back"—Shaman Nokyung pursed her lips—"and each time he returned to the mainland, he forgot that promise. But I believe that he'd truly meant it this time. A pity."

I jerked up a glance. "A pity?"

"A pity that he is dead."

"He's *not* dead!"

Her eyes went round, likely stunned by the viciousness in my voice. "The police closed the case."

"Until there is evidence," I said, calmly this time, "he is not dead, ajimang."

"Maewol is not like you." She slid her hands into her sleeves, and her gaze roamed my face, observing every angle and line. "She accepts things for face value. It is better that way, rather than living haunted by what could have been. And it would be better if you returned home, Hwani-yah. In a few days villagers will gather here for a public kut; Maewol and I will both be busy preparing for that ritual, too busy to help you. Leave before then. The last time your aunt corresponded with us, she said you were betrothed. Get married and move on with life; don't wander out here in the wilderness. Your father would have wanted this too—"

She stopped and her expression crumpled.

I looked over and saw my sister watching me from the latticed hanji door. A sister I hadn't seen since I was thirteen, she ten. In the slant of shadow, I saw the disheveled sweep of hair, braided down her back. Dark eyebrows that slashed low over her mismatched eyes. And like the shaman, her eyes were also outlined in black, a stark contrast to her paleness. So pale her skin seemed to glow.

Without even greeting me, she walked off.

A sheen of ice frosted my heart, and my voice as well: "I crossed a thousand li of seawater to come here," I said. "I at least deserve *some* kind of answer."

The wind howled outside, but there was a stillness inside the squalid quarter, the room attached to the fortune-telling hut that I was to stay in just for a few nights. Someone's chamber pot, tucked against the corner, reeked of dried urine.

I lit a greasy candle; light spluttered in the darkness, and my shadow swayed against the wall as I opened Father's burnt journal for the thousandth time.

While more than half of the book was incinerated, the first few pages were legible. With my mind I filled in the missing words, burned away by fire, and skimmed through Father's report of the thirteen missing girls. On the last page was a list of female names, the names of fourteen girls—and next to the fourteenth name was an inky dot. It was as though Father had tapped the tip of his calligraphy brush there, again and again. He must have been deep in thought while staring at the name.

Eunsuk.

Who was Eunsuk? Was she one of the missing thirteen? But then why were there fourteen names in total? The shaman had told me that Father had come to Jeju to solve two potentially related cases. Perhaps he was right and the past had been resurrected.

A past I wished I could remember.

I slid out my own journal from my sack and opened it onto a fresh page. A bamboo calligraphy brush in hand, I rolled up my sleeve and dipped it into the ink. In small letters, I wrote:

Forest Incident, five years ago.

An ache pounded behind my left eye. My vision blurred, and the ink bled before me, branching out like twigs until I saw not my own writing but an entire forest blooming on the page. I pressed my fingers into my eyelids, hard, then looked again and everything had returned to normal. A neat vertical row of Hanja characters stared back at me.

I let out a breath and collected my thoughts. Father had

found me in the forest of Mount Halla five years ago, close to the scene of an apparent suicide. Dipping the brush into the ink, I took note of what I knew were facts:

I ventured into the woods with Father and Maewol.

Little sister ran away, we tried to find her, and I ended up getting lost. We both got lost.

Father, with the help of servants, found us unconscious hours later, a few paces away from the corpse of a young woman.

Seohyun was her name.

Father is now missing, and a woman named Boksun sent me his journal.

I tapped the end of the bamboo handle against my lips. One thing was clear: I needed to find this Boksun woman. I would worry about everything else afterward—

The brush stilled in my hand. But where would I even begin my search for her?

I jumped to my feet and stepped out of my quarter—not through the door that faced the yard, but the one that led me to the sangbang, the main living space that linked to all areas of the house. My sister's door was on the opposite end. The candlelight was still burning, but no one was inside.

I roamed the hut looking for her, silent except for the whistling wind and Shaman Nokyung's snoring. Then I heard it—the sound of shuffling somewhere outside.

I followed the noise out of the hut and into the open yard

that whirred with gusts of crisp freshness, tinged with the smoky scent of aged pine from the nearby forest. The sound of someone busy at work led me into the kitchen, where Maewol was crouched on the dirt floor, stirring a wooden spoon around in an earthenware pot.

"Maewol-ah," I whispered, so as not to startle her.

She continued to stir, and I smelled something medicinal. Maewol had written in one of her letters about Shaman Nokyung's aching limbs and how she often boiled for her the root of a jeoseulsari, a plant that remained green through winter and was said to contain magical properties.

"Maewol-ah," I called again.

She jolted up, clutching the spoon like it was a knife. Then she let out a breath. "It's you." And she returned to her crouching position, sticking the spoon back into the pot. "What do you want?"

I opened my mouth to speak, but closed it, wondering how to greet a sister I hadn't seen in years. My mind floundered about for a moment before I heaved a sigh and decided that I'd just get straight to the point. "I'm looking for a woman named Boksun. Who in this village do you think would be able to help me?"

Maewol covered the pot with a lid and cast the spoon aside. She walked right past me without saying a word.

A tendril of anger unfurled in me. *"Maewol-ah."* I walked after her, into the yard. "I came all this way. I need your help. I need to find our father—"

"Your father. Not mine."

I didn't know what to say to this. "Father came to Jeju for *you*."

Maewol stopped so suddenly that I nearly walked into her, and she whirled around to face me. Her mismatched eyes bored into me, one larger than the other, but both filled with deepwater black. "He came because of the *Forest Incident*. He came because he made a *mistake* that day."

"What mistake?" I said, irritation pinching my voice. "What are you talking about?"

"He made a mistake that day, and if he hadn't, our lives would have turned out so different."

"The only mistake that was made, Maewol-ah, was *you* throwing a tantrum and then running away."

"Oh, is that what Father told you?" she retorted. "That I got lost because I'd *run away*?"

The knowing edge in her voice sent a wave of anxiety through me. I could not remember anything about that day, and so I'd always relied on others to fill in my memory—and this reliance came with an undercurrent of fear that I was being fed lies. But surely not Father. He would never lie to me.

"Why should I doubt what Father told me?" I demanded. Before she could answer, the fear in me spiraled. "In fact, why should I believe *anything* you say? You lied to me so many times. You stole my belongings and lied about it. You always ran from home and lied about where you went, and I'd always be in trouble for not having watched you better!"

"Who do you think turned me into a liar? Father gave you *everything*. But me? Father was always teaching me a lesson. Nothing came easily to me. I never got away with mistakes, no matter how hard I tried. The good things you had, I wanted too, so I borrowed them."

"Borrowed." A dry laugh escaped me, and I stared out at the sky streaked with red and blackish blue, wondering what madness had seized me into thinking that I could work with my sister. I had thought that Father's disappearance would close the gaping chasm between us, that it would make things right.

"Five years," Maewol said at last. "I haven't seen you for five years. And then you suddenly barge into my life without so much as a 'have you been well?'"

Her words sank into me and sharpened into guilt, but I pushed the feeling aside. Father was missing, and all she could think about was her own feelings. "Dwaeseo," I snapped. "I'll investigate on my own."

"Do whatever you want." An angry blush stained Maewol's cheeks as she opened her mouth to say something more, but then she stilled, her attention snatched away by whatever was behind me. I followed her gaze, looking over my shoulder.

Past the yard and the stone gate surrounding the hut, at least a dozen stars twinkled against the shadows of the rolling hills. They were lights of torches swishing. As the torches grew brighter, closer, I saw the orange glow of firelit faces, wrinkled with deep lines of grief. They pushed against the wind and pressed forward in one direction, northward toward the black ridges of Mount Halla.

"They must have found her," Maewol whispered. "The thirteenth girl."

three

WATCHED MAEWOL RETREAT INTO THE hut. I was now alone, standing in the yard, as the torchlight grew brighter and brighter until the villagers were gathered before the jeomjip, a crowd of haggard faces.

"What brings an entire village to Shaman Nokyung's gate?" I asked, voice lowered.

No one seemed to recognize me; my parents had always made sure to hide us, either by disguising us or burying us deep within a palanquin. It was what other parents in Joseon had done and continued to do—partly to preserve their daughters' purity, and partly out of fear that our names might end up on the government's human tribute list. So it should not have surprised me, seeing the question in their eyes. Yet the urgency straining their faces left no time for them to make inquiries as to my identity.

One villager, a tall girl, held a torch high, and its light

flickered across her countenance—an ashen face and a pair of eyes so dark with despair they looked like pits. For a moment, I felt like I was looking at myself. She looked just as I had when I'd learned of Father's disappearance.

"Not an entire village, only family and relatives. Is Shaman Nokyung inside?" she asked. Her voice was weak, as if she were about to faint, and all the while she kept her gaze lowered. "We would like her to follow us to Mount Halla."

"Why?" I asked.

"My—" She blinked hard, like she couldn't believe what she was saying. "My sister . . . She's been found there. She is dead."

A chill crawled up my spine. A dead girl on Mount Halla— the vast wilderness where bodies could easily be lost and never found. It was the place Father had entered but had never walked out of.

My gaze strayed northward as my heartbeat quickened. There were secrets hidden inside the mists there, a connection between all these incidents of the missing and dead. A connection that might become clearer if I could figure out what had happened to the thirteenth girl.

"I'll go get the shaman," I said. I turned to make my way toward the hut and found myself standing face-to-face with my sister. Maewol had changed out of her rags into a white hemp gown. Her knuckles were also white, clenching on to the bronze spirit-summoning rattle that all shamans had.

She walked right past me and made her way to the villagers. They were all a head or two taller than she.

"Shaman Nokyung retired early for the night," Maewol said. "Let her rest. I will go."

"Then come quick," a villager at the far end of the crowd called out, "before the storm arrives!"

Maewol left with them. No one asked me to follow, but I did.

We traveled through the darkness and whistling wind, across the stretch of barren land covered in rocks and tufts of grass. After perhaps an hour or more the path disappeared into the mouth of the mountain.

A villager at the front motioned at the torch-wielding crowd. "This way!"

Maewol and I glanced at each other. The moment we stepped in, the forest shuddered awake in the firelight, creaking trees swaying in every direction. So too did the questions in my mind.

"Who found her?" I asked the victim's sister. Her name was Koh Iseul, I had heard someone say, and she looked to be twenty years of age. Perhaps a bit older. "And when?"

Iseul spoke to the hem of my robe, her voice nervous and so quiet I could hardly hear her. "A villager named Chul came to the mountain to collect firewood, sir."

"And *when*?" I asked again, walking closer so as not to miss her murmured response.

Iseul avoided my gaze and glanced at my sister, supplication in her eyes. She was uncomfortable, splotches of red forming on her cheeks, made redder by the torchlight. At once, I remembered who I was pretending to be: a young nobleman. This disguise had kept me safe on my journey, but it raised walls between me and Iseul. I took a few steps away from her until her tense shoulders eased.

At length, Iseul replied, "I think he said it was around sunset when he found . . . found my sister, Hyunok."

"What condition was she in?"

"He was too scared to examine her closely and rode over to tell my mother about his discovery." Her voice thinned into a trembling whisper. "Hyunok was only fourteen. I can't believe she's dead."

Suddenly, the forward movement of the crowd stopped. I stood on my toes and looked from side to side, but all I could see were people standing frozen. Then a wave of whispers arose, punctuated by a piercing scream.

"Hyunok-ah!"

My steps quickened, and Maewol followed. Soon we stood at the edge of the crowd of people pressed shoulder to shoulder, craning their necks to snatch a better look. I peered through the human wall and saw a downhill slope ahead, ending in a steep drop-off. At the edge just before the descent lay a woman's shoe.

A cold sensation billowed inside my chest. Only those who were running for their lives lost a shoe and never returned for it.

I squeezed through, and finally the view opened before me. The slope descended for about thirty paces, a cluster of sharp rocks at the bottom. And there lay the pale figure of a girl, face up, both legs twisted at an odd angle.

A woman behind me kept crying out, "Hyunok-ah! Hyunok-ah!" The sharp pang of grief in her voice seemed to cut across my skin. "Get up! I am here. Your mother is here!"

But Hyunok did not move.

I borrowed a torch from a nearby peasant, then, grabbing hold of a tree, I gingerly slid down the slope, steadying myself against protruding roots. Once I reached the bottom and climbed over the rocks, I stopped before the body. My insides roiled, and my knees nearly gave in as I stared down at a girl who was younger than me; her lips were slightly parted, and her eyes were wide open, staring up through the branches and into the ocean of stars splashed across the night sky.

"Hyunok," I whispered, the name her mother had called her by. "Hyunok-ah?"

She did not blink.

My throat was so parched my tongue stuck to the roof of my mouth. I hadn't stood so close to death since Mother's passing—when I had held on to her until her flesh had grown cold. The finality, the absoluteness of death . . . it frightened me.

"Talk to her," someone whispered. It took me a moment to realize that a villager was standing nearby, talking to my sister. "Mistress Maewol, commune with her spirit. What does she have to tell us? Was it an accident?"

Maewol looked pale, terrified—she'd likely never seen a dead body before. She'd never had the chance to look at Mother after she'd died giving birth to our stillborn brother.

"Mistress Maewol?"

At the prodding of more villagers, Maewol looked up at the sky and shook the rattle, an eerie and sharp clanging noise in the night. In a low chant, she beseeched the spirit of Hyunok to listen to her prayers. Then, as though someone had leaned in to whisper to her, Maewol turned her ear to the left.

"I sense her spirit," Maewol said. "She is angry, filled with much han. She is asking for justice."

Of course her spirit is angry, I thought. *Who wouldn't be angry after having their life cut so short?* Instead of listening to Maewol, I stood before the body and tried to remember my father's lessons.

What would Father do if he were here? While other police officers hurtled in and out of cases based on hunches, searching only for evidence that would bolster their assumptions,

Father had collected details and let those tell him the story behind the crime. Standing tall in one place, beginning to his left he would slowly turn in a complete circle, taking in the scene and documenting every detail in his black notebooks.

I hadn't brought anything to write with or write in, so instead I recorded everything into the blank pages of my mind—the shoe above the drop; the disturbed plant life that left a gash down the slope, perhaps the direction Hyunok might have tumbled down.

I turned to ask Iseul when her sister had last been seen, but I couldn't find her among the shadowy crowd of people who must have all filtered down the slope at some point. As I spun around to search for her, something strange flickered in the corner of my eye.

A light twinkled among the trees, small as a firefly, and then disappeared.

"Who is this boy?" a male voice demanded, and I looked to see a stranger pointing at me. Perhaps the father of Hyunok, or an uncle. "Who brought him?"

"I'm from the mainland," I said, and glanced at Maewol, hoping she would play along. "Come to look for my uncle, Detective Min."

The villagers stared with shuttered expressions, and some looked at me as though I'd grown another pair of eyes.

Keep your shoulders straight, I ordered myself as sweat dampened my brows. *Whatever you do, don't look down.*

"We don't need the help of an outsider. How can we trust him?"

A grumble of agreement followed.

I could see they'd raised their guards against me, as they had been doing for centuries against powerful invaders. I would need a better disguise to fish information from them. Instead of becoming stronger, I needed to become weaker, to seem vulnerable . . . People only tell secrets willingly to those who cannot do them harm.

"But any help is *help*," a villager said. "We must find the beast that is taking our girls!"

As the onlookers argued among themselves, I focused my mind and returned to the memory of my father. At the end of his initial procedure, his gaze orbiting around, he would examine the corpse and its immediate surroundings.

I crouched before the body of Hyunok, only fourteen winters old. She was dressed in a jeogori jacket worn over a long skirt. The whiteness of the fabric made it easy to see the countless little tears in it—perhaps from running through a forest of sharp branches—along with mud stains and blood.

But then I noticed something else. Beneath a thin layer of leaves, right next to her wrist, was a rope.

Look carefully; think carefully. One must interpret evidence correctly. The memory of my father seemed to hunch over me, examining the evidence by my side. *Failure can prove injurious, even fatal.*

I pulled up Hyunok's sleeves. There were linear abrasions

on both her wrists. I moved my gaze down, to where her skirt had hiked up slightly to reveal ankles with the same marks. But there was only one rope—a rope cut through cleanly—and it was only long enough to have tied either the wrists or the ankles, not both.

Hyunok's still face glowed brighter as a young man approached, holding a torch over his head. He was dressed like a nobleman, with a forest-green silk robe, yet the hem and collar of his robe were worn out with loose threads fraying at the edges, as though he had worn the same garb for the past several decades. He couldn't have been older than twenty-five though.

"Did you find something?" he asked. He looked at me as though he genuinely wanted to hear my thoughts, so I answered him.

"Look closely at her wrist—someone had her tied up. And her ankles as well. But there is only one rope, which someone clearly cut with a knife. I don't know where the other rope used for binding her could be—"

The man crouched before Hyunok's body, the fire from his torch blazing too close to my face; I staggered back onto my feet. What was he doing, touching the body, squeezing her limbs? Such concentration crinkled his brows, and then he ran a hand over his short black beard, as though in thought.

"Look here," he said, hovering the torch along the dark purplish hue blossomed across on her arm. "This is where the blood pooled, and when I press on it, like so, the discoloration does not blanch easily. Her limbs are also stiff. By this, I would say her time of death was early this afternoon."

I watched him quizzically. How did he know all this?

He gazed up at me, revealing a brawny face with chiseled features and dark brows that lay low over a deep-set pair of intelligent eyes. The corner of his lips twitched, barely concealing a smile. "You look bewildered, young master."

"Begging your pardon, but who are you?" I asked.

"You may call me Scholar Yu."

"You mean *ex*-scholar," someone mumbled. "Now only an alcoholic and troublemaker who gambles or sleeps all day."

"No amount of alcohol can erase the memory etched into my bones." Yu smirked as he ran a finger across the brim of his tall black hat, but it was dusty and slightly slanted to the side like the drunkard that he was called. "My knowledge will always be intact. I am the son of a third-generation physician."

I was about to return my attention to the corpse when the clanging of Maewol's rattle suddenly stopped. The complete silence that followed was louder than a scream. I glanced up, and Maewol was staring wide-eyed at the dark forest with her mouth open.

A haze edged the corner of my vision. Hallucination or memory, I could not tell, but I found myself staring at a scene from five years ago, of my ten-year-old sister wearing the same ominous expression as she whispered, *Oshyutda*.

The back of my neck prickled eerily. As though the

ten-year-old sister had stepped out from that memory, Mae-wol uttered the very same words now: "It is here."

"What?" I asked, clutching the torch tighter. "What is here?"

"Evil."

With the body carried away on a wooden stretcher, the crowd dispersed to search the surrounding area for witnesses or suspects, leaving only Maewol and me—along with Scholar Yu, who could barely disguise his thrill. He seemed genuinely excited to assist with my clandestine investigation, and I was genuinely grateful for his presence. I would have been terrified in the forest alone with my sister, who wasn't any less frightening herself with her wide eyes and trembling rattle.

"It was there," I said, pointing toward the space between the tree branches. "I saw light coming from that direction earlier."

I had enough common sense to know that if I ventured there alone, I would not know how to find my way back to the shaman's hut. I would get lost, just as I had five years ago. I turned to Scholar Yu, a friendly face. "We could go there together. Perhaps we could find out what happened to the victim?"

"Of course I will accompany you"—he twirled his hand in the air—"for who else will watch over the young?"

The young. He seemed to see me as a naive child who knew nothing about the world. Yet he had no idea, did he, the secrets I carried—heavier than his own, I'd wager. Raising my torch, I took a step forward, then remembered my sister, who was standing so quietly behind me that I'd forgotten her for a moment.

"You can return to the hut if you'd like," I said.

Without a word, Maewol passed me in a few long strides, heading in the direction I meant to go myself.

I bit my tongue, and together with Scholar Yu, we followed behind and wove our way through the forest.

Twigs cracked like bones beneath our steps.

The scent of moss and dew, soaking the misty air, filled my nostrils.

Then sounds of hooves echoed somewhere in the distance. Horses? Villagers? We paused to watch a herd of shadows moving through the bluish-gray mist, tinged with the orange of flickering torchlight. It was a herd of Siberian roe deer, quietly descending the mountain. Once they were gone, Scholar Yu was the first to break the silence.

"So you came to look for Detective Min?" he asked. "I knew him."

My chest cracked open. Hearing Father's name was like seeing a ghostly trace of him, his reflection shimmering on the surface of a stranger's memory. I tried tempering the eagerness in me as I asked, lowering my voice a notch, "You know my fath—Detective Min?"

"He questioned people about the missing thirteen girls. And also the suicide of Seohyun."

Seohyun. The woman who had died in the forest of Mount Halla, around the same time that Father had found Maewol and me in the woods.

"What do you know about her?" I asked.

"What everyone knew about her," he answered. "She worked in Nowon Village selling baskets and the vegetables she'd grown. She didn't have family here, though people claim she had a Jeju accent, so she must be a native of this island."

"What was she like?" I prodded.

"No one knew her when she wandered in seven years ago, all bruised and in rags. I never did see her myself, as I was thrown onto this island only one and a half years ago. But people tell me they still remember that haunted look in her eyes—the most haunted eyes they had ever seen. Then one day the villagers here in Nowon began saying she was a tribute girl, that she must have escaped Ming."

The kingdom where she would have been given over to aristocrats, men from Ming and Joseon alike . . . This, I knew too well.

"Most tribute girls who find the chance to return often never do—they kill themselves before they reach Joseon," Scholar Yu continued. "But Seohyun chose to live, and perhaps she thought that by coming to a village where no one knew her, she'd have a chance to live an ordinary life."

"But she didn't," I guessed.

"No. The moment everyone discovered that she was a tribute girl, they began treating her differently. She could have still been a virgin, untouched—she may have escaped Ming China in time. And yet the villagers avoided her like the plague. She was always alone and lived so quietly for the two years that she resided here . . ." His voice trailed off as his gaze lowered, but not quick enough to hide the distress filling his eyes.

"Is that all, sir?" I asked. "Was there anyone that would want to hurt her?"

His brows crumpled, and for that brief moment, I saw not an alcoholic jester but a solemn man. "She lived quietly, as I said, but whenever anyone got too close to her, she would lash out, saying that there was a monster among us. Her mind was troubled. She lost half her weight each full moon; she was as thin as a bone right before her death."

"How do you know all this? You have been here for only one and a half years, you said."

"Everyone kept an eye on her," he replied, "and I keep my ears open to what everyone says. They still talk of her. Some believe that her spirit is stealing their daughters out of revenge."

Of course some villagers would believe that. The people here were so superstitious. "Then based on everything you've overheard, what do you think happened to Seohyun?" I asked.

He gave me a long, quizzical stare. "I don't want to think about it. Would you?"

We spoke no more after that, but on my own, I continued to wonder about Seohyun as I lost myself in the rhythm of climbing over protruding trunks and around rocks. My knees rising and falling, rising and falling, leaving me in a trancelike state where all my thoughts were pinned to Seohyun.

So she had been a tribute girl.

She had lived through my worst nightmare.

I'd grown up with my parents hiding me and Maewol from being detected so that even close neighbors could not see us. They told me stories of soldiers rounding up screaming girls, leading them by ropes. These wailing daughters would be loaded onto vessels, taken away to a faraway kingdom by orders of Xuande Emperor of Ming. I had thought these to be distant tales, only stories that affected the girls on the mainland.

Until the day our maid had scrambled into our home.

Hide your daughters! she had ordered my mother. *You must hide the girls well!*

Mother had asked why, only to be answered by flickering torchlight in our yard—a troop of soldiers stood outside. They were led by a greedy-looking man, an emissary come to Jeju to seize maidens. Someone must have told him that Father had beautiful daughters, and so the emissary had come to our home in search of one more maiden who would be a worthy tribute.

In the end, the emissary had changed his mind; he'd decided to withdraw his soldiers and retreat from our home. It was a small mystery I still wondered about.

"There!"

My pulse leaped at Maewol's voice. She was pointing at a small hut, only large enough for one or two people to reside in, made of lava rocks that had ancient moss crawling over it. Scholar Yu went in first, pushing against the brushwood door; it creaked open onto a small, drafty space of dirt floor and cobwebs.

I followed him, passing Maewol, who looked reluctant to go in. No, not merely reluctant—she looked faint with horror. A part of me wanted to stay close to my sister, to wait out her trembling at her side . . . but I needed to find out where that light had come from.

"Scholar Yu." I stepped into the hut, examining my surroundings for signs of life. "How long was the victim Hyunok missing for?"

"A year, from what I hear. But I doubt she was kept in this hut for that long. She would have been easily found."

"Hm." I worried my lower lip.

All I could think about, surrounded by these four cold and damp rock walls, were the dead girls—surely the other twelve girls were dead as well. Where could they have gone for so many months, and without a trace?

There was a filthy old mat and blanket laid out along the wall. Crouching, I examined the place where Hyunok might have slept, and found a single strand of hair, long and black. Past it, at the end of the mat where she would have stretched out her feet, I found a rope with frayed edges. She must have gotten hold of something sharp, perhaps a sharp rock, to cut the rope loose while her wrists were still tied. I also noticed on the wall, near the dirt floor, were nine circles—scratched out with the same rock, most likely.

"What did you find?" Scholar Yu asked.

"Something drawn on the wall and a frayed rope." I patted my hand along the mat and felt a bump. I pulled it aside to reveal a small, jagged rock. As I had suspected. "She cut the rope around her ankle and escaped her captor."

"But what about the rope around her wrists?" he asked. "You said it was probably cut with a knife after she'd fallen down the drop. Are you saying she cut it herself?"

"The captor might have done it."

"Why?"

I tried to sound like Father, always so sure in the way he connected evidence, even though I was certain of nothing. "Perhaps the captor found the body with her wrists still tied . . . but for some reason, he did not wish Hyunok to be *found* tied up. Yet the sliced rope was left there, right next to the body, which would have defeated that purpose . . ."

"So, what are you saying?"

I ran my thumb across the sharp edge of the rock, then a thought sparked. "Whoever cut the rope was surprised in the act and left it on the ground next to the corpse."

"Surprised? Could this have been because a witness came into view?"

"Perhaps the captor heard *us* approaching." The words rushed out of me, and I tried hard to quell the flame of excitement. "Maybe it took him that long, nearly the entire day, to even find Hyunok's corpse, and just as he was cutting the rope loose, our search party arrived. Do you know what time the body was *first* discovered?"

"You should ask Chul, the man who found her. But I would say it was late in the afternoon, five hours before we arrived . . ." His voice dropped into complete silence. I glanced to find him peering at me with the most bewildered look. In a whisper, he asked, "Why do you say 'he'?"

"What do you mean?"

"You referred to the captor as a 'he.' How would you know that?"

I returned my gaze to the dirty mat, to the strand of hair, to the frayed rope. "A woman wouldn't do such a thing to a girl."

I didn't want to even imagine what Hyunok had endured. But the magistrate would have Hyunok's corpse examined, and we would learn of what had happened to her—whether we wished to know it or not.

"You were right!" came Maewol's voice from outside.

I peeked outside the hut to see Maewol crouched over something—a paper lantern dropped on the earth.

Scholar Yu rushed past me and lowered himself next to

Maewol. He closed his thumb and forefinger over the wick of the candle inside, then slowly lifted his gaze to mine. Gone was the teasing glint I'd seen in his eyes when he'd called me "young one." His eyes were wide and solemn, sharp with fear.

"It is still warm," he rasped.

four

I **WOKE UP TO FIND MYSELF** hunched over the low-legged table in the shaman's hut, eyes swollen from crying over a dream I couldn't remember. My chest was sore, my heart so bruised, like an overripe persimmon smashed. I sat up, my back stiff and aching, and rubbed my eyes.

A single word was written over and over again down the sheet of hanji I'd fallen asleep on. I couldn't remember writing it, yet there it was, staring at me.

Father
Father
Father
Father
Father

There were days when I'd hardly think of my father, but there were other days—days like now—when the reality of his disappearance lurched into my mind, sinking sharp grief into me. I still had a sliver of hope that he might be alive. But what I'd witnessed the previous night made me waver . . .

I could picture Hyunok's corpse too well, the awkward angle of her broken legs, her gaping eyes. What had terrified her so much that she had so blindly run to her death? And who had kept her all these months?

A rustling sound disturbed my thoughts. I looked up from the hanji paper, wondering if an animal had snuck into my room, but instead I saw my sister crouched in the far corner near the screened door. She seemed to have no idea that I was awake, so busy as she was rummaging through my sack of belongings. She was like a raven, always stealing everything of mine that shone.

Maewol paused in her search, then drew out a bronze hand mirror. It wasn't a common item, it was a luxury. She drew it close to her face, as though wanting to examine the very pores in her skin.

I thought of ordering her to put it down; it was mine. But then I remembered something else I wanted more, answers to questions that had been bothering me since the night before. Was my sister truly able to commune with spirits? And if so . . . couldn't she just commune with the dead and tell me who the killer was? Couldn't she confirm whether Father was alive?

"Do you want it?" I asked.

She jolted and tossed the mirror back into the sack. "No."

I rose from behind the table and walked over. "If you want it, I'll give it to you."

She paused, picked the mirror back up again, and held it against her chest. Her face remained blank—I couldn't tell whether she felt grateful or not. And with that unfaltering look, she rose to her feet and would have walked out if I hadn't sidestepped, blocking the entrance.

"I'll give it to you," I said, "if you give me something in return."

Maewol narrowed her eyes at me. "What do you want?"

"Tell me the truth," I said to my sister. "Do you really sense spirits?"

"I can't hear what they say," she replied slowly, as though her words were treading with caution. "I can't really see or hear anything clearly. It's like seeing shadows through the fog. A very *thick* fog."

"So you don't know how to summon them or chase them away, do you?"

She glanced at the door, and I could tell she was about to say something that the shaman would have disapproved of. Maewol shrugged a delicate shoulder. "I don't know if the chants work. Shaman Nokyung says they do. But I do know for certain that I'm bringing people hope. And I do know that spirits exist."

I stared long and hard at my sister. In Father's account of the Forest Incident five years ago, he'd said that Maewol had thrown a tantrum, refusing to go into the forest for our annual visit to Grandfather's grave. She had sensed something ominous in the forest.

When Seohyun's body was later discovered, Father came to believe that Maewol did indeed sense spirits, but I had a hard time believing. I'd often catch myself brooding over the spirit world with suspicion, this world Maewol would write to me about in our sparse letters. Most people in Joseon accepted this other dimension as a fact, and yet, I still wondered. How could I believe the spirit world existed when it was invisible?

"I don't believe you," I said, so quietly that Maewol didn't hear, busy as she was polishing her new looking glass.

I tightened the sash belt around the robe I'd worn since the start of my travels. Then I combed out my knots until my hair flowed like silk, twisted it into a topknot, and pierced the knot through with a silver pin. Father's pin. I reached for my black gat and donned it, and as I tied the straps at my chin, I could feel Maewol's gaze. I could feel the question in her eyes: *Where are you going?* I wanted her to ask it, so that I could invite her to come along with me. But she didn't.

She turned the mirror around once in her hand, then she said, "I need to help the shaman prepare for the public kut. There's so much that needs to be done; it's going to be the largest ritual this year."

I watched her stride across the room and leave, taking the mirror with her.

"Very well, leave me," I muttered under my breath, and reached into my sack of belongings. I pulled out the necklace I always wore like a pendant—hanging from it was Father's wooden police whistle. "I'll investigate alone, then."

I had read through all of Father's investigative journals, sixty volumes in total. Journals that hadn't simply reported on the facts of the crimes but had evaluated all the information, evidence, and patterns. I'd watched as small details at the beginning of his investigation sometimes became essential elements in a crime, and it was sometimes a detail as small as a phrase uttered by a witness. *Testimonies*, he'd written at the end of one report, *are crucial to create an accurate history of the incident. It is often the only way to fill in the blank spaces of an investigation.*

So testimonies were what I needed, and there were two in particular that I keenly wanted to hear.

The first was from Koh Iseul, the victim's sister. I'd met her the day before, but there had been no time to ask questions. Now I needed to hear her side of the story while everything was still fresh. As to where I might find her, I knew all I needed to do was ask a passerby for directions. In a village as small as Nowon, everyone knew everyone.

The second was from Boksun, a woman I'd never met before. She was somehow at the center of Father's disappearance, and I didn't know what role she'd played in it. All I knew was that she had paid a traveler to send me his burnt journal. I would have hounded the courier with questions, but he had delivered the journal through my servant, and she had asked him nothing.

Drifting strands of thoughts tangled in my mind as I borrowed one of the shaman's horses; she had a stable of four. It came as no surprise to me—every family on this island raised horses. Surely she wouldn't mind if I took one for the day.

By foot, it would have taken me two hours to reach Nowon, but by horseback, I reached my destination in a fragment of that time. As soon as I rode into the rocky village, everywhere I looked were faces like pages from a memorial, filled with death and horror and pain. And when I stopped one passerby to ask where I could find Koh Iseul, the old man replied in a voice as lifeless as his expression.

"Madam Oh's Gaekju Inn," he whispered. "Koh Iseul is a servant there."

I continued on my way, and then stopped at the sight of a zelkova tree that was said to be hundreds of years old. I'd always pass this tree as a child on my way home . . . My gaze inched toward the path I knew would lead to the house filled with childhood memories. After a moment's hesitation, I steered the pony around and found myself traveling through the curvy alleys that blocked strong gales, past the pen of squealing black-haired pigs, until I saw my old home.

Three large stone houses stood in a wide yard, its thatch roof gleaming white with streaks of gold in the sunlight. Green trees towered behind, their leaves rustling in the cool autumn breeze, a familiar sound I'd grown up with. A low fence made of black rocks walled in Father's estate, an estate that looked the same as it had five years ago: humble and small. Father had been wealthy, but not wealthy enough to afford the cost of bringing material over from the peninsula to build a giwajip. And it was also unwise to build such mansions here, for Jeju was known for its wild wind and rain, a powerful force that could ruin houses not meant to persevere in such harsh climates.

But while Father's old estate was not a fancy, tiled-roof mansion, it still felt more like home. It felt like a well-loved book with all its creases, tatters, and worn pages. A mixture of warmth and grief-tinged nostalgia spread through me as I rode over to the jeongnang, two stone pillars where a message would be left according to the number of logs set between them. I saw that all three logs were on the ground, telling me that the owner was home, *please come in*.

My muscles went rigid.

No one should be home.

I quickly tethered my horse to a post, then rushed past the stone pillars, past the large gate with its thatch roof and wooden double doors that had been left open, beckoning me into its spacious yard. There were no weeds, no collection of dust. *Someone is caring for this place.* Perhaps this was all a grand jest, a cruel jest by Father; perhaps he had been home all along.

I ran over to the nearest room, a storage area; it was filled with pots of fermented vegetables. Another door, unlocked, led me into the sangbang—the main room, where we had taken our meals together as a family.

There, I stopped.

The room was empty, completely empty . . . and yet, as though I'd stepped back in time, life blossomed before me. The sun shone against the wooden floor, glowing against the bowls left on a low-legged table. Mother's skirt was bright blue, and she sat on the floor, sewing. Father sat next to her, wiping the blade of his cane-sword. I was thumping around after my sister, yelling something at her.

I blinked.

At once the darkness returned. The living space was empty again, and the delight I'd felt in that moment faded away until all I had was a pit full of ashes. Every corner of the house was now haunted with what had once been and would never be again.

"Is anyone home?" I called out, my voice wavering under the weight of disappointment. I made my way across the floor, reaching out for the brass handle that would lead me to Father's quarter. "Abeoji?"

Then I heard familiar footsteps—long, confident strides. I hurried back to the front of the house and looked out at the yard. An old woman was bowing to a male figure of the same height and build as my father.

Delight exploded in my chest once more.

I dashed down the steps and hurried across the yard toward the man whose back was to me, the man I knew to be Father. How I yearned to see his face again. The wrinkles along the sides of his eyes, which I knew deepened when he smiled; the short beard that would leave my forehead itchy when he placed kisses; and the great, towering height of his that had always cast a warm, protective shadow over my life.

"Abeoji!"

This time Father heard me. He turned, and I found myself staring up at a man with chiseled cheekbones and intense black eyes. His dark hair, which was tied into a topknot, had streaks of white, and he was garbed in an onyx silk robe with gold embroidery. Next to him was a woman who appeared to be a servant, by her dress.

I touched my brows, confused.

Father was still missing.

My heart tightened around a sharp ache. And when I breathed, pain fissured through me.

"Detective Min hired Maid Kkotnim. All these five years he made sure to keep this house intact," the strange man explained, as if sensing my flustered state. "He'd always intended to return the family to his hometown and have a homecoming feast here. But then he rose in ranks, didn't he? *The greatest detective of Joseon*, they called him. Even I've heard of his reputation all the way here in Jeju."

I realized that my eyes were watering, the disappointment too intense. Yet I somehow managed to whisper, "Who are you?"

"Village Elder Moon," he said. "I am the bridge between the villagers and the magistrate."

"Why have you come to—" I paused, the words *my home* hanging on my lips. "Why did you come to this place?"

"I came to ask the maid to inform me if she sees you." He paused and turned to dismiss the old woman. Once we were alone in the yard, he said in a low and gentle voice, "I've heard rumors that Detective Min's daughter might come to investigate. What a coincidence to find you here."

A flutter of panic brushed by me. "What do you mean?"

"Commander Ki sent a letter asking after you, Min Hwani. He must have known you'd come here too. He requested that I send you back to your aunt."

Min Hwani. The sound of my name sent a jolt of cold through me. He'd called me by my name—my *real* name.

I took a stumbling step back. "You know me . . ."

"You look mostly like your mother," he said. "But your eyes—they are your father's eyes."

I couldn't believe he'd recognized me. I'd thought, growing up so sheltered here in Jeju, that no one would be able to recognize my face. That had been Mother and Father's aim.

"Why are you dressed as a boy?" the village elder asked.

I stood straighter as fire crawled up my throat and spread across my cheeks. "I heard about other women traveling as men, for safety—" I blinked, unable to shake off the bewilderment. "Have we met before, sir?"

"It was a brief encounter," he replied. "The villagers reported the suspicious Forest Incident to me, so I went to visit your father to collect his testimony. I wanted to interview you as well, but apparently you couldn't remember anything."

"I don't even remember your visit," I whispered. "Did you know my father well?"

"Quite well. He was a good man, and had stayed good despite having spent years dealing with hardened criminals." Village Elder Moon let out a breath and gazed across the yard, over the black stone gate and at the vast sky ahead. "He was not like the other officers who, in chasing monsters, became vicious themselves. No, he laughed when people laughed and cried when people cried."

That was my father. The one I was so desperately searching for, the one I would give up my own life for.

"Please, sir," I whispered. "Do not report to Commander Ki of my whereabouts."

He hesitated, and the silence that stretched between us left a cold sheen of sweat on my brows. "It isn't me you should be concerned about," he said at last. "You should worry about your uncle."

"My uncle?" I had several relatives living here in Jeju, but not in Nowon Village. He had to be mistaken. "Which uncle, sir?"

"Well, a distantly related uncle. Your father's sister—Lady Min—was married to a high-standing gentleman before his passing," he said, and I knew that. "And that gentleman's sister's husband is Magistrate Hong."

That is a very distant connection indeed, I thought. And then it struck me that I had encountered a Magistrate Hong on the vessel. I tried to wrap my head around this coincidence—but then again, here on Jeju such coincidences were frequent. Everyone knew each other and were often connected through a web of ancestry. I had no time to further speculate, though, as the village elder spoke on.

"Whatever the case, I would do my best not to catch the magistrate's attention if you wish to remain here. He knew your father."

My interest sparked. "How well, sir?"

"Very well, I would think. Your father briefly mentioned that, many years ago, he had once admired Hong for his strong sense of justice. But Magistrate Hong is changed now, and if he learns that you are here . . ."

"He won't, sir," I assured him. "As long as you do not inform him."

He gathered his hands behind him, a contemplative look shadowing his face. Then finally he replied, "Very well, I will not inform him."

I boldly added, "Or my aunt."

"You have my word," he said. "But on two conditions. First, if you are in danger, you must tell me. And second, once the case is solved, you must return to your aunt."

"Thank you, sir—" I rushed to say, but then paused. This seemed too good to be true. "Why would you help me like this?"

"I may be a mere elder over a meager village, but I share ancestry with the Nampyeong Moon clan through Moon Jang-pil. Have you heard of him?"

"He was a great military figure."

"Geuleochi!" He seemed very pleased that I knew who Moon Jang-pil was. "So, you see, bravery and honor is something our clan has always valued." He paused to examine me, so long that I felt my cheeks heat up. In a kindly voice, he continued, "And you . . . You came all this way to find your father . . . If you were my daughter, I would be proud of you. And if your father were here, he would be proud too."

I stood still as his words sank deep into me, into the cold and hollow space that Father had left behind when he'd suddenly vanished from my life. "Would he . . . ?"

"Of course he would be. Now, you should go."

I looked up. *Go where?* Then I realized—I wasn't really home, and this man was not family. Yet I wanted to linger for a few moments longer; perhaps it was the stillness of the day, without rain or gusty wind, and with the sun beaming high in the sky.

"You must go find your father, daenggi mŏri tamjŏng. That was the nickname your father gave you, is it not?" He smiled, a gentle and barely visible curve of his lips. *Young detective with braided hair.*

five

DAENGGI MŎRI TAMJŎNG WAS THE name Father had given me because of the way my hair was fashioned, braided down my back, then tied with a silk daenggi ribbon . . . and because I was always picking apart information, refusing to believe anything without evidence.

Young Hwani—the girl who had sought after and had solved many petty crimes, like the case of the stolen jade ring or the case of the dead hawk—would have stayed hopeful, and not allowed herself to be overwhelmed by the fear that had awoken in me at my old home. A fear that told me that perhaps Father was truly gone, and no house, no room, would ever be filled with the sound of his laughter, of his voice calling my name. Ddal-ah. *Daughter.*

But he is not dead, young Hwani would have hissed at me. *You have no evidence; he is simply absent!*

I wanted to believe that. Fathers weren't supposed to disappear. Fathers were supposed to stay forever.

"He is simply absent," I whispered to myself. "Until you find evidence, Min Hwani, he is not dead."

I repeated this over and over until the heavy weight in my chest eased. It was true; there was no point preparing a funeral in my heart when there was no corpse to bury.

Feeling the strength return to my limbs, I kicked the pony's sides, urging her to quicken her pace. We raced through the village streets, my ears filled with the sound of hooves thundering across the dirt, and finally arrived at Gaekju Inn. Tethering my companion, I took my journal and writing utensils from a traveling pouch and entered through the gate into a vast yard containing eight large straw-roofed stone houses. The place was packed with customers lounging on a platform covered in low-legged tables strewn with bottles of rice wine and bowls of stew, as well as merchants streaming in and out of the yard with their A-frames loaded with goods. Gaekju Inn was the center of all merchant activities in Nowon, for the owner of this establishment was the middle person between the mainland and Jeju merchants.

"Oi."

I turned to see the chiseled face of Scholar Yu, his mustache twitching as his lips perked into a smile. He seemed to be the only one in this entire village who remembered to smile—who thought it *appropriate* to smile—when there was a serial kidnapper wandering loose through the shadows.

And perhaps that was why he was bound up, a red rope wrapped around his torso, and with a stout guard keeping watch over him.

Together the men lounged on the platform, a table before them—as well as a bottle of rice wine. The guard poured himself a drink and emptied it in one swallow. He warily eyed Scholar Yu, who was gesturing at me to approach.

"In case you are wondering," Yu said as I drew near, "I was brought here to be scolded for trying to run away this morning. I've always dreamed of getting on a smuggling boat to escape this damned island."

The guard mumbled, "For a man who claims to be eager to escape, you seem most determined to stay and overly curious about the goings-on here in Nowon."

Yu, whose wrists were also tied, flicked his fingers, as though waving the guard's voice away. "And you?" he asked me, his voice bright and loud. "What brings you here?"

"I'm looking for someone. I heard Hyunok's sister, Koh Iseul, works here."

"Ah, I do indeed know her."

"You do?"

"He knows everyone," the guard grumbled. "The nosy drunkard."

Scholar Yu ignored the comment. "I saw her in the work-room at the end of the main house—"

My stomach grumbled, audible enough that both Scholar Yu and the guard dropped their gaze to my abdomen.

"Have you eaten?" Yu asked, and when I shook my head, for the barest moment, I saw concern cross his smiling face. "It's well past noon. You must take care of yourself, or you will be unable to take care of others."

Hunger sharpened in my stomach, and I suddenly noticed how my hands trembled, as they often did when I missed a meal. "I *should* eat," I mumbled.

I sat down on the raised platform and ordered a seafood stew from a passing servant. The bowl that arrived was filled with hairtail, squid, shrimp, and vegetables. I leaned forward and took a whiff; it smelled like the sea. I ate the soup along-side coarse grain rice, savoring the chewy white fish, until my thoughts drifted away. The taste of food weakened, turning as bland as ash in my mouth, then tasting like nothing at all, as I lost myself in worry. Village Elder Moon knew who I was. Could I trust him?

I wolfed down the rest of my meal and wiped the corners of my mouth. "Do you know anything about the village elder?" I asked.

Scholar Yu arched a brow. "Why this sudden curiosity?"

"I encountered him on my way here."

"Well, well." He shifted, trying to get comfortable despite

the rope tied tightly around him. "I only know of him because of the library he keeps. A vast one in Mehwadang. Books on medicine, law, history, everything. But mostly poetry."

Just like Father's library.

"Oh, and of course there is his daughter. I once caught a glimpse of her on one of her rare visits to Nowon, and I forgot how to breathe seeing her remarkable beauty. I simply had to learn more about her. Apparently, Village Elder Moon is preparing his daughter, Chaewon, for the crown princess selection—she is one of the thirty candidates. She qualified despite her family's humble roots as poor nobles, and also despite her age."

What felt at first like acidity deepened into the sharp prick of envy. *How fortunate she is*, I thought, *to be someone's daughter*. She could call out "Abeoji!" whenever she desired, and he would always answer in his warm voice, "Ddal-ah." It was pathetic, this ache in my chest, but it was there. Of all the fathers in this kingdom, mine was missing, and I felt Father's absence more than ever.

"How old is she?" I asked brusquely.

"Nineteen."

I nodded as I struck my palm against my chest, pretending that my heartache was indigestion. Once the pain subsided, I said, "That is indeed late." And it was. Noble-born girls between the ages of eleven and twenty could be selected, but most were merely twelve or thirteen years of age. The most important duty of a queen—the most important duty of *any* woman, my aunt had pointed out to me too many times—was to provide an heir, and the older a girl was, the more value she lost. I'd managed to avoid being forced into marriage for the entire year, for I—along with other young ladies—was forbidden to marry during the royal selection period.

"She is old and also a noble from Jeju, disadvantages to be sure. But Lady Moon is a special case. I have seen many beautiful women in my life, but she is the most exquisite. I call her 'the Pearl of Joseon.'"

"*The* most beautiful?" I wondered what she looked like, this daughter of Village Elder Moon.

"Yes, but, as the village elder said, it is dangerous for a girl to be so beautiful in this time and age."

I remembered also the words of the magistrate, that the one thing in common among the missing girls was that they were pretty. "With a beautiful daughter like Lady Moon," I said slowly, "would he not be concerned for her safety? Girls are going missing here in Nowon. What has he done to stop that?"

"He has made several reports, submitted them to Magistrate Hong's office, but each time his reports were dismissed due to lack of evidence."

Lack of evidence. A thought lit up in my mind. If I could find enough evidence, I could assist the village elder in convincing the magistrate to cooperate . . . I clenched my fingers tight, trying to douse my excitement. My main concern about investigating had been that I had no power—no power to arrest, no power to interrogate. But the village elder? He had the authority where I had none.

"Last night, what was it you told Iseul's family in the forest?" Scholar Yu asked. "I followed her family to see what the commotion was all about and heard you explaining something. You are related to Detective Min in what way?"

I opened my mouth to reply with a lie—about being young Master Gyu, about how I'd come to find my uncle. But I remembered Village Elder Moon's promise to protect me from being sent back home. I also remembered the hostility of the villagers toward me, a foreigner to the Jeju people, even though we were of the same kingdom. And there had been Iseul as well, unable to meet my gaze when speaking to me. If I wanted her to open up, I could not be a nobleman from the peninsula.

"I am Min Hwani," I whispered, clutching the journal tight. "Daughter of Detective Min."

At the end of the main house was indeed a workroom; the wooden doors were opened onto a girl with sunburned skin. She sat cross-legged on the wooden floor, weaving jipsin—straw shoes. At her feet lay a bundle of straw and loops of saekki rope. She worked slowly, like she wanted an excuse to stay alone in this small room for as long as possible.

My journal tucked between my arm and side, I waited for her to look my way. But when she didn't, I called out—as gently as I would to a wounded bird. "Good afternoon."

She looked up, her lips pale. She didn't look glad to see me.

"I wasn't able to ask you many questions last night, but I'd like to continue, if you would let me."

She rose to her feet and hurried down the stone steps to stand before me, hands gathered and head bowed in supplication. "Please excuse me, young master, I should go—"

"I am Hwani. Min Hwani," I said. "I am Detective Min's other daughter."

Confused suspicion clouded her face.

"It is dangerous for a young woman to travel alone," I explained, "so I had no choice but to disguise myself, though I have no need for it anymore."

Understanding seemed to dawn in her eyes, and as it did, her expression softened. "Detective Min did mention a second daughter . . . Now that I think of it, your eyes look exactly like his. Mistress Min."

I'd never thought I resembled Father, but two people today had already mentioned this. "Then you must understand why I am most determined to find answers. If I can find out what happened to your sister, I am sure I'll also discover what happened to my father."

She shook her head and, in a despondent voice, said, "I had so much hope when Detective Min approached me, promising to help find my sister." She dug her nail into her thumb, as though attempting to ease her inner turmoil with pain. "But now there is no point investigating my sister's death, Mistress Min."

"Why not?"

"The detective is gone. And when I requested audience with the magistrate this morning, he said he'd heard rumors of the way men looked at my sister, that she was one of the prettiest in this village. He said my sister must have run away with a man. That she must have plunged herself down the slope out of guilt. He said"—her nostrils flared as she took in a deep, aching breath—"that such cases were unworthy of his attention."

An incompetent magistrate who ignored suspicious circumstances. Clearly, he was the local tyrant of this village, whom no one—not even the village elder—seemed capable of challenging.

"She would be fourteen now," Iseul said, a muscle in her jaw working. "She was thirteen when she went missing. How could someone so young have a lover? And if she did have a lover, how could she still be a virgin after having lived with her lover for an entire year?"

My hand that clutched the journal weakened. A pretty girl, missing for an entire year. I'd assumed the most gruesome and abhorrent crimes would have been committed against her during that time, but she was still a virgin. "Are you certain?"

"The midwife is my aunt, and she examined Hyunok quickly. We knew Magistrate Hong would have buried her without an examination; he is like that. So we did it ourselves. We examined Hyunok, and my aunt concluded that my sister hadn't been harmed in . . . *that* way. Besides the bruises caused from the fall, there were no marks on her person, no signs of violence at all."

"Gone for an entire year, held captive by a stranger . . ." I spoke my thoughts aloud, unable to process them. "Untouched. Unharmed. How curious . . . Surely the strangeness of this case would draw the magistrate's attention?"

"The magistrate cares for naught. He is an idle man who has no interest in wielding justice." A quick, bitter laugh escaped her. "But he is very diligent about finding all the ways to steal from us."

"How so?"

A look of hesitation crossed her face. Then she shook her head. "I shouldn't say more. I could get in trouble."

"If you think I would expose you," I rushed to say, "I promise—I promise on my mother's grave and upon my father's life—that your secrets are safe with me."

Her knuckles had turned white; she was digging all her nails into her palm now. Nervous. Untrusting.

"Please. I don't care about the magistrate," I said in a quiet voice. "I just want to find who is behind all the disappearances."

Her hesitation lasted for a few more moments. Then she

looked around before ushering me inside the workroom. Once I stepped in, she finally whispered, "He is a callous man, the magistrate. He burdens us with heavy taxes for all sorts of reasons. I do not even think it is allowed. A few years ago, Mr. Cho went around collecting petitions begging the magistrate to remove the taxation injustices. But, of course, the magistrate ignored the pleas. He even had Mr. Cho executed. It is *this* man, Mistress Min, who is in charge of justice here." Iseul shook her head, then, in a sign of defeat, threw her hand in the air. "My sister is gone, and no one will find the killer."

"I *will* help you," I said.

Her clear brown eyes met mine. A bold move of a servant to stare her superior in the eyes, but I didn't care.

"I promise."

A pause ensued, then determination sharpened in her eyes as she ushered me to sit down. "No one will hear us here, Mistress Min," she said, settling beside me. "What did you want to ask me?"

I set up the inkstone and held my brush tight, ready to jot down her responses. "Were you close to your sister?"

"We were born eight years apart, my sister and I. So I was old enough to . . ." She closed her eyes, her jaws clenched as though she were fighting for composure. And when she spoke, her voice sounded raw, prickling with grief. "To hold her when she was just born. She was so tiny. I could hold her in the palms of my two hands."

"When did you last see your sister?"

"The night before her disappearance, a year ago."

I jotted this information down in my journal. "Did anything stand out to you that night?"

"Yes," she whispered. "I told this to Detective Min as well, but before my sister disappeared, two odd things happened. The first is that on the night of her disappearance, there was a report of a horse and wagon filled with hay, sighted right outside the village tethered to a tree. No one knew who it belonged to."

"And the second . . . ?" I said.

"My sister told me someone was following her. I noticed it was Convict Baek, and I told Mother of this. Mother, of course, was terrified by the rumors going around—that someone was kidnapping girls. So she confronted Convict Baek, and he growled at her that one ought to hide their daughters. 'Don't let them wander the island. There are bad people out there,' he said. And then he walked off. I thought it so odd."

My pulse quickened. "Who is Convict Baek?"

"Lord Baek Hyosung. But he was stripped of his title and exiled to Jeju after his father attempted a coup. His father was a large, angry man, and when the king sent his servants to execute him with arsenic, he wouldn't die. So Village Elder Moon had to find more arsenic. It took an entire week to kill the man. And like the father, his son too is an angry man. We began referring to him as Convict Baek."

I twirled this new information around in my mind.

"Would you have any reason to think that Convict Baek would want to harm your sister?"

Iseul froze, and I could read the signs of distress surfacing on her—the red staining her cheeks, the way her chest rose and fell in quick succession.

I asked again, slowly, "Did Convict Baek have any reason to hurt Hyunok?"

She wiped her brows. "It's all my fault," she whispered. "I shouldn't have . . ."

"Shouldn't have what?"

"We borrowed so much that it couldn't be easily paid back."

"From him? What did you need all that money for?"

"For Shaman Nokyung."

My heart froze. "What? Why?"

"Hyunok was born with an ominous prophecy over her, and the fate-changing ritual is costly. We soon fell into debt, and Convict Baek offered to loan us bags of rice to pay the shaman with—as long as we paid it back in increments. But he never told us about the interest that would end up growing faster than we could catch up to."

"What was the prophecy?"

"Shaman Nokyung told Mother when my little sister was born: *When the cloud hides the moon, and the sea rages in the wind, the man whose face is covered will come, and your youngest daughter will be lost.*"

"And you believed the prophecy?"

"Yes." Her voice had dwindled into the barest whisper.

I worried my lower lip, and a string of dread unfurled within me. *Belief.* From what I'd learned from reading Father's old journals, belief was the oldest story ever told. It was a desperation, a need to cling on to something that gave our life meaning, something that would help us find our place in this kingdom. But to me, belief without evidence was superstition, and superstition was what the weak clung to. Shaman Nokyung had chosen to either profit from the fear of others without truly knowing their future, or there was another reason why she had known, years in advance, that Hyunok would one day meet a terrible end.

"Begging your pardon, Mistress Min, but you are so young," Iseul said, a note of hopelessness sinking her voice. "Do you really think you can solve what your father was unable to figure out?"

It was the first time anyone had asked this of me. I blinked, struck by the weight of that question. And without thought the answer came out of me: "He may not have solved it, but he must have found an answer—that is why he disappeared. I just need to find the trail he left behind and follow it."

"Yes, he must have found the answer. The greatest detective in Joseon, they called him . . ." As her voice trickled away, a strange expression shifted across her face; it began with a twitch, then the furrowing of brows, punctuated by the widening of eyes. "I remember."

"Remember what?" I asked, my heart oddly picking up speed.

She stared at me, her eyes so wide I could see the whites. "When Detective Min was investigating, he stayed here at this inn, and I remember which room, for we had to inspect it several times for insects. He swore his room was infested, but it was not—there is a new customer staying there, and he has not seen a single insect in it. Then on the day your father disappeared, he acted so strangely, looking ill and telling us how tired he was from insects keeping him up all night. We were sure that he was going mad. I also overheard him tell the innkeeper he was going to a place with hostile and remembering eyes, to cleanse his conscience and hopefully face his daughter one day without shame. I could never figure out what he meant by this."

A chill ran down my spine. Iseul had echoed the riddle Father had left behind in his chamber. *Hostile and still, with remembering eyes* were the exact words Father had used to describe the eyes watching him from the forest. Had he been referring to the Forest Incident? The incident I could not remember, and there was a growing fear in me that all the answers to Father's disappearance were in the blank space between where my memory ended and began.

I needed to remember. If the truth behind Father's disappearance was somewhere in my mind, then never remembering might mean never finding him. And it would be my fault.

Panic fluttered in my chest. I looked down and noticed

I'd unconsciously written a note in my journal: *Go to the forest.*

I pressed my fingers into my eyelids, hard, then looked around. I could see the workroom, the bundle of saekki rope, and Iseul's round face. I turned, glancing over my shoulder, and saw the sky, so clear and blue. It was the perfect weather to venture into the woods, even though I'd promised Father to never enter it alone.

But I had to. It was for him.

SIX

HAD NO MEMORY OF ENTERING the forest five years ago, nor of leaving it. But I did recall the morning of the incident: I'd woken up to Father's plan to pay respects to our grandfather at his burial mound, and on the way we would visit Shaman Nokyung. We owed her payment for the pudakgeori, the ghost-ridding ceremony meant to save Maewol from her shamanic calling.

Mother would have joined, but with her being ill, she'd stayed behind while the three of us—Father, Maewol, and I—rode off. Father wore his black robe with gold embroidery; Maewol and I were dressed as boys.

That was all. The next thing I remembered was blinking up at the frightened eyes of my parents.

You're awake, Father had whispered, then had glanced over his shoulder at the sound of horse hooves rumbling to a halt outside. *He's here—the village elder. He needs to put together a report of the incident, so he will have to question you.*

What happened? I'd asked. *What did I do wrong?*

And that's when Father and Mother had discovered that I had absolutely no memory of the Forest Incident. That must have also been when I first encountered Village Elder Moon; the confusion of the moment must have wiped him from my memory.

I kicked the pony's sides, clicking my tongue. I'd spent too much time roaming the village, trying to reacquaint myself with its people and streets. There was no time to waste now. I rode for at least an hour, past the shadowy ridges of oreum hills, past the shaman's hut with its glowing paper screens, and continued on for a half hour or so. The damp cold soaked into my skin, and the sky had darkened even though it was early yet. The night always descended quicker in autumn; I hadn't accounted for that on my journey here.

Biting my lower lip, I glanced over my shoulder. The hut was now so far away I couldn't see it in the distance. It was too late to turn back.

"It's just a forest," I whispered to myself, running my finger over the whistle that hung from my string necklace. I urged the pony faster until we reached the foot of the mountain.

The wind-whipped trees grew tall as we approached, and soon I had to crane my neck to stare up at the shadowy treetops swaying against the sky, surrounding me in all directions. Surely I would find the memory I'd left behind in the forest if I tried.

Once the forest grew too dark, I dared not venture in any deeper, lest I lose my way.

I dismounted, and with the pony's reins securely tethered, I took a few steps forward and stood still. I examined everything—the silhouettes of ancient trees, the wild mushrooms and crawling roots that embraced large boulders. Thick moss carpeted the forest floor, my feet sinking with each step. I peered into the cracks in the woodland, the deep crevices filled with shadows, wondering if I'd find my memory within. Would I see Maewol throwing a tantrum, refusing to venture any farther? Would I see her running away? Would I see Father and me searching for Maewol, only to get lost myself?

Or would I see something else entirely?

I waited. I couldn't tell how much time had passed, but it was growing so chilly that my teeth were chattering. No memory drifted into my mind, and I didn't know how much longer my stubbornness would last.

"Min Hwani," I whispered to myself, "you *need* to remember what happened." I squeezed my eyes shut and pressed my fingers into my eyelids. Under them, shapes of light rippled across the darkness. Still I waited, listening to the disorienting noises around me: the crashing cascade of creaking trees, snapping limbs, and the roar of the wind through treetops.

Then, slowly, the white shapes under my eyelids branched

out into trees that arched over three riders. It looked like Father, Maewol, and me.

I frowned, my eyes still closed. Was this a memory or a figment of my imagination?

The shapes shifted, and I noticed a large tree covered in what looked like warts and wrinkles. It reminded me of the Grandmother Tree, a nickname my sister and I had come up with for the tree we would hide our secret messages to each other in.

I pressed my fingers deeper into my eyes until they throbbed with pain. I waited for the streaks of light to shift again, to show me something more. But the forest would not budge. It wouldn't let me enter deeper into the memory—if it was a memory at all.

A startled neigh pierced the night.

My eyes shot open and I whirled around to see a silhouette standing before my pony—a tall figure with hair tied into a topknot. When he raised his torch, the blazing light illuminated a face that wore a painted-white mask with three red dots—one on the forehead, and one on each cheek. I'd seen this mask before. My mind scrambled through all the books I'd read and stopped at a memory. It was a hahoetel mask named the punae, the concubine.

Breathless with fear, I took a step back, my gaze unwavering on the mask—the closed eyes, the smiling red lips. The mist and darkness of the forest seemed to accentuate the mask's mischievous and cruel glint.

"Wh-what do you want?" I asked. "Are you lost—?"

A sword flashed out from a scabbard, and my hands flew to my mouth, muffling a cry. I hadn't seen it in the dark, but now the blade swung through the torchlight with one quick slash, cutting loose my pony. At once, the frightened creature galloped away, leaving me behind among towering trees and a sword pointed at me.

I took a step back; the Mask moved forward. That blade was meant for me. Without a second thought, I turned and ran as fast as my legs could take me.

I turned a sharp corner around a boulder, slid and stumbled down a slope. I kept running, blood roaring in my ears, so loud that it took time for me to realize that footsteps were not chasing after me. When I glanced over my shoulder, I saw nothing but mist tinted blue in the moonlight. My legs wobbled, and I crawled to hide behind a tree; I pressed my back hard against the trunk, my heart pounding rapidly against my chest. Who was this person? Why was he wearing a mask?

Then realization struck me.

The evidence tying the two cases together, of the Forest Incident and the missing thirteen . . . was the masked man. He had been sighted in both cases. And now he had come for me.

I clenched my shaking hands together, resisting the icy wave of panic that lapped against me. *I am safe*, I told myself, *I am safe now*. By the time I'd counted to one hundred, my heart beat steadier and I was no longer gasping for air. I shifted, the leaves rustling under me as I moved to make sure I was alone. Craning my head, I glanced beyond the trunk—and a cold sharpness touched the bottom of my chin.

My stomach dropped away. A silent scream filled my chest as I stayed still. But the icy object pressed my chin upward until I was staring, wide-eyed, along the gleaming blade up to the smiling mask, flickering orange in the torchlight.

"Please . . . ," I whispered. "Please let me go."

The sword hovered by my neck.

"Please," I tried again.

The blade flashed as he swung the sword, and I squeezed my eyes, waiting for the slash of pain.

But I felt none.

I opened my eyes to see the blade stuck on a thick piece of wood—a branch held by my little sister.

Maewol . . . What was Maewol doing here?!

She pulled away, and the Mask swiped his sword at her chest, only missing by a sliver. A sliced piece of Maewol's sleeve fluttered as she staggered away. And she should have stayed away, yet she came running back, yelling, and with all her might—the might of doing chores all day for Shaman Nokyung, going up the mountain and collecting wood, lugging around large brown jugs of fresh water—she swung the stick across the man's face.

His mask fell off, and he whirled away to collect it, hand covering his face.

My sister grabbed my wrist. "Run!"

At once we were fleeing, leaping over roots and rocks, leaves and branches scratching us. We reached a steep slope, and without a thought, Maewol hurtled down, steadying her footing on roots and clinging onto trees as she went. I tried to do the same, but I tripped over a rock and went whirling and thumping down like a sack of rice. It all happened so fast I couldn't feel anything until my body hit the slope's bottom. Pain pulsed where my skin had been gashed open. But the pain felt like nothing compared to the stabbing fear.

Run.

Maewol grabbed my wrist and dragged me up, slinging my arm around her shoulder to steady my whirling universe. We staggered forward, constantly glancing over our shoulders, convinced that at any moment, the fog would part for the smiling white mask. But instead, a phantom memory formed before my mind's eye:

Father holding me in his arms, staggering through a veil of fog as thick as the one before me now, ducking sharp branches as he leaped over snowy mounds down the slope. Bloody scratches across his pale, pale face, though none on mine. His arms tight around me, a girl small enough then to fit into his embrace. His large hand covering my ear, pressing my cheek close to his heart. Next to him was his manservant, carrying Maewol in the same way, looking as terrified.

As though my thought had beckoned it, the fog parted. Tendrils of smokelike wisps curled away as the Mask stepped through, walking so slowly, so surely, as though he knew with certainty that it was only a matter of time before he found and killed us. But he hadn't spotted us yet.

Seeing a large tree, I clamped my free hand over Maewol's mouth and shoved her to the side. I forced her to crouch next to me, shoulder to shoulder, behind the tree. Her wild eyes demanded answers as I removed my hand.

She tried to speak, but I quickly placed a finger to my lips and pointed back to the direction we'd come. She glanced around the tree, then whirled back, slamming against the trunk.

We both remained still. Unmoving. Behind the trunk, barely wide enough to hide us both. I realized the edge of my robe was sticking out. I tucked it back in, rustling the leaves.

His footsteps, crunching down the slope, paused.

Blood roared in my ears.

My sister's hands were trembling.

We remained this way for what felt like an eternity. Then the footsteps continued, but not toward us. Soon all we could hear was the forest thrashing in the wind. Still, we couldn't be too cautious. I placed a hand on Maewol to prevent her from moving and counted all the way to three thousand in my head.

"He's gone," I finally whispered, my voice still shaking, my eyes still surveying the darkness. "We're safe now."

"Gods," Maewol said, "gods, we nearly died."

We fell silent, both of us in utter disbelief.

Then I stared quizzically at her. "How did you find me?"

"I sensed something ominous," she said, like it was a matter of fact. "Then I saw you pass by the hut. And I know you—you always get lost. So I followed. Why did you come *here*?"

"In Father's note, he wrote that hostile eyes watched him from the forest," I said, calmly at first, but soon the words rushed from my lips. "He *had* to have meant this forest, where the incident occurred. The note he left, along with Hyunok's body also being found in this area—there has to be a connection. And now the masked man appears here too! There is something terrible indeed occurring in these woods. If I can remember what happened five years ago, I think I'll be able to find Father—"

"You need to stop looking for Father."

At the strained note in her voice, I turned my eyes to her. Shock punched my chest at the sight of her red-rimmed stare, burning with anger. "Why?"

Her voice thinned into something quiet and dark. "You used to always call him the greatest detective in Joseon."

"Because he is."

"He's not as great as you think him to be."

"How could you say that? Father came back for *you*," I hissed, resentment sharpening in my chest. I had done everything for Father, and he had come back to this horrible place for this ungrateful daughter. "You really can't think or see beyond your own feelings, can you? You only see your own hurt; it blinds you to how much Father sacrificed for you."

A humorless smile curved her lips, making her look mean. "Do you know what the forest taught me that night?" she asked, her bitter voice thick with honey. "That in my next life, I would not want to be his daughter."

"What?" My skin prickled with cold, horrified that my little sister could speak so ill of a father who'd gone missing. "How could you say—"

"And I would not want to be your sister either."

seven

THE FATHER I KNEW MADE no mistakes. He calculated his every move a thousand times before making a decision. Yet the acidity in Maewol's voice made me question him for the first time in my eighteen years of life.

I lifted my bronze hand mirror, a new one I'd purchased from a merchant at the inn, and saw a stormy cloud had descended upon my brows. It felt like everything in me was crumbling; soon I might even see cracks form across my own face.

"You mustn't," I whispered to my reflection. "You mustn't doubt him. He's your father. Your *father.*"

I repeated the words over and over until the doubt quieted in me, for now. Letting out a breath, I dipped a cloth into a bowl of warm water and wiped the blood that had smeared from the deep scratch on my right cheek.

When Maewol and I had limped our way back to the hut,

we'd found my pony had returned home; Shaman Nokyung was securing the frightened creature in the stable. She'd caught sight of us, bloody, our clothes torn.

"Min Hwani," she said, "I knew the trouble you would cause when you came." Then she turned her stern eyes to my sister. "And you, Min Maewol, you come with me."

They were now in the room across from me, the shadowy wood-floored sangbang between us. I'd left the door to my room open, allowing me to see the candlelight illuminating my sister's paper-screened door. Shaman Nokyung's silhouette moved as she tended to Maewol with the gentleness of a grandmother.

And I was here, alone.

I forced my gaze away. The longer I stared, the wider and emptier the space around me seemed.

I dipped the cloth back into the water, twisted it and watched blood unfurl. I'd never seen so much of my own blood. Raising the mirror again, I pressed the cloth against the deepest gash right above my left eyebrow and winced. A sharp branch must have smacked my face while Maewol and I had run and stumbled through the dark forest. Right then, I thought I saw darkness shift against the bronze reflector. I blinked and quickly set the mirror back down, afraid that if I stared too long at the space behind me, I'd see the white-painted mask materialize in the shadows, eyes closed and lips smiling.

I kept myself busy, trying not to remember. I continued to

wipe my face until the wounds felt clean, no longer covered in dirt or flecks of tree bark. I then slowly lifted the skirt of my robe. My undergarment, torn, revealed skin ripped and scratched. It didn't hurt too much, but never had I seen so much blood. There weren't too many opportunities that would leave me with deep slices while sealed within a mansion, packed with cautious and bowing servants. Except when I upset my aunt.

I pressed the wet cloth against the long gash that ran down my knee, down the calf, stopping right above my ankle. It stung, yet the pain was a mere pinch compared to Aunt Min's beatings. When she was upset, she would wait for Father to leave before striking my calves with a thin stick, and the humiliation of it had made the cuts all the more excruciating. She would always say, "Your father spoiled you, so it is my duty to instruct you on how to be a good woman, or else your husband will beat you instead."

I'd never told Father of these incidents; I'd never shown him the thin scars on my legs. I couldn't. Father had lost our mother; I didn't want to be responsible for him losing his sister too—

The door slid open, and I quickly pulled the robe over my torn undergarment and struggled to my feet, clenching my teeth against the ache. Shaman Nokyung stepped out with a tray that carried a wet cloth and a bowl of bloody water. Maewol's blood. I lowered my gaze, ashamed of what I'd gotten my sister into, and I waited for the shaman to walk past me. But she paused and said, "Maewol told me what happened."

"Yes, she must have," I whispered. "A masked man attacked us. His mask fell off, but I didn't get the chance to look at his face . . ."

It had to be Convict Baek, I thought. Everyone in the village was scared of him, that was what Iseul had told me. But—

I lifted my gaze to meet Shaman Nokyung's unwavering and angry stare.

But Iseul had also mentioned the shaman's name, the debt she'd put the family in. Dread coiled in my chest. The villagers had no idea, did they, of how the shaman was using their grief for her own gain. They trusted her. And Maewol trusted her too.

Perhaps too much.

"Do you know," Shaman Nokyung murmured, "the last thing Maewol said before running out was that her sister needed her? I told her not to get involved, and I was right to worry."

"Why do you care about her so much?" I asked. "You know, ajimang, my aunt has mentioned bringing her back to the mainland." It was a lie. Aunt Min had barely agreed to take care of even me. "To live with us."

The shaman's stare wavered, and she suddenly appeared fragile and disoriented. She was imagining, perhaps, life without Maewol. "You wish to know why I care so much . . ."

I stared, waiting.

"I once had a daughter, but when she left me, I felt a pain that would never go away. I used to set the table for two. But then there was only one." Her lashes lowered, drawing a curtain over her eyes, over her agony, or perhaps her lies. "One day Maewol snuck into my life and has not left it since. She takes care of me in my old age; she boils jeoseulsari roots every week to make herbal medicine for my aching limbs." She finally looked up and examined me—my eyes, my nose, my ears. "You know, you can lose family, Min Hwani. Family whom you loved more than life. But you can also find family—those who come into your life a stranger yet make you feel as though you've known them for all your life . . . Go home, Hwani-yah. Move on. Find your place and your true family. Your father is not here—I sense it. The gods have told me."

If I could, I would have taken the bowl of blood-water she carried and thrown it in her face. But Aunt Min had taught me over the span of five years how to be a lady.

A quiet laugh escaped me. "Did you also sense the victim Hyunok's fate? Did you know she would die in the forest?"

"I sensed something terrible would happen."

I couldn't believe her, this thief, this con woman.

"You are on Jeju, the island of eighteen thousand gods, and yet you do not believe in the spirit world?" the shaman said. "Have you never caught the scent of a faraway land in the wind? I always sense that there is far more to this world than what our two eyes can behold. I swear to you, beyond the folds of the earth, sea, and sky resides an invisible realm."

"You sense that another layer to this world exists," I retorted. "Perhaps you're right. But that means nothing to me. Can you actually foresee which girls will go missing? Then give a list of all the girls to me now. Let me deliver the names to the magistrate to keep them safe."

"I sense darkness over people and places," Shaman Nokyung explained, "but I cannot determine what the darkness is made of. I had no idea Hyunok would end up murdered."

"Yet you still put villagers in debt. They believe that you're able to change their future—"

"Enough," Shaman Nokyung snapped. "You can investigate all you want, but I came to you to say this: Don't get Maewol involved. The masked man killed your father. Don't think he will not kill you and your sister if you are not careful. And do not even consider taking Maewol back to the mainland. Her shamanic calling will rebel against that, and she will also not accept it so easily. Maewol has not yet forgiven her father."

I stood still, disturbed by the same haunting question from earlier: What *had* my father done? Both Shaman Nokyung and Maewol spoke of a wrong that had occurred, which I knew nothing about.

"I don't understand," I whispered, and half regretted that I'd interrogated the shaman. For she knew the truth about my sister, a truth I was desperate to understand. Sliding a note of politeness into my voice, I asked, "Why does Maewol resent my father so?"

"I will tell you if you promise to convince your aunt not to take her."

I turned her request over in my mind. There was nothing to lose in agreeing to this. After all, I'd never imagined Maewol living with Aunt Min and me. Such a life would have left her miserable, as it had left me. "I will."

She hesitated, then glanced over her shoulder at the room where Maewol was. She must have realized Maewol could easily eavesdrop. She put down the tray. "Follow me. Let your sister rest. We have a long day tomorrow—the public kut I told you about."

A public ritual where many of the villagers would gather— to be scammed, all at once. I didn't say anything though, and quietly followed her into her personal quarter. Shaman Nokyung sat down and lit a candle, which illuminated the pile of coins on her low-legged table. She'd been counting them, it seemed. Money fished from starving villagers.

I'd always heard that shamans possessed great fortune, even on this harsh and lonely island. I hadn't realized how true this was until now.

With a sweep of her hand, she slid the great heap of coins into a pouch and placed it inside the drawer of a lacquered cabinet. Inside, I caught a quick glimpse of a small object, but before I could examine it any longer, she shut and locked the drawer, hanging the key around her neck.

"Sit down," she ordered.

I obeyed, carefully crossing my wounded legs, back straight, hands folded in my lap.

With her twig-thin fingers, she slid open another drawer and took out a pipe, silver like those belonging to nobility. She lit it, and smoke curled from her lips, the tobacco easing the lines of pain etched into her face.

"Every year your father told Maewol that he would bring your family together. Perhaps he truly did mean it, but he'd forget it as soon as he returned to the police bureau, drunk on his title. As everyone would say, he was the greatest detective in Joseon," she muttered, her lips twisting. "Yet he forgot how to be a great *father*."

"He *was* a great father," I protested.

"To you," she said pointedly. "To you, his favorite, his most obedient and filial daughter, of course he was. But to Maewol?"

"I know Father left her behind in Jeju, but that was because *you* told us her shamanic calling would be deadly if resisted! And after the Forest Incident, Father believed you. But he had to leave; he knew how powerless he was. An officer who serves in an idle and corrupt police bureau has no real authority to investigate. So he had to accept Commander Ki's offer to be promoted, to try to protect us," I said. "But he still visited Maewol as often as he could. He's missing now because he came back for her."

Shaman Nokyung watched me. "So . . . *do* you want to know the truth of what happened in the forest five years ago? Or will you raise a protest over everything I say?"

The outrage in me lost its steam. "I do," I said sheepishly. "I do want to know."

"Very well." She took a few puffs from her pipe, as though trying to calm her nerves. Despite the steadiness of her gaze, her hands were shaking, and it took a while before she said, "The day of the incident, Maewol threw a tantrum. She didn't want to go into the forest. She was scared and sensed something"—a frown flickered across the shaman's brows—"something terrible would happen.

"I was once a mother too. I had a girl who always threw tantrums, like Maewol. When my daughter was a child and cried too long, I would always tell her tales about a tiger that would descend into the village to devour crying children."

"Where is your daughter now?" I interrupted without meaning to. The urge had been too powerful. I had never seen her daughter before.

A ghost of a shadow crossed her face. "Gone. Disappeared. Back when I lived elsewhere." She waved her hand, as though to disperse my curiosity. "As I was saying, I told my daughter stories of child-eating tigers so she would stay quiet. But . . . children cry. They misbehave. It is to be expected. But your father, unfortunately, did not just tell his daughter a tale.

Your father was a militant man, a man of strict discipline. He punished Maewol."

The muscles in my body had stiffened to the point of pain. "How did he punish her?"

She didn't answer me. Instead, she said, "It would always hurt my heart, as it did your mother's, seeing how harshly he raised you two—always expecting perfect obedience. He was unforgiving, Hwani-yah. And Maewol still remembers that incident as though it were yesterday. She is still trapped in that forest where her father abandoned her, to teach her a lesson. The forest of his wrath."

I remember, once, finding the doors to Father's study locked. No one was to enter—not the servants, not my aunt, and not even me. Later, when he'd come out, I'd caught a glimpse of his eyes: red, puffy, wet. And frightened. I had dared not ask why my father, who had braved hundreds of cold-blooded murderers, had been weeping alone. It had been the day he'd returned from his first trip to Jeju, to visit Maewol.

He was the greatest detective in Joseon, Shaman Nokyung's words echoed in my ear. *Yet he forgot how to be a great* father.

I closed my eyes, lying on the sleeping mat of my room. *Father must have known*, I realized. He had known that he'd failed Maewol that day in the forest. He had tried to undo his errors, to undo his sins, but he had failed again. Now he was missing, and Maewol was still angry. And weight of it all sat heavy on my chest. I was the eldest; I should have known, I should have written more letters to Maewol. Letters that might have stitched the gap between her and Father.

I gave up on sleep and left my room, wandered down the veranda outside, breathing in the air that was cool enough to soothe the uneasiness in my chest. I stopped before my sister's quarter. The lights were on inside her room, even though it was long past midnight.

I leaned toward the hanji door and said, "Maewol-ah?" I waited, but no one answered. "I need to talk to you. Are you asleep?"

Silence continued on the other side. Then a note slid out from between the door: *No.*

I stared down at the note, remembering when we were young. When Maewol would write me notes, detailing her concerns, requesting the wisdom of her older sister. Even then, we hadn't talked much to each other outside of our letter exchanges.

"Why not?" I whispered.

Another pause, but this time I strained my ears and could hear the faint sound of paper rustling, of the calligraphy brush tapping against inkstone. Another note appeared, Maewol's brushstrokes splotchy and smeared: *What if the Mask comes? We need to stay awake and keep watch.*

I chewed my thumbnail, something I'd stopped doing over the years because Aunt Min would dip my fingers into a nasty-tasting rice vinegar. But ever since I'd come to Jeju, the habit had returned with a vengeance. My nails were cracked and bleeding from the anxiety of looking for Father—and now, the sinking sensation that I should never have dragged my sister into this.

I took a retreating step. I had no right to ask her about the Forest Incident. I'd nearly gotten her killed today.

I turned, meaning to leave, when the sound of paper sliding against wood caught me off guard. I looked to see yet another note:

I overheard you and Shaman Nokyung speaking.

My hand dropped to my side, and I tried to reply, yet no word would form. I didn't know what to say.

Maewol wrote: *If I told you what happened, would you even believe me?*

"I promise I will. Just this once . . . please let me prove to you that you can trust me."

I'll tell you, she wrote, *if you tell me what you'll do if you find Father dead. Will you go back to the mainland?*

The weight of her question settled heavily upon me. I wanted the truth from Maewol; it was only right that I give her my own. Raw and honest, all my defenses down.

I lowered myself to the ground and stretched out my legs—carefully, to avoid touching my wounds—and stared up at the pitch-dark sky. "Yes. I'm going to get married to the man of Aunt Min's picking and move across the kingdom to his home. I will be expected to care for his elderly parents."

Do you love him?

"I don't even know him."

You never listen to Shaman Nokyung or me. Why listen to Aunt Min?

"Because I saw Father's delight," I whispered. His smile had stretched from ear to ear, the widest smile I'd ever seen since Mother's passing. "A young man, whose father was a retired military official and a family friend of Aunt Min's deceased husband, had shown interest in asking for my hand. They must have wanted to forge an alliance with Father. As for Father, he simply wanted a grandchild . . ."

The birth of a child is a new life for everyone, he had said, *and I've not held a baby in my arms since Maewol was born.*

"After seeing him so glad, I just couldn't say no. Besides, it is the way of life for women to marry and bear children."

Behind the door, I could hear Maewol furiously scribbling away. A note was shoved through the door's side: *Your life isn't meant to be used up to fulfill another person's dream. That's what Mother told me. And I'm sure if Father had known your true feelings he would have said the same.*

A long and heavy blanket of silence settled around me, and I sank deep into my own thoughts. I didn't know how to *be* if I was not pleasing Father or my elders.

I closed my eyes for a moment, my eyelids scratchy from the sudden wave of exhaustion, but when I opened them again, my limbs were freezing and the sky had lightened into a grayish blue. Surprise shot through me. It seemed a few hours had passed. "Maewol-ah?"

She didn't answer, but the candle was still burning. I rose to my feet, wincing against the sting of my wounded legs, and knocked on the wooden frame of her door before sliding it open, realizing it had never been locked.

Maewol was curled up on the floor, sleeping on a sheet of paper, calligraphy brush in hand. The floor creaked under my step. She woke with a start, her head jolting up, revealing cheeks covered in ink stains and cuts. Her shoulders eased at the sight of me.

"It's cold, Maewol-ah." I blew out the candle, then helped her onto her sleeping mat. I took the thick blanket folded in the corner of her room and spread it out over my sister. "I'll make sure nothing happens to you. I'll sit outside your bed-chamber until the sun comes up."

I owed this to her.

"No, you don't need to—" But after a moment of resistance, she was so tired she gave in easily.

The floor creaked as I tiptoed over to the door. Before I could leave, Maewol whispered, "Do you think we'll die?"

"No," I said, and I meant it. "I won't let us die."

I stepped out, closed the door, and sat on the veranda. The night's biting cold deepened until I could no longer feel my toes. But I stayed still; I stayed near. I wanted Maewol to know that no harm would come her way—not without facing me first.

Wrapping my arms around myself, I watched the sky. Hours must have passed; slowly, the darkness lifted. A bird chirped, twirling through the air, then perching on the stone gate. The rising sun painted the land in shades of purple, and a sheen of mist hovered over the golden grassland.

Then I heard the familiar sound of paper sliding out. A note fell against my feet. At once, I picked it up.

Five years ago, I sensed something wicked in the forest. I told Father we shouldn't go in. But he wouldn't listen. I was so afraid I tried to ride away, but he took my pony's reins and made me follow.

I screamed at him, I think. Father got so angry with me, he told me to get off my horse. When I didn't, he dragged me off and he said to you, "Hwani-yah, let's go. We are leaving your sister behind for the wild animals to eat."

I tried running after, but he yelled at me not to follow. So I stayed by the Grandmother Tree and counted to a hundred three times. When he didn't come back, I tried looking for him, but I was crying so hard I didn't know the direction I was going.

And then I saw a man in a mask wandering through the forest. He was holding a sword, so I ran as fast as I could and hid, and stayed in my hiding place until I heard your voice calling out my name.

After we found each other, we were making our way down the mountain when we stumbled across a young woman at the bottom of a low cliff. You went to inspect her; she was still alive, her legs broken. She told us someone was coming, she told us, "Hide." So we did; we ran and hid behind a rock and listened to the sound of footsteps, followed by her scream. We must have passed out, either from the cold or from terror. It's the only possible reason I could think of as to why Father found us both unconscious by dawn.

That is what happened five years ago. And for five years, Father has visited Jeju eleven times. He would go to speak with the village elder and magistrate, always trying to find out what happened that day in the forest. But he never did try to speak with me. He never even looked at me.

My back stiffened as I read her note, then reread it again, chilled by her words. I felt like I was witnessing someone else's story—not my sister's, not my father's. He wasn't like this. Maewol had to be mistaken—

A whisper tickled my left ear, an echoing memory: *Go bring your sister back now.*

I frowned ahead as the vision of branches moved at the back of my mind. They twisted and snapped, and I could hear the sound of heavy breathing—my breath, ragged from urging my pony to gallop faster. I could remember thinking, *I can't hear my little sister crying anymore; why is she so silent?*

When I had arrived at the spot where we'd left Maewol behind, next to a large ancient tree, I remembered stopping dead in my tracks. She should have been there. She should have known we were going to come back.

But she was gone.

eight

I ROUGHLY TOSSED ASIDE THE ROBE I'd worn the previous night—my disguise, no longer needed, torn to shreds—and pulled a spare hanbok out from my traveling sack: a chima dress and a jeogori jacket, both made of silk. Angrily I shoved myself into the two-piece garment, grabbed my hair and plaited it, tying the end too tightly with a red ribbon.

I didn't know how to wrap my mind around what Father had done. I didn't know what to do with the thorny truth Maewol had placed into my hands. I didn't want to think about it.

The disappointment was unbearable.

For the rest of the morning, I hunched over my journal, gathering my strength to focus on the investigation and only the investigation. I documented everything that had occurred, then tried thinking of all the names that circled around the Forest Incident and the case of the missing thirteen. Whenever my attention drifted back to Maewol's story, I pinched myself hard. *Focus.*

Dipping my calligraphy brush into the ink, I rolled up my sleeve and wrote out the first name I thought of. *Seohyun.* She had died on the day of the Forest Incident.

The next name: *Koh Iseul.* Sister of Hyunok, the victim recently found in the forest.

Convict Baek. Known for his violence and for stalking Hyunok. He was also tied to Hyunok's family in that he'd lent them—and likely others—money that would soon be steeped with interest.

Shaman Nokyung. The reason behind the family's debt. She had claimed to have foreseen Hyunok's doomed future, and had made her family pay for an expensive ritual that was meant to change her fate. In the end, she had still died a horrible death.

Village Elder Moon.

I paused, remembering his promise to help me investigate. He was responsible for reporting to the magistrate. He was the voice of the villagers, yet he'd failed to find enough evidence to sway the magistrate's interest. Or perhaps he had found plenty of evidence, only the magistrate had still ignored the people's pleas to find their daughters.

And, of course, there was the tyrant. *Magistrate Hong.* I wrote his name and circled it. He oppressed his people with heavy taxes and neglected his duty to wield justice.

Boksun. She was the piece to the mystery I couldn't

understand at all, the questions about her still unanswered: Where was she? How did she know Father? She had sent me Father's journal, burnt and hardly legible. And in that journal there had been the fourteen names of likely victims.

I bit the handle of the bamboo brush. To solve a mystery spanning five years, I needed more. Thirteen girls had gone missing; behind each one, there had to be mothers and fathers, sisters and brothers, friends and rivals, acquaintances and witnesses.

I dipped the brush into the ink, hesitated, then wrote: *Father.* What had he discovered? Where had he disappeared to? And why?

As I stared down at the page, my attention drifted and I could hear sounds coming from far away. At first I thought I'd imagined it, but the longer I strained my ears, the clearer it became. The sound of pounding drums. Was this the public kut Shaman Nokyung had referred to?

A memory drifted into my mind: *Learn everything you can. Collect every testimony, every rumor, every suspicion.*

I closed my journal, then tucked it under my arm, picked up my satchel filled with writing equipment, and stepped out of the hut. I needed to gather as much information as I could, and where better to collect it than from the site of a kut? If many villagers were to be there, then among them was bound to be family, friends, or acquaintances of the missing girls. The more stories I had, the clearer it would become who was right, who was wrong, and who had the most reason to be suspected. That was what Father—

I flinched away from the memory of him.

I followed the noise to the foot of Mount Halla, where I saw white charm papers fluttering from a rope, marking the space that housed the ritual. Row after row of women on their knees rocked back and forth under the wide sky as they rubbed their palms in supplication. They moaned and wept, and a man fervently clashed the gong as Maewol beat the drum with all her might. She looked possessed the way her head swung from side to side. To this beat, Shaman Nokyung danced in circles, her hanbok flying around her, as did the red-and-white fan she held.

"We pray to my ancestral spirit!" she chanted. "Please listen to our prayer!"

The noise was so loud, so oppressive, I had no room to think, so it took a while for me to notice the obvious: Many of the kneeling women had pregnant bellies swelling out from their dresses. And Shaman Nokyung, I realized, was supplicating to the gods for sons. She prayed against the curse of daughters being born. A prayer that was uncommon among those living in the coastal areas of Jeju, where survival meant having daughters—for daughters became haenyeo divers who provided for the families, while men stayed home to watch the children or to drink their days away. But Nowon was not a coastal village. People of the mid-slope farming communities had adopted the ways of the sophisticated political convicts sent to live among them. The way of Confucius—one that was rigid and obsessed with sons. Daughters meant hardship and tragedy, which was proving to be the case here in Nowon. Too many mothers had loved and lost their daughters to the beast lurking in this village.

"Con woman," I said under my breath. I opened my journal and took out my calligraphy brush and inkstone. Carefully I circled Shaman Nokyung's name. Thanks to the lurking beast, to the disappearance of daughters, she had a public ritual packed with frightened villagers—and the jingling of coins.

I looked up to see what other details I ought to record, and it was then that my attention caught on a young man swaying through the crowd of villagers, the folds of his dusty robe billowing, a white ceramic bottle clutched in his hand, likely full of wine. It was Scholar Yu. He was irrelevant to my investigation, yet I couldn't look away, observing the way he would pause now and then to eavesdrop on conversations.

When he wandered in my direction, I caught his sleeve. "What are you doing here?"

"Ah, good morning." His eyes twinkled . . . too sharp and aware for a man who ought to be drunk. "Why am I here? As I always say, where there are large gatherings, there will be gossip." He raised the bottle. "I must maintain my reputation somehow as Nowon's gossipmonger."

Taking a swig of his foul drink, he continued on his way, sauntering around the crowd of villagers. I watched him for a few moments longer, at his complete lack of respect for those who were grieving. What a waste of a life, and what a waste of my attention. I crossed the thought of him out from my mind.

I returned to my journal to record my observations of the people around me. When the ritual ended, the women lingered on their knees, still rocking back and forth with their hands pressed to their chest. *How many here have already lost a daughter?* I wrote in my journal. *A sister? A niece?*

Shaman Nokyung had disappeared, and Maewol was running back and forth, collecting and putting away the instruments, but she paused and looked up. Our gazes met for a moment, and I saw young Maewol again, standing alone in the forest.

One, two, three . . . I tore my gaze away, but I could still hear her small voice. *Ninety-eight, ninety-nine . . .*

"Why are you here?" Maewol's voice startled me back to the present, and I glanced up to find that she'd drawn near, only a few steps away. Her face was pale, almost translucent, like there was a secret light glowing within her. And along her cheeks was a constellation of the faintest freckles. I'd forgotten about those.

I cleared my throat. "I need more testimonies."

"Do you want help?"

I blinked at her, unsure of what she meant. She stared at me like nothing had happened this morning, like our honest exchange of words hadn't affected her—

No, Maewol *had* changed. She had offered me assistance. The old Maewol would never have tried to help me.

"How?" I asked.

"Whom do you want to speak with?" she asked.

"I already spoke with Hyunok's sister, so a family member of one of the other missing girls."

Maewol surveyed the crowd, then pointed to a woman with a long, oval face. "Speak with her. She is the mother of Mija, one in the first group to go missing."

"Group—?" Before I could ask my full question, I sensed a prickling sensation that told me I was being watched. When I turned, I saw it wasn't one person watching me, but a whole crowd of women.

Maewol scratched her nose, glancing at me, then back at the crowd. She slipped out a cloth and began to wipe one of the cymbals while she walked away, retreating from me—the target of all eyes.

"Min Hwani," the women whispered. "Is she Min Hwani?"

"She looks just like Detective Min," one of them said. "She must be the elder daughter."

"Kkotnim did say the elder had returned," said another. "It has to be her."

So the servant keeping Father's house had a light mouth; she'd blabbered to the entire village already about my return. I just hoped word hadn't reached Magistrate Hong.

"I am Min Hwani," I said, but the crowd continued to whisper among themselves, as though they hadn't heard me speak.

I pressed on. "My father came to Jeju to help find your daughters, only to go missing himself. Please help me find him."

I turned to look at the woman with the oval face, Mija's mother, but she grabbed the wrist of a young girl—her other daughter perhaps—and whispered, "Let's go home now." She walked off in long strides, her daughter following along at a light run to keep up.

The crowd slowly dispersed as well, eyeing me suspiciously. It appeared everyone would leave, completely ignoring my request. But at length an old, lanky woman hobbled forward, hands gathered behind her back. Her wispy white hair was tied into a bun, and loose strands of it were dancing across her sunburned face. Her pale brown eyes shone like honey, and she seemed to stare into my soul.

"Do not mind the villagers," she said in a loud, raspy voice. "Do not mind their silence. Over the years, they have grown silent in their fear for their children and for themselves. Our village was once warm and kind, but now everyone points fingers at each other. Everyone suspects everyone. So they dare not talk, not when everyone is watching."

"Do you dare not talk as well?" I asked quietly.

"No," she replied. "I have lived too long to be afraid."

"Then . . . whom do you suspect, halmang?"

She pursed her lips and walked closer. "Some days, I think *this* is the person . . ." Her eyes darted to one side of the crowd, then shifted again. "Other days I think it is *that* person. But every day there is no answer."

A long pause ensued as a faraway look glazed her eyes. Her gaze remained there, somewhere in the distance, or even farther than that—perhaps she was looking at someone from five years ago.

"Did . . . did you lose someone?" I dared to ask.

In a bare whisper, she said, "I have become skin and bones because all I can think of is my granddaughter and her friends. I wonder, over and over: How do five girls disappear at once?"

My stomach dropped. "Five at once?"

"They were all friends; they grew up together, our huts near one another. One morning, my twelve-year-old granddaughter runs in to grab her oojang. I ask where she is going with that straw cloak, and before rushing out, she tells me she is heading to the mountain to look for eggs. She didn't come back."

As she spoke, others drifted forward until I was surrounded by a small circle of haggard-looking women, shadows in their eyes, yet eagerness gleamed there too.

One woman with a forehead creased with deep wrinkles spoke next. "I remember that incident. Your granddaughter was one of the first few girls to go missing, wasn't she?"

"She was," the old woman replied. "We searched everywhere, then finally rushed to tell the village elder. He assured us the girls would likely come back the next day, yet they never did. So he reported the disappearance to Magistrate Hong. But when has he ever helped us? That wretched man."

Another woman joined in. Her nose flaring, she angrily gestured at the air. "That wretched magistrate, I can't stand him," she spat. "He told Mija's mother that the girls had run away. Then a year later three more girls went missing. Then one girl, and a few months later, three more. Hyunok was the thirteenth. They were all last seen near the forest, and a few times, witnesses claimed to have seen a man in a white mask nearby. Suspicious, truly suspicious. But do you know what the magistrate kept saying? That they'd run away, that they'd come back. Do you know why? Because he knew that if the girls had truly run away, it wouldn't be his responsibility!"

"Do you remember the names of all the girls missing?" I asked, flipping to the page where I had transcribed the fourteen names from Father's journal.

"Of course, their names still haunt me," the flaring-nose woman said. Raising her hand, she ticked off each finger. "Mija, Dawon, Jia, Yoonhee, Boyeong." She paused before moving on to the next group of missing girls. "Jiyun, Heju, Gayun." She paused again to think. "Eunwoo. Then Bohui, Kyoungja, Mari."

"And the last girl, the thirteenth girl. Hyunok," I whispered as I crossed her name out. I'd crossed out all the names now . . . except one. "Is there a girl named Eunsuk in this village?" I asked.

"Eunsuk?" Flared-nose pursed her lips. "No, no Eunsuk."

The women around me exchanged glances, all whispering among themselves.

"There is no Eunsuk, is there?"

"No, no, I don't think so."

"Isn't that the name of Moonsun's eldest daughter?"

"No, that girl's name is Eunju—"

"I have lived in this village for seventy years," the first old woman interrupted. "There is no Eunsuk."

I rubbed the base of my neck, back and forth over my necklace string, back and forth as my mind narrowed in around a baffling question. Then who was this person, this Eunsuk whose name had made it into Father's list of female names?

"Then," I asked, "does anyone know a woman by the name of Boksun?"

Faces immediately lit up with recognition. "Yes, Boksun used to live in Nowon," Flared-nose said, "but disappeared five years ago."

A shiver ran across my skin, and it took me a moment to find my voice. "When exactly did she disappear?"

"The nineteenth day of the twelfth lunar month," the old woman replied.

I wrote the date down, then paused. Most people couldn't even remember the year the Joseon dynasty had begun, yet this woman remembered a date as obscure as this. Without glancing up, I asked as politely as I could, "How did you remember that date so easily?"

"Because it was two days before that tribute girl named Seohyun died in the same forest that you and your sister were found unconscious in. We all remember *that* date."

I kept my eyes pinned to my journal, suddenly feeling naked.

"Boksun?" A small voice rose from behind the circle of women. "Why does everyone want to know about Boksun?"

The crowd parted, revealing a woman who looked so frail, she might have been made from bird bones.

"I work at the inn, and Convict Baek has been asking around there, asking each merchant and traveler whether they've seen Boksun. He even has a sketch of her face."

Tension gathered in my shoulders at the mention of his name. "I suppose Convict Baek hasn't found her yet, then . . . ," I murmured, half to myself. Then in a clearer voice, I said, "If I wanted to find Boksun, who should I go to?"

"Her hometown is somewhere in the far east," the bird-boned woman said. "But from what I hear, a traveler who visited the place a few years ago said she is not to be found even there. It's like she's vanished from this earth."

Just like Father.

The old woman grunted, and a wisp of her white hair blew across her face. "There is one person you could ask," she said. Her gaze locked with mine. "You could ask the man obsessed with finding her, if you dare. Or . . ." Her gaze strayed to Scholar Yu, who I realized stood at the edge of the crowd, his ear turned to our conversation, even though his gaze was fixed on the hills as he took another swig of wine. "Or you could speak to our gossipmonger. He likely knows a little about everyone here in Nowon Village, even the dead and missing."

"So, are you going to speak with Convict Baek?" Maewol said during our walk back to the shaman's hut. "That halmang is right; he would be the best person you can speak with to find out where Boksun might have disappeared to."

My mind was still lingering on the second name the old woman had mentioned: Scholar Yu. I had tried speaking with him before leaving the public kut, but he had been too drunk by then to assist me. It made me question whether I should rely on his testimony at all, for his knowledge was likely as wobbly as his own knees. "What do you know about Scholar Yu?"

Maewol shrugged. "A drunkard and gambler. He's also very nosy, as you must have noticed. I always see him nosing about at the inn. And he has a soldier that visits his hut every day, to make sure he hasn't tried to escape the island. He's tried several times, apparently."

"Why *was* he exiled to the island?" I asked.

Maewol waved her hand in the air. "I don't know. Something to do with his father, a physician. Poisoned someone important. So they punished the family by sending them here."

"And where is the rest of Scholar Yu's family?"

"In another village. That's what the soldier told me."

Why had Scholar Yu left his family? And why was he so hungry for village gossip? It couldn't be from sheer curiosity.

As I silently brooded, Maewol eagerly said, "You are going to speak with Convict Baek, are you not?"

I shook my head. "I doubt he'll tell me anything—"

"You should search his house." Maewol spoke so fast I knew she must have been thinking of this for a while. "I can't think of any other way to find the truth from him."

I restrained myself from rolling my eyes at this ridiculous notion. But then it occurred to me that she just might be right. Convict Baek might not tell me the truth, but his house would. At the thought of invading his home, my knees weakened and an uneasy laugh escaped me.

"*Of course* you'd think of this method," I said, trying to hide the nervousness that twitched the corners of my lips. "You're an expert at going through my things. You always did leave my room with my most hidden valuables."

"I mean it. He won't talk. He sliced up his daughter's face when she was only twelve, and no one knows why still," Maewol said, and I winced at this information. "A man with too many secrets doesn't open up so easily. It would take time to coax them out. But you don't have time, do you?"

"I'll try speaking with Scholar Yu again, he's the gossip-monger—"

"A drunk gossipmonger," Maewol pointed out. "Not a truth teller."

I took in a few deep breaths until the nervous twitches in my face calmed. "You're right; I didn't say you weren't. But you're not coming with me."

She walked on ahead. "I absolutely will come. You need my help more than you know."

I quickened my steps, trying to catch up with her. "Why are you even helping me?" After all, I was trying to find the father she so despised.

"If I don't help you, you'll get yourself killed, and then in the afterlife you'll haunt me forever. I'm going to help you; don't try to stop me." She halted in her steps, her white hanbok billowing against the vast gray sky. "*Then* you'll leave Jeju. And in one piece."

nine

THE RAIN CAME DOWN, FIRST in dribbles, then in sheets that swept across the rugged contours of the land. But Maewol and I were dry, protected under the canopy of a towering tree with roots that sprawled out like the legs of a spider. A few paces through the blue haze of rain and mist was the hut I'd disgruntledly followed Maewol to—the house of Convict Baek.

"All three logs are down," Maewol whispered.

I glanced at the jeongnang, the two-stone-pillared gate. There were indeed no logs hooked into the gate, which meant *I am home.*

My sister and I waited, and the silence between us left me tense. *One, two, three . . .* I kept thinking of her lost in the forest, of Father's mistake. *Ninety-eight, ninety-nine . . .*

"Do you remember . . . ," Maewol said suddenly, but her words trailed off.

"Remember what?" I asked, my muscles knotting tighter.

"I'm the youngest, but Father always told me to take care of you whenever we went out. You'd always get lost or nearly die from falling off something. That's why I'm here," she said. "To keep you alive."

She was so determined. Since arriving at Convict Baek's hut, she had reminded me three times already that she was helping me *not* because she cared about Father or the investigation, but because she worried I might get myself killed and turn into an angry ghost that would haunt her for all her days. The more she tried, the more I sensed that Maewol was lying through her teeth. Yet I couldn't put my finger on what her truth was.

"I know," I said, playing along, grateful for distraction. "But if I do die, I promise not to haunt you. I have a long list of others I'd rather scare."

Like my aunt.

I returned my attention to the jeongnang fence. A part of me hoped he would remain home so that I could retreat from this dangerous idea, but another part of me waited on the edge for Convict Baek to step out of his home to slip a log or three in between the two pillars. I knew there was no better way to find Boksun—and Convict Baek's secrets.

For if he was anything like me, he would keep his darkest self locked away. I kept mine in the form of a letter, hidden at the bottom of a drawer filled with a stack of blank hanji paper. A farewell letter, apologizing to my aunt and stating how I'd like my inheritance to be used. I had written it when Father had still not returned even when Chuseok had arrived last year—the festival when people traveled all across the kingdom to return to their birthplace to reunite and celebrate with loved ones.

I'd written the letter in the whim of the moment, in need of a way to express my grief—but I knew myself too well to believe I would actually end my life. Even if my worst nightmare came true, I would still do what I was best at doing: live in obedience. I would marry and bear children. It was Father's dream.

When you return home, Hwani-yah, I thought, *you should burn that letter.*

A drop of rain filtered in through the canopy and plopped onto my forehead, dribbling into my eye. I blinked it away and continued to stare at Convict Baek's house. What secret had he hidden inside—perhaps under a piece of furniture, or written out in a dusty journal, or squeezed into a crack in the wall?

"Why do you need to find Boksun anyway?" my sister asked, drawing my attention back to her. She was crouching on the grass, plucking the heads off little white flowers.

"She's the one who sent me Father's journal."

Her head shot up. "*Now* you tell me. Why do you think she sent it to you?"

"I have no idea."

"Maybe she was trying to send you a message . . . Or maybe Father gave it to her to give to you."

I withheld a sigh. "Why would Father send me a burnt journal?" I asked patiently.

"Perhaps it wasn't burnt initially, but something happened . . ."

Maewol went on, whispering every single theory that came to mind—and she had many. Her mind was, as ever, bursting with imagination. I tuned her out, as well as the sound of the rain still pitter-pattering against the leaves above us, and focused on the house. Some time passed, and around noon, when my hands trembled with hunger, I saw movement.

A man walked out of the hut, his face covered by a conical straw hat, with a straw cape tied around his neck. He was tall, and his back was wide; he certainly looked strong enough to swing the sword that had nearly killed me. With ease, he picked up a long, thick log and placed it in between the two stone pillars, meaning *I will return home shortly.*

My pulse thrummed. I glanced at Maewol, whose arms were crossed as she sat napping against the tree. "Jjing-jjinga," I whispered, using the old nickname I'd given her for her frequent whining. "Wake up."

At once, Maewol's eyelids cracked open. "I was just resting my eyes."

"He just left." A flush of tingles raced across my skin. "Let's go."

Rain hit our straw cloaks, held over our heads, as we dashed toward the hut. There was a chance that Convict Baek had servants, so I stopped before the jeongnang and called out, "Is anyone home?" Rain tapped madly upon the straw roof and sluiced across the empty yard. "Anyone?"

"No one's in." Maewol lifted the gleaming wet log off the jeongnang, ushered me to walk through, then lowered the log behind her before catching up with me again. We made our way to the storage room, hid our dripping-wet cloaks behind a large ceramic pot, then wrung the rain out from the hems of our skirts.

"Remember," I whispered, "we get in, then we get out as quick as we can."

A minute later we were wandering through the main house, shoeless. I slid open a door and stepped into the very first room we encountered; it was a small quarter, and there were blankets folded—perhaps the room where their servant slept. In fact, where *was* their servant? I hoped the hut was as empty as I assumed it to be . . . Worrying my lower lip, I stepped out, hurried deeper into the house, and opened the next door.

Maewol peeked into it. "I think this is Gahee's bedroom."

"Who is Gahee?" I asked.

My sister, as though she hadn't heard me, wandered into the room. I ducked inside and quietly closed the door behind us. The white wallpaper was torn here and there. There was a sleeping mat sprawled out on the floor, along with a blanket, twisted as though someone had thrashed awake from a nightmare. There was a worn-out cabinet that reached up to my torso, and when I opened it, I counted ten drawers. But the drawers proved to be empty, save for a few articles found in one: a binyeo made of brass, decorated with bright red glass stones.

"Who is Gahee?" I asked again.

"Convict Baek's daughter."

I nodded slowly, remembering. The daughter with the sliced-up face.

"I know lots about her." Maewol took the binyeo in her hand and raised it. "This hairpin probably belonged to her mother."

"Deceased, I'm assuming?"

Maewol nodded. "Gahee visited the fortune-telling hut many times before. She had nightmares and told us about her poor mother, a Jeju woman she'd never met before. She died giving birth to Gahee, and everyone says it's because Convict Baek worked her so hard—in the kitchen, in the mountains, in their plot of land. And he beat her too. So Gahee asked us to convey a message to the spirit world, to her dead mother."

"About what?"

"To beg her mother to stop giving her dreams . . . dreams of killing her own father."

I frowned, taking the binyeo from Maewol and placing it back in the drawer. "What is Gahee's relationship with her father like?"

"He sliced his daughter's face up when she was twelve, as you know. Apparently, when the villagers demanded answers for his cruelty, he said, 'Perhaps we understand love in a different way. But I do love my daughter. I would give my life up for her. I would kill for her.'"

I shuddered. "He sounds terrible."

Maewol shrugged a small, delicate shoulder. "A father can be both your protector and your worst enemy."

Her words pricked at me. Wanting to get away, I walked off to examine the room some more, then said brusquely, "How old is Gahee now?"

"Nineteen."

I didn't want to be in this room any longer, my sister's remark still lingering in the air. "Let's move on."

We searched through a few more rooms, then finally opened the double doors that led into what appeared to be Convict Baek's quarter. I could already feel the hairs on my arm rising. The quarter was drenched blue in the stormy light. As I examined the soiled handkerchief left on the floor and the half-full chamber pot forgotten in the corner, a disturbing sensation crept up my skin. I was spying into the life of this unsuspecting man, a possible killer.

It didn't take long to find one of his secrets. I opened the scroll of hanji resting on a low-legged table. Maewol crouched next to me, so close I could smell her breath—the scent of sweet persimmon. *My* dried persimmons. Now I understood why they were missing when I'd last inspected my traveling sack. Pushing my annoyance aside, I focused carefully on unrolling the paper and realized there were two papers scrolled into one. One sheet held a detailed map of Jeju, and on it were names of different villages, many of which had been crossed out. The second was a picture of a woman.

"That must be Boksun!" Maewol blurted.

"*Hush*," I said, startled by her loud voice. "It looks like Convict Baek has searched almost all of Jeju for her. Except this area." I pointed at Seogwipo. "We should look for Boksun ourselves, starting here."

I rolled up the scroll and placed it back exactly where it had been: on the desk, angled toward the left, close to a red-lacquered case. Convict Baek would have no idea that his room had been searched.

Right then, Maewol picked up the lacquered case and examined the shiny brass lock plate.

"Stop," I said in a harsh whisper. "Put it down."

"There might be something inside—"

"Look at the lacquer. Your fingerprints are all over it. There was none before. Here," I said, grabbing it from her. "Give it to me."

"Stop it! Let me see what's inside!"

In our bout of tugging, I finally managed to pull it out of her grasp, but the force of the release knocked the small case against the table. A loud *clack* fractured the silence. Maewol and I froze, straining our ears at the silence that returned.

The silence persisted.

My thundering pulse eased. At once, I narrowed my eyes at Maewol and hissed, "That can*not* happen again—"

"Abaji?" A female voice came from outside; a Jeju woman by her dialect. Then the double doors opened. "I thought you'd left—"

The case dropped from my fingers. Maewol and I stood frozen as though knives were pointed at our faces. For a long moment neither of us spoke, and neither did the young woman standing by the door. Her face was covered with scars that rippled across her cheeks and down her eyes, the skin sliced on either corner of her lips, widening her mouth.

"What are you doing here?" Gahee asked in a thick Jeju dialect. She should have been frightened—we were strangers in her home—but instead she just stared at us. "What are you doing in my father's room?"

"We—I—" Maewol stammered.

I dug my nails into my palm, anchoring my composure, then said in a steady voice, "My father went missing, and I am simply making sure that your father wasn't involved. Everyone thinks he was, but I don't. Still, I need to make sure of this before I cross him out—"

"You're suspecting the wrong person," Gahee said. "My father told me it wasn't him."

So naive. "Of course your father would say that."

She stared at me, her eyes as blank as the eyes of a dead fish. "Father told me the killer was the last person who saw Seohyun alive: Shaman Nokyung."

Her words slammed into my ribs.

"Liar," Maewol snapped, and then I could feel my sister's wild eyes on me. "Older Sister, let's go."

I couldn't move. I couldn't stop staring back at Gahee. "Tell me more."

Maewol grabbed my wrist. "You told me yourself, we're not to linger! Let's go—!"

I knocked Maewol's hand away. "You go first."

It was only after Maewol stormed off, her feet thudding across the hut, that I glanced at the space she had occupied a short moment ago. And then I knew; if I had looked at my little sister, I would have seen the same look of hurt that had gleamed in her eyes five years ago.

"From what I heard, Shaman Nokyung told the village elder during his interrogation that she hadn't seen Seohyun that day," Gahee said. "But then a witness later testified that she'd seen them together."

"How can I believe you?"

Slowly, Gahee untied the ribbon securing the end of her braids. A strange thing to do. "You don't need to believe me. The witness testified in a public interrogation, so go look at Village Elder Moon's reports on the case."

Dread curdled in my stomach as the weight of Gahee's gaze constricted me, or perhaps it was the truth of her words. Shaman Nokyung had lied about seeing Seohyun. She was hiding something, something dark and frightening.

"Does it not make you wonder?" Gahee whispered as her

fingers slipped around the brass handles attached to the double doors. "What could Shaman Nokyung have possibly said to Seohyun that day? What could have pushed Seohyun into killing herself? I wonder . . . And I think you should too."

Before I could move, she stepped out of the room and jerked the two doors shut behind her, then tied the handle with her hair ribbon.

I rushed forward and tugged hard at the inner handles, hoping the ribbon would loosen. But before it could, Gahee returned; her silhouette moved across the hanji screen as she tied the handles again with something thicker. Rope. I hurried over to the other door, the one that should open onto the yard, but it was also locked from the outside.

My heart pounded. I was trapped in the home of the prime suspect.

ten

FEAR FILLED ME LIKE THE thundering of a thousand wings. I had invaded someone's home; now I was trapped in it. I paced the room, drenched in cold sweat, then ended up back at the door where Gahee was. She was still on the other side, just sitting against the door.

"Please, let me go," I tried again, as I had been trying for the last hour or so. "Tell your father I was here, do whatever you want. But there's no need to lock me in here."

My words were only met by silence.

"Gahee."

Still no response.

Trying to calm the panic in me, I ran my fingers down the string around my neck until I felt Father's wooden police whistle. I clung to it. Father had given this necklace to me when I was a child and constantly afraid whenever he'd left for the police bureau late at night.

134

In as gentle a voice as possible, I tried again, "Just as you are trying to protect your father, I was simply trying to search for mine—"

Gahee rose to her feet. I thought she'd finally open the door, but instead she rushed away down the hall. I pressed my ear against the latticed screen, my chest tightening as I sucked in quick, shallow breaths. I heard a tree outside creaking in the wind. Rain was still pattering against the screened doors. Then I heard footsteps.

Finally, I saw Gahee returning, her silhouette growing. But the silhouette grew too tall, the shoulders too wide, long limbs moving as the door shook, the rope being untied. It opened, and I nearly fell to the ground at the sight of Convict Baek.

His hair was tied into a topknot, strands falling over his eyes. There was a tear on his sleeve, revealing his muscled arms, veins running down and entwining around the wrist and stretching out through his fingers. He had hands that could kill someone.

My gaze darted behind him. The door was open. I took a few steps forward.

"If you run," he said, his voice as sharp as a blade, "I will catch you and drag you over to the village elder, thieving wench."

"I wasn't—"

"Sit *down*."

I took a hobbling step back and found myself sitting on the floor.

He sauntered forward and crouched before me, and his head turned to one side, at such an extreme angle that the bones of his neck cracked. "I have ears everywhere," he said, so close that his breath trailed down my cheek. "Among every few households there is always one who serves as my eyes and ears. And my little birds have been telling me that Detective Min's daughter is here in Nowon, and that she is asking questions about me. I don't like people digging into my life."

"My father is missing," I said with some force, my voice cracking. "Everyone says you are to blame."

"You believe what everyone says?"

"No, but I—"

"Then I suppose you believe Seohyun killed herself. She did not."

"How would you know—"

"Someone murdered her, and the last person seen with her was Shaman Nokyung."

He sounded so sure, too sure. "Let us speak outside, not here." I pressed my hand against the floor and struggled to my feet. I made for the door, but he sidestepped, blocking me. "You have no right to keep me here!"

"Just as you had no right to break into my house?"

"My father, a detective of the sixth rank, will never stand for this. When he hears of how I've been treated, he will have you arrested—"

He barked out a laugh. "You are no daughter"—he took a step closer, and I retreated—"for you have no father. He is dead." He took another step, and with his large hand he shoved at my shoulder with such strength that I went toppling. My head hit the corner of the low-legged table, my hair coming undone and falling over my face. "Now, who are you again?"

I pressed my forehead against the floor, squeezing my eyes tight against the explosion of stars and fear. My bones—my life—felt brittle under the shadow of his towering height.

Wherever I am, Father had once promised, *I will never be too far to hear you.*

My trembling hand shook as it reached for the whistle and pressed it to my lips. I blew, so hard the desperate trill carried into my mind memories of when I had used it before. Those days and nights when Father would work long hours at the bureau, leaving me alone in a mansion filled with creaking silence and an aunt who clicked her tongue at my very existence. I had called for him, and he'd never come.

But now—would Father ever return to me?

Wiping the wetness from my eyes, I blew on the whistle a second angry time before Convict Baek ripped it from me.

"Give it back!" I screamed, rising to my feet and rushing at him. I grabbed his arm, my nails digging into his skin, as I tried to reach for the necklace he held high above me. "Please!"

A smirk slid across his lips.

"Please—!"

"Convict Baek," came a commanding voice outside, and Baek's grip over the necklace loosened. "We know you have Detective Min's daughter in there. Bring her out at once or bear the consequences."

Convict Baek stood still, his bemused expression frosting over. He then pointed his burning black stare down to me. "Oh, I have *been* bearing the consequence for years," he said; then, leaning closer to my face, he spoke in a whisper. "You want to find your father? Then here is a riddle: What bribe is large enough that a beautiful maiden will be set aside?"

I did not have time to decipher his words. His hand was close enough that I grabbed the whistle and bolted out the door.

I stumbled and ran down the living quarter, threw open the entrance door, and stared out at the face of Village Elder Moon, standing in the light shower. My sister was behind him, wide-eyed and openmouthed. My knees wobbled as I hurried down the steps, into my sister's arms.

"It took you long enough," I croaked as gratitude rushed through me.

"I would have come sooner, but it took me time to find Village Elder Moon!" Maewol said in her defense.

"Twice," I whispered. "You've helped me twice."

"That's what little sisters are for."

Convict Baek sauntered out, his head bowed, and with him came the memory of his whispered words. *What bribe is large enough that a beautiful maiden will be set aside?* He was

138

sly and conniving, this man. I didn't know the answer to his riddle, or if there was one at all. But I did know that whatever bribe he spoke of, he was wealthy enough to corrupt others with secret gifts. For his wealth was apparent. Baek wore the garb of a nobleman; his robe was made of deep blue silk with silver-threaded embroidery.

"Village Elder Moon," Baek whispered. "How good of you to grace my house with your presence again."

I held on to Maewol tighter as Convict Baek finally lifted his head, glowering at Village Elder Moon.

In a sweet, soft voice, he said, "Do not be upset with me. I was simply disciplining this slip of a girl who decided to invade my home. She frightened my daughter." A smile curved. "The things we do to protect our daughters; I'm sure you understand."

Rain sprinkled over us as silence ensued.

Then the village elder's lips twisted into a stern and angry line. His eyes were so cold that a shudder ran down my spine. And under his breath, he uttered a single word, and I'd never heard the word filled with so much disgust and abhorrence. "Chunhangut."

Lowlife.

He waved a hand at me and Maewol. "Let us leave."

Only once we were off Convict Baek's property did Village Elder Moon turn to face me. His eyes lingered on my face, and it took a moment to realize that blood was dripping down my forehead.

"Did he hurt you in any other way?" he asked.

"No, sir," I replied.

"Your sister told me that you'd come to confront Convict Baek," he said, and an edge of disapproval slid into his voice. "If she hadn't come running to frantically tell me about your predicament, I'm sure I would have regretted ever promising to assist you with your investigation. Perhaps it is better if you returned to your aunt, Mistress Min."

"Please, sir—"

"I will speak with you tomorrow." He then called out to his manservant, who was waiting nearby. "Dukpal-ah, accompany Mistress Min and her sister safely back home."

I stared at the village elder as he turned to leave, wishing I could grab ahold of his sleeve, to somehow regain his favor. My desperation peaked as Maewol held my wrist, ushering me away from him toward our own ponies, which she'd tethered nearby. She freed the reins and handed them over to me. "We should go now. Shaman Nokyung is likely worrying about us."

Convict Baek's words clung on to me: *Someone murdered Seohyun, and the last person seen with her was Shaman Nokyung.*

I couldn't leave now. There was so much I needed to report.

"Village Elder Moon," I called out, shaking myself free from Maewol. He stopped in his tracks and cast a frowning glance my way. "I would like to speak with you—about what happened today."

"*That*," he said, the disapproval deeper in his voice, "can wait until tomorrow. Do not make me repeat myself twice. You and your sister ought to return home."

Everything in me drooped like a withered flower. "Yeh," I whispered.

Once Village Elder Moon was gone, it was just Maewol, the manservant Dukpal, and me.

"What were you going to speak to him about?" my sister asked.

"Like I said," I replied weakly. "About what happened today."

"Only that?" Suspicion lurked in her voice. "What Gahee told you . . . you don't believe it, do you? That Shaman Nokyung might be involved?"

I lowered my gaze. "No," I lied, my voice a whisper. "I don't."

"Good. You better not believe her," Maewol muttered. "She's the daughter of that monster who locked you up in his house. What was he *thinking*? It's even more obvious now that he must have stolen the other girls."

"We don't know anything for sure yet."

"I do know for sure that the shaman is innocent. I *know* her."

And I thought I had known Father.

Listlessly, I asked, "Does she mean that much to you, the shaman?"

"Of course. When Father left me, Shaman Nokyung was all I had. She's the only person in this entire kingdom who would never leave me." Climbing onto her pony, she added, "If she ends up in a prison block, you'll find me there also. Next to her."

It was a warning: If I turned the investigation against Shaman Nokyung, I would lose a sister as well. I wanted to cover my face and fall apart. I'd come to Jeju to look for the truth, and in doing so, everything seemed to be going wrong.

I wanted to spiral into a deep and dreamless slumber, but sleep evaded me that night. Exhaustion seeped into my mind as the hours dragged by, numbing me as the sky transitioned from black to blue-gray. Then with the morning sun came the sound of distant hoofbeats; it took me a moment to realize I wasn't hallucinating.

I crawled across the floor and looked outside. The empty land, cold and dry, shifted with moving light as clouds rolled across the morning sky. And in the distance approached a black-robed rider. I couldn't tell who it was, but I remembered Village Elder Moon's remark that he would visit me today.

Retreating across the floor, I brushed my teeth and washed my face, then inspected my reflection. It wasn't covered in blood anymore, nor in tears. I quickly plaited my thick black hair down my back, then slipped into my hanbok. I meant to head for the door, but etiquette stopped me. *You must never leave the house alone*, Aunt Min's words drummed in my head, *and if you do,* always *hide your face.*

I took out my silk jangot of azalea purple and wore the overcoat-like veil over my head as I would a hood, the shadows cast by it meant to hide my face. I also noticed the norigae I'd brought with me, a tassel from which a decorative sheathed dagger hung. An extra touch of respectability. Quickly, I tied it onto the upper part of my hanbok. Perhaps Village Elder Moon would be more forgiving of me if I presented myself to him as a delicate flower.

By the time I stepped out into the yard, Village Elder Moon was waiting outside.

"Good morning, young mistress." His voice was reserved and solemn. "I have come to take a report on what occurred yesterday. Is the shaman in?"

"She is sleeping. As is my sister."

There was a pause. On the mainland, such a circumstance would never have occurred. A maiden would never have needed to make a report, but then again, no decent young lady would have left the safety of her aunt's home to begin with.

"Then I will have to speak with just you for now. May I come in?"

"Of course." I showed him into the main living space,

where Village Elder Moon seated himself before a low-legged table. His whole presence seemed to fill the room. He did not make a comment about what the hut looked like, filled with charm papers and small statues of gods and incense. But I knew what he was thinking: how odd it was that the daughter of a well-educated detective had ended up in a hut full of delusion. That is what Father had once called this jeomjip.

My skirt puffed around me as I sat before the village elder, tightly holding on to the two silk strips of the jangot under my chin, as though a strong gust of wind was about to blow the veil off. From deep within the shadows cast over my face, I silently watched as he opened a notebook and took out a brush and inkstone.

"Yesterday, your sister informed me that you'd gone to confront Convict Baek. Why is that?"

"Because I think he is involved in the two cases. Everyone thinks he is involved."

"Everyone?" He wrote down my words, and as he did, he murmured, "Perhaps not everyone. I do not think so."

"But . . . witnesses say they saw him stalking Hyunok, and he is tied to at least one of the victims by debt."

"Perhaps you're right. But don't you think it odd?" His brush paused in midair as he glanced up at me. "You were here for a few days and already think you've found the suspect. If it were that easy, wouldn't your father—who was in Jeju investigating for a week—have come to that same conclusion within a day or two? Why did he not have Baek arrested? Or at least interrogated?"

My shoulders sank under the weight of his words. It would be a lie to say I hadn't wondered about this myself, but I had been so convinced by the testimony of others.

"The most obvious suspect," Village Elder Moon whispered, "is not always the perpetrator."

"I can't think of who else would be behind the mask. The masked man was witnessed both times, in the Forest Incident and the kidnapping cases . . ." I placed my knuckle against my lips, remembering the list of names I'd written into my journal.

Village Elder Moon gently cleared his throat. "Regarding yesterday's incident," he said, his voice low, "it seems you did more than confront Convict Baek. According to him, you and your sister invaded his home. Is that true?"

My hand dropped back down onto my lap and the silk jangot slid off from my head. "He threw me against a table."

"Yes, I can see that."

"That must be some kind of violation of propriety."

"Convict Baek has chosen not to report you. He told me he'd misspoken yesterday, that nothing had happened. You, however, may choose to report him, and should he accuse you then, I doubt you will be found guilty. You belong to the ruling class, Mistress Min. And unfortunately—or perhaps fortunately for you—the magistrate sways in favor of those in power. *However*," he added, giving me a pointed look, "I must write to your aunt to inform her of this incident."

"But you promised me! You said you wouldn't!"

"It's becoming too dangerous for you, and I cannot take that kind of responsibility—"

"I'm close to finding the truth, Village Elder Moon," I lied. It was a half lie, for I sensed I was close to finding something—but whether that something would serve to illuminate or further complicate my investigation, I did not know. "I'm so very close to the truth that I can feel it in my bones. I can't leave yet."

He set down his brush and studied my face. "What truth?"

"I spoke with Convict Baek's daughter yesterday, and she thinks it is"—I lowered my voice, glancing around me to make sure no one was present—"Shaman Nokyung. I don't want to suspect her, but . . . you're right, sir. Convict Baek is too obvious for a case still unsolved."

"Isn't the shaman like a grandmother to your sister?"

An ache sharpened in my chest. "Yes."

"Yet you would investigate her?" he said, and there was no judgment in his voice. There was only curiosity.

"I follow facts, sir, not feelings."

He considered me for a moment, then said, "Come, let us talk outside."

I glanced at my sister's door. She had saved me twice—yet I was using Shaman Nokyung as bait to get the village elder

146

into letting me remain in Jeju. She'd never forgive me if she knew.

Once we were outside, he said, "What is it that makes you most suspicious of her?"

"Gahee told me that Shaman Nokyung was last seen with Seohyun. Is that true?"

"It is. I remember this testimonial; I keep a record of all reports made by the subdistrict administrator. You may come visit the library I keep at Mehwadang next time to read it yourself." He paused, his gaze far away as he searched his memory. "If I remember correctly . . . on the twenty-third day of the twelfth lunar month, that is when a female witness testified that Seohyun had been seen with Shaman Nokyung."

So Gahee had told me the truth. "Did the witness say anything else, sir?"

Village Elder Moon gathered his hands behind his back and paced the yard. At length, he said, "The last witness claimed Shaman Nokyung and Seohyun were having an intense argument. After waiting for a few minutes, she decided their row wouldn't end anytime soon, so ended up leaving the fortune-telling hut . . ."

I waited, my pulse beating hard.

"I had inquired as to what the two were fighting about," he continued, "and the witness told me she'd only overheard a little. But she had heard Seohyun say, 'I am not Eunsuk anymore. Eunsuk died in the kingdom across the sea, where her dignity was taken.'"

147

Eunsuk.

The pieces clicked together, and I finally understood why Father had written Eunsuk's name on the list of the other thirteen missing girls. Eunsuk was Seohyun; Seohyun was Eunsuk. But who was she to the shaman?

Another thought clicked into place. Shaman Nokyung had mentioned a daughter who had disappeared.

"Seohyun is Eunsuk," I whispered as realization dawned. "I believe she may be the daughter of Shaman Nokyung."

"I had a similar assumption."

"You did, sir?"

"There is little I think of, day and night, besides the masked-man incidents." He paused. "My daughter does not sleep. We've tried everything to ease her mind. My wife took her to visit every shaman in Jeju, but of course, to no avail. I do not believe in witchcraft; such superstitions are for the ignorant. But I did have hope that acupuncture would help her, as it is known to treat nightmares. Yet she continues to go for days without sleep."

I waited, holding my breath, wondering how this story connected with the Mask.

"My daughter wasn't always like this," he continued. "She wasn't always tormented by her irrational fears of being kidnapped. But I suppose it is not so irrational."

"What do you mean, sir?"

"My daughter nearly was kidnapped once. But we do not talk about it."

My gaze darted up to his face, but I forced it back down. Even in the midst of disorientation, I knew not to stare my elder in the eyes.

"I built a second home just for her. Yeonhadang. I built it in the hopes that she would recover, for it is quiet and serene there. The state of her mind would disqualify her from the crown princess selection, which she desires far more than anything. So I trust you will keep this information to yourself."

"Of course, sir," I promised.

"So you see, I often wonder who the masked man can be, this man who steals girls. And as suspicious as I am of the shaman and her possible connection to Seohyun, she has no motive to kidnap the girls. Nor the strength."

I had no idea myself, but it occurred to me that Seohyun-Eunsuk had been a stranger when she'd first wandered into Nowon; this village was not her place of birth. If Shaman Nokyung was indeed her mother, then wouldn't that mean she too had come from elsewhere?

"Do you know how long Shaman Nokyung has lived in Nowon, sir?"

"Seven . . . eight years. She suddenly appeared in Nowon Village, saying the gods had called her here."

Only seven or eight years . . . that meant the other five decades of her life were not accounted for. She could have been a criminal, a murderer, and no one in this village would have known better. Perhaps, whoever it was who wore the mask, she had known him in her life before Nowon.

Village Elder Moon gestured at me. "What is it that you most desire?"

I blinked up at him. "Sir?"

"In every human being, there is always something too important, something one must have at all costs."

"My father," I whispered. "To see him again."

He paused, and gently, he asked, "And if he is dead?"

I didn't blink this time. "Then to give him a proper burial."

He bowed his head and let out a breath. "There are few in this kingdom as devoted as you are."

I shifted, my ears burning, both with delight and embarrassment. "And you, sir?"

His lashes lowered; his brows crinkled. "The day my daughter was nearly kidnapped, I realized that what authority I thought I had was an illusion. I desire to never feel so helpless again—a helplessness you must undoubtedly be feeling." He considered me for a long moment. "Very well. For one more week, I will keep myself from telling your aunt. Solve the case by then, or I will have to write to her. And I will not stop her from bringing you back to the mainland, whether or not you find your father."

I lingered outside after the village elder had left, trying to think of all I needed to do, how long it would take. When I returned to my room, I gasped, surprised at the sight of my sister sitting behind my low-legged table. "What are you doing here?"

"I was waiting for you." She slipped a scroll of hanji paper out from her sleeve, rolled it open, and held the corners down with stone weights. "Look."

I sat down across from her. "It's a map—of what?"

"I wanted to tell you yesterday, but you looked so distraught I thought it would be better to wait until you'd rested."

"So," I said, feeling the exhaustion of a sleepless night settling over me, heavy and oppressive, "what did you want to tell me?"

"He found her first."

I sighed. "Who found whom?"

"Father," she said, and a flash of cold jolted through me, as though she'd splashed water in my face. "He hired Merchant Rhee to look for Boksun. The merchant spent over a week searching, had requested help from other merchants, and finally found her."

I could hardly breathe, clinging on to Maewol's every word.

"Father paid him a handsome sum to tell no one of this discovery. That was what Scholar Yu told me when I went to make inquiries at the inn, while also inquiring about the village elder's whereabouts."

"Wait." I must have misheard. "Scholar Yu, the drunkard?"

"Yes, a year ago he saw our father and Merchant Rhee

whispering together. So he finally got so curious that he coerced the merchant into having drinks with him. Several enough to make the merchant confess a few things, like the fact that Boksun lives near Jeongbang waterfall."

"That's in Seogwipo," I whispered.

Maewol nodded. "Yu didn't think this information was important until he found me asking around about Boksun. He also drew this map for me."

I stared back down at the map, so sparsely illustrated, yet I could imagine the route we'd have to take, drawn out in ink, of oreum hills and trees, massive slopes where wild ponies grazed, of hidden entrances into lava tube caves, the fields of swaying grass . . . The route Father had once taken. I pushed the stones away from the paper with one sweep of my arm, rolled the map up, and rose to my feet.

"What shall we do now?" Maewol asked.

"We?"

"Yes, we."

"All right . . . *we* are going to find Boksun first."

eleven

ON HORSEBACK, MAEWOL AND I rode through gusts of fresh wind, following the path outlined on the map. My sister was dressed in her shamanic garb of flowing white and the bright red of her sash belt. Her face was hidden under the shadows of her white cone hat. She'd even brought her fan and her ghost-summoning rattle. "In case I need to summon the gods," she told me, then in a quiet voice added, "but really, it's to show whoever crosses our path that I'm someone to reckon with." As for myself, I had worn my hanbok, along with a silk jangot covering my head, in the hopes that my meek appearance might lighten the lips of any secret keeper we might encounter.

But for the first few hours of our travel, we didn't encounter a living soul. There was no one to ask if we were heading in the right direction; there was only the wind, the persistent wind, driving the clouds across the sky, ruffling through the grassy landscape and pushing at our backs, as though urging us to make haste.

I held on tight to the fluttering map, trying to find my place, and then I looked around. Every direction looked the same. My attention stopped before a high oreum hill, one of the hundreds of small ancient volcanoes now covered in overflowing grass, shrubs, and trees. I steered my pony, ignoring Maewol's "Where are you going?" as I followed the memory of Father's words up the slope.

Study anything too close, he'd said, *and you'll get lost.*

Father had gotten lost many times before, blown too far away by his investigations. At night he would travel by the stars and during the day by the sun. If he ever became absolutely lost, he'd find his way by climbing to the highest point to get a broader idea of where he was.

Look at everything around you from a distance, and you'll find the way back home.

Once we reached the top, I found myself staring down at a deep pocket in the hill, a crater covered in grass and a circle of trees. Ponies were grazing below. Sometimes holes were found around these oreum hills—entrances into an extensive system of lava tubes, of abysses and endlessly long caves with ceilings decorated in limestone, and of mysterious lakes hidden deep in the earth. But that was the world below me, and perhaps it was only make-believe, these stories made by those with an abundance of imagination. I forced my gaze up and looked ahead. All that mattered was the world I could see, an undulating land carved by fire and marked by the wind, and beyond it, the faintest glimmer of blue, which was where we were heading toward. The seaside.

"We're still far from the coast." I urged my pony forward again. "What did you tell the shaman? She'll have noticed your absence by now."

Maewol ran her hand along her pony's mane. "I left her a note. I told her I was going somewhere with you, and would return in two days at most."

"She'll be worried about you . . ." I paused. "You're like a daughter to her."

"We only have each other."

"Didn't she used to have a daughter?"

"She's dead."

"And you must know how she died . . ."

"No." Maewol slowly shook her head. "She never did tell me. But she often has nightmares, and I see her weeping with such anguish. I sometimes worry she'll die from heartbreak."

"People don't die from heartbreak," I murmured, while wondering what fueled Shaman Nokyung's nightmares. Grief . . . or guilt?

"You should hear it yourself. When she cries," Maewol added sheepishly, "it sounds so painful I feel like crying myself."

I forced my gaze back onto the map, afraid she'd see guilt flickering in my eyes. The old woman Maewol so cared for was the prime suspect listed in my journal. At some point, I would have to tell Maewol the truth about Shaman Nokyung's possible connection to the disappearances. Gripping the map tighter, I fixed all my attention onto the illustration—

A rabbit dashed across, frightening my pony.

I nearly fell off, both my hands clutching the map, but I managed to steady myself at the last minute.

"Stop staring at the map." Maewol snatched the crinkled paper from my hand, and the rudeness of her behavior left my face hot.

"Give. That. Back."

"Follow me, Older Sister." She urged her pony into a gallop. "I *know* how to get around."

I rode after Maewol, the heat spreading to the tips of my ears. I chased her down the slope to the foot of the hill. The path continued on, winding into the distance, but Maewol disappeared into a field of swaying reeds.

"Maewol-ah!" My anger peaked as I waited before the reeds. "We're supposed to follow the *path*."

Silence.

Heaving out a sigh, I followed her in, the silvery-white plumes towering over me. It was loud here. The wind swept through, and the reeds rustled in all directions, as though I were surrounded by the crisp sound of hushing waves.

"Maewol-ah," I called again, less angry now. "This isn't the way we're supposed to go."

"It is, trust me!"

I followed her voice and caught glimpses of her, of inky strands of hair flying, her skirt loose in the wind. And a glimpse of her eyes, gleaming like black pearls as she glanced over her shoulder. "It's a shortcut. The path will reappear on the other side."

Reluctantly, I rode deeper into the field after my sister. Uneasiness knotted in my chest. I told myself that if we got lost, we could always turn back, and yet the field stretched on for longer than I would have liked. When we reached the end of the reed field, I quickly retrieved the map from Maewol and inspected it. I couldn't recognize any landmarks in our surroundings.

"So?" I asked. "Do you know where we are?"

Maewol shrugged. "I don't know."

I sat up, tall and stiff. "We had a plan! We've traveled for at least five hours, all the way here, following the map." I shook the paper in my hand. "We were supposed to *stay* on the path. We don't have time to waste like this!"

"I'm sure we'll find our way to Jeongbang waterfall," she said. What gnawed at me most was that she sounded utterly unaffected and much too calm.

"You do *not* find the place you need to reach by *wandering*."

"I do all the time." She pushed strands of her hair away from her face, tucking them behind her ear. Then she urged her pony forward. "How are you ever going to solve a mystery when your nose is buried deep inside books or right up against that map?"

"Maewol, it doesn't work like that. Maps are meant to be *followed*."

"No, a map is meant to be used when we're lost, and we are not lost."

Maewol continued to ride on, and I continued to follow. Our argument went on in circles, myself convinced that we were lost, and Maewol convinced that wandering a bit would do our travels no harm.

I shook my head, trying my best to restrain myself from yelling. "We need to turn back. If you won't, then I will—"

A faint *hush* sound expelled every thought from my mind.

I frowned, then exchanged a glance with Maewol. "It can't be . . ."

I urged my pony into a gallop, passing by a line of squids left to dry out under the sun. Soon the grass turned to sand, and the sand into froth-capped waves that rushed toward me, then receded into the vast stretches of rolling waves. And on either side of where I stood were stone pillars that rose straight out of the sea, guarding the island's edge like fangs.

Hoowi!

Hoowi!

I glanced farther ahead. The turquoise water turned a deeper blue, and I could hear the whistling sound of haenyeo fish-divers as they rose from the depths—a breathing technique passed down from woman to woman for generations. On this forsaken island of poverty and starvation, where the king sent his most unwanted ones, haenyeos had still found ways to survive by free-diving into the turbulent sea.

Some distance away, a group of haenyeos sat on the beach, clad in their swimming outfits of loose white cotton that bared their skin. Women who weren't from the coastal villages of Jeju were often scandalized by their openness, but not me. I was more preoccupied by their ability to plunge into the unknown depths.

Nervously tugging the silk jangot over my head, I climbed off my pony and pulled the reins as I made my way toward them, hoping one of them might know the way to the Jeongbang falls.

"Excuse me." I stopped before a middle-aged woman. "Could you direct us to Jeongbang waterfall?"

As though she hadn't heard me over the crashing waves, she continued to sort through her mulgudeok. The bamboo basket was heavy with her catch, of abalone, sea urchins, sea snails; a blend of slimy, squirming things. Next to her was a wooden walking stick.

I raised my voice a notch. "My sister and I have lost our way."

"Keep walking that way." She gestured southward without looking up, like she was too busy to spare a glance my way. "You cannot miss it."

A shadow fell next to me. "Ajimang!" came Maewol's voice, and it was then that the woman looked up, revealing a square face with a pair of strong jaws, and an even stronger gaze. "Have you heard of a woman named Boksun?"

The ajimang's hands stilled. "Why do you ask . . . ?" Her attention drifted from my sister and fixed on something yonder.

I glanced over my shoulder at the wind-ruffled sea; some-one was swimming to shore. At first, I thought it was a young woman, by the speed and strength of her strokes, but out from the waves rose a grandmother with dripping gray hair tied into a coil at the nape of her neck.

The ajimang next to me called out, "I'm coming, Halmang Sunja!"

Grandmother Sunja walked with a stagger and a bamboo basket full of her catch. She wasn't the only old woman out at sea. I'd heard of haenyeos older than eighty still diving for fish. The sea made their limbs youthful again; that is what I had been told. In the sea, these old women knew no pain nor exhaustion, though they still maintained the wisdom that came with age and experience. That was why, even though Halmang Sunja looked like a frail woman on land, she likely claimed a high rank among the haenyeos as a sang-goon, the chief of the collective.

She might even be able to help us.

Eagerness thrummed in my blood as I watched the ajimang reach the shore, bringing the walking stick over. The stick went to Halmang Sunja, and her heavy bamboo basket went to the ajimang.

Both women made their way toward us now, and when they arrived, Halmang Sunja turned to me. A thousand wrin-kles were carved into her face. "Nuge-kkwa?" Her Jeju dialect was strong, and it took me a moment to realize that she was asking who I was.

Before I could reply, the ajimang said, "They were lost

and asked for Jeongbang Fall. They also asked about Boksun. Coincidentally."

Coincidentally? Bewilderment beat through me as the two women exchanged glances, not only between themselves, but with the other haenyeos who were watching us. Suspicion lurked in their eyes.

"I am Min Hwani." I lowered the jangot, letting the old woman's gaze rest upon my bare face, and I knew what she saw: the deepwater-black eyes I'd inherited from Father. "Daughter of Detective Min Jewoo." I cast a sideways glance to my right. "And this is my sister. Maewol. Our father went missing last year, and we're trying to find him."

"He went missing, did he?" The old woman pushed the dripping ringlets of hair away from her face. "A good man, he seemed like. Your father rode over to us haenyeos last year to ask the exact same question. 'Where is Jeongbang waterfall?' he asked. And he also asked if we knew of a Boksun."

I held my breath, afraid that if I exhaled then this moment would vanish like the mist. It was hard to believe that in my sister's off-course wandering, we had found our way to the very trail Father had walked. My skin pebbled as I glanced to my left, at the stretch of sand and twigs. Empty, and yet I could almost imagine Father standing there alongside us.

We rode far along the coast and up a steep slope until we reached a hamlet of lava rock huts. It was deep enough inland that I could hardly hear the thundering waterfall dropping into the sea. In fact, I couldn't hear much at all. It was quiet here, like we'd stepped into a deserted and forgotten settlement, but then I heard a squeal of laughter.

Following the sound, we rode up to a large nettle tree with sprawling branches. Under it lounged those who did not dive, those who had stayed behind to watch the children; they were all men, except for one young woman. Shadows of branches seemed tattooed onto her pretty face. Then the wind stirred and the shadows swayed away, revealing a pair of watchful eyes. Eyes that weren't observing the infant on her lap; they were observing us.

I urged my horse closer. The trotting hooves sounded too loud, drawing all attention my way. The male chattering shushed into silence, and all ears seemed to strain as I said, "We are looking for someone named Boksun." My eyes locked onto the young woman's. "Perhaps you could help us."

The shadow seemed to move into her eyes, filling them with a horrible depth. "Who are you?" she whispered as she rose to her feet, clinging to the infant. "I said, who are you—" She paused, her gaze stopping on Maewol and her outfit. Her knotted brows loosened. "You are a shaman?"

My sister leaped off her horse, her conical white hat nearly falling off her head as she landed on her two feet. She set it right. "I am Min Maewol, the assistant to a shaman you must know. Shaman Nokyung." She waited as recognition dawned in the young woman's eyes. "And this is my sister, Hwani."

"Hwani?" the young woman said. My name lingered on her tongue as her brows lifted, a spark of familiarity illuminating her face. A spark that seemed to light the faces of all those who had once encountered Father, as though Father had prepared them to greet me one day. "Hwani, yes. I know that name." Her tight shoulders eased. "Detective Min's daughter. You both must be his daughters."

"Are you Boksun?" Maewol asked.

"I am . . . What are you both doing here?"

A mixture of relief and dread washed through me. "You sent me Father's journal." I dismounted, and with hurried hands, I searched the traveling sack that dangled next to my pony's side. At last, I pulled out the charred book, clutching it tight to still my trembling. "That is why I am here."

Boksun stared at the journal for a long moment.

My stomach churned, and I wanted to puke. I'd run away from Aunt Min, crossed an entire sea, driven by the questions sparked the moment I'd received this journal. Why had Father given his journal to Boksun? Why had she then sent it to me? Had he given her something more, like the answers to this investigation?

"Come." Boksun led us away from the crowd of vigilant men. Shifting the child onto one arm, she reached out with her free hand and held the journal, pocked with fire holes and browned at the corners. "I should have sent it to you sooner," she said, still in a whisper. "I hesitated for too long. And then a fire broke out. It nearly burned our hut to the ground, and it burned the journal too."

"Surely . . ." I clung to a remnant of hope. "Surely you at least read the journal before the fire?"

"I cannot read." There was real remorse in her voice. "I wish I could have sent something more to you than this ash of a journal."

"So," Maewol finally said, tilting her head to the side, her eyes filled with curiosity. "Why *did* you withhold the journal from my sister?"

Hesitation flinched across Boksun's face. "Because . . ." She swallowed. "I was scared."

I shook my head, frustration straining against my voice. "Why? In fact, why did he even give the journal to *you*?"

"Follow me," Boksun said under her breath. "There is something I need to show you two."

I tried to imagine what it was Boksun had to show us, but soon thinking became difficult as we climbed down the cliff-side, the edge that dipped into a lashing of wind and clouds of misty waterdrops that rose from Jeongbang Fall. The wind blew so hard that my silk veil almost flew away several times; I clutched it tight against my chest, letting it flutter in a wild dance as I tried to take in quick sips of the air.

"Let me start at the beginning," Boksun said at last. She was leading the way and she kept her gaze fixed ahead, the infant secured to her back in a wraparound blanket. She locked her arms behind her, under the child's bottom, for added safety. "While your father was investigating into Seohyun's case, he heard about how I had disappeared two days before her death. He'd also heard that Seohyun and I were friends. So he had someone search for me. He thought I'd run away because I perhaps knew something about how she'd died."

"Did you?" Maewol asked.

"No. I didn't even know of her death until Detective Min told me. But that was how he came to find me in the first place."

"Then why *did* you run away?"

Boksun paused. "I haven't told anyone, except Seohyun and the detective . . ." Another beat of silence passed. "I was collecting wood in the forest when a man in a white mask accosted me. He struck the back of my head so hard I could barely see, and when my world finally steadied, my wrists and ankles were tied up. And I was in a shed."

Maewol and I exchanged glances. We'd been to that shed.

"He didn't lay a finger on me. He just sat quietly with me, as though he were deep in thought. So I asked him where he was taking me, and he replied with such an odd answer."

"What was that?" Maewol and I both asked.

"To the Ming kingdom."

My brows slammed low. Ming? That was far across the sea. "Did you recognize his voice?"

"No."

"Do you know Convict Baek?"

"Yes. But I never heard him speak, only saw him a few times."

"What else happened?" Maewol asked.

"The masked man did leave the hut once, I think to scout the area, and that's when I noticed he'd left a piece of paper behind. I managed to crunch it up so small that it could fit concealed in my hand . . ."

She was forced to pause as we struggled down the steep and uneven slope, covered in a twist of camelia trees, prickly pine trees, and dozens of other plant species, all so thickly gathered around us that I couldn't see anything through the ripe green. But I could hear the great, thundering rush of the waterfall, growing louder and louder with every passing moment.

Once the climb down became easier, Boksun continued. "Then, when the masked man came back, I told him I needed to empty my bowels. He hesitated, but he untied me, and when he took me to a bush, that's when I managed to escape. I immediately ran to Seohyun. She was like a secret older sister to me and other girls. Very protective. Convinced that our village housed a monster. She told me to come live here, that no one would find me in Seogwipo. I'd be safe in the village she'd grown up in. She told me to tell her relatives that 'Eunsuk' had sent her."

"Wait." Maewol came to a sudden halt. "Isn't Eunsuk the name listed in Father's journal?"

When had she snooped through it? "It is." Dread hardened in my stomach, sensing that Maewol was about to discover what I already knew. Right as I thought this, Boksun said:

"Seohyun was Eunsuk. Shaman Nokyung's daughter."

"What . . . ?" Maewol's voice tapered away, and I glanced behind at her to see the color draining from her face. As she struggled to process this information, I asked Boksun, "So you live with Shaman Nokyung's relatives?"

"Yes. Her whole family is comprised of generations of shamans. They are famous in this region, so much so that even Magistrate Hong heard of Shaman Nokyung all the way on the other side of Mount Halla."

My interest piqued. "Did they ever meet?"

"Long ago, he would apparently send her a palanquin to bring her to his estate. He struggled to sleep at night. Perhaps ghosts were keeping him awake."

Shaman Nokyung knew the magistrate, and something about this did not sit well with me. *Figure it out later*, a voice in me whispered. For now, I returned my attention to Boksun. She had to be in possession of evidence that might lead me to Father; I needed to know all that I could before answering other questions.

"So why did you wait to send the journal to me?" I asked.

"Because I didn't want to stand out. I thought that if I tried delivering a parcel to Detective Min's daughter, the masked man would be able to hunt me down—and do with me whatever he'd planned to do five years ago."

I bowed my head, understanding seeping in. Boksun had lived for five years in the daily terror of being discovered. And someone had indeed been furiously searching for her: Convict Baek. Whether he was the masked man or not, I could not say, but he'd had a detailed map of Jeju, all the villages he'd probed for Boksun marked off.

"But why did Father give his journal to *you*?" Maewol repeated, impatiently this time.

"Please. You'll understand everything soon." Boksun waved at us, urging us to walk faster. "You'll see."

The trees thinned and opened onto a rocky shore. I shivered at the cold that seeped into my skin, for not only was the air damp with white mist, but it was further chilled by the cliffs that engulfed us in shadow. I could not fathom why Boksun had brought us here, but without asking, Maewol and I followed her until we were standing before the fall—water hurtling down from high above, crashing onto a rubble of giant rocks and the cobalt blue of where fresh water hit the sea.

"Wait here." Boksun's face, as pale as the bone-white sky, turned to me as she passed the baby into my arms. She then climbed the rocks and skipped from one to the next until she was so close to the waterfall that I could see the left side of her hanbok turn dark, drenched with water. She reached toward the pile of rocks, and her hand disappeared into a little crevice.

"She's hidden something there." I looked down at the infant's face. "I wonder what this has to do with the journal—"

"So Seohyun is Eunsuk," Maewol interrupted, her voice aggressive. "That doesn't mean anything. It doesn't make Shaman Nokyung a criminal."

"Well, we'll find out soon, won't we?" I said, gesturing ahead with my chin.

Boksun was now skipping over the rocks toward us. Perhaps she had a secret message from Father, a map to his whereabouts. Or perhaps it was a page from the journal, an explanation of who was innocent and who was guilty.

Boksun landed safely on solid land, holding a little box in her hand. "I told Detective Min about the paper I'd taken from the shed. When I showed it to him, I begged that he take it far from me. I didn't want anything to do with it. But he refused. He told me to keep it here."

I passed the baby to Boksun and took the box from her, my hands brushing against her wet fingers. I opened the box, slipped out the paper and unfolded it.

"The moment your father saw the illustration," Boksun whispered, "he seemed to understand it."

Maewol leaned close to me, our heads nearly touching as we both stared down. On the thin, fluttering sheet of hanji were nine circles, circling one another. There were other symbols too, winding lines and dots that looked more like ink splatters.

"Oddly enough," Boksun continued, "when I showed this

to Seohyun the last time I saw her, she also seemed to understand. I asked her what it meant, and she said only two words: *dusk* and *fog*."

Maewol's gaze snapped to me, and a knowing, frightened look gleamed in her eyes. But before I could ask her anything, my sister turned her attention to Boksun. "Why would he leave evidence like this with you? And his journal . . . why didn't he try sending it to my sister himself?"

A shadow of distress darkened her eyes, and I watched as she tried diverting our attention. "Now I remember! Maewol was the name Detective Min mentioned." A sheen of sweat glimmered on her brow. "So *you* are the reason for his return to Jeju. He told me that those we love the most are often the ones we hurt the deepest—"

I didn't want to hear any more of her babbling. "You keep deflecting this particular question," I said. "Why did Father leave this evidence with you?"

Boksun lowered her gaze, like she couldn't meet our eyes anymore, and at this, Maewol snapped, "You *do* keep avoiding my question. You said I'd understand everything, but I don't. I don't understand at all. What are you hiding from us?"

"I—I just didn't want to tell you both," Boksun whispered. "I've dreaded this moment for months. It's the worst thing ever, having to do this . . ." Her voice was heavy, almost trembling under the weight of whatever secret she bore. "Detective Min left the evidence with me, because . . . because he didn't think he would live much longer."

A thousand needles slid into my chest, so deep I could feel the tips scraping against the bones of my being. "What—" I swallowed hard, barely able to speak. "What do you mean?"

"Your father didn't look too well when he was here." Her brows pressed together, distress knotting her expression. "He collapsed once and lost consciousness. He vomited twice. Your father . . . I—I'm sorry."

"What was wrong with my father?" I asked, my voice cracking.

"Your father was poisoned," she said.

twelve

MY EYES REMAINED DRY AS I sat straight on my pony, gripping the reins so tight my knuckles ached. Whoever had harmed Father, I was going to make them pay. As my mind circled around this oath, thoughts I had never entertained before crept to the surface, thoughts of the ways in which I could take a life.

Knife.

Rope.

Cliff.

Water.

Poison.

"Did you hear what Boksun said? Father really did come back for me," came Maewol's voice, a bewildered whisper. "For *me*? I couldn't believe it when the shaman told me."

I didn't turn to her. I couldn't bear to see her face. "Father is likely dead." My voice sounded so sharp. "And you're just thinking of yourself?"

Maewol rode closer. Her voice grated at me as she said, "I don't think he's dead. Poisoning doesn't always kill you. And if it had, I would think it odd that no one managed to find him. He would have passed away in the middle of the road, or in his room, or somewhere conspicuous like that. I wonder what happened. What should we do?"

We. "It ends here."

"Eung? What ends where?"

"You helping me with this investigation." I kept my eyes fixed ahead at the oreum hills. "I want you to stop."

"I told you, I need to help you so you can leave Jeju sooner and in one piece—"

"Just *stop*!" I bellowed. It wasn't even Maewol I was angry at, but the fire burning in my chest couldn't be contained, seeping out from the cracks in my voice like molten rock. "You don't even *care* about Father, so stop pretending like you do! He wronged you, I'm sorry, but he's *dead*! I'm going to investigate on my own now."

Maewol rode ahead, then steered her pony sharply to block my path, bringing my horse to a prancing halt. Maewol's eyes narrowed and burned into me as the tips of her ears glowed red. "No, you will not," she whispered, the obnoxious veneer falling away to reveal a solemn young woman. "This is not just your case."

I couldn't stop myself. "It is my case. I began it. I ran away from Aunt Min. I left my old life behind, I crossed an entire sea. I gave up everything to search for Father." I gritted my teeth, trying to hold back the words, but I couldn't resist the force of it. "You didn't even care to search for Father until I came. Why—is it because I'm investigating the case? Does this investigation suddenly look so appealing to you? You take everything from me."

A stunned silence followed. I hadn't known such thoughts existed in me, thoughts that made me feel slimy and pathetic.

"I take everything from you?" Maewol said, her voice flat, her stare so pointed I had to look away. "I only saw Father once or twice a year, and even then, he stopped looking at me when I wanted to be seen by him. He stopped speaking to me when I wanted to be spoken to. But you?" She paused as shame prickled my cheeks, like spits of fire landing on my skin. "You had Father's sole attention for five entire years. You were always the center of his world. I only got a few grains of his affection. Is it that wrong I feel a bit of joy at the thought that Father truly had come to Jeju for me?"

A drop of rain splattered onto my eyelid. I blinked it away, and when I reluctantly looked at my sister again, Maewol's face sharpened before me, her skin so pale, made paler by the inky blackness of her hair and the grayness of the skylight. Her mismatched eyes, one larger than the other, watched me from above the scattering of freckles. Her face, I realized, was no longer round and glowing like the ten-year-old girl I remembered, but sharp and all angles, as though the fierce gales and sharp rocks of Jeju had carved her bones. This was Father's other daughter, the one Father loved dearly, the one he had wronged most truly.

And me? I tore my gaze away and gripped the reins tighter. *Did Father even think of me when he disappeared?* I was the elder, I was supposed to be more generous. But at the thought that, perhaps, Father had secretly loved Maewol more, it sent a crack through my bones.

"I am Father's daughter too," Maewol said, a little less forcibly. "And I am your sister, unless you've forgotten."

I wished I had forgotten. We were two starving children scrambling for the few grains of affection left behind by our father. For surely a man only had so much love to give. But Maewol was right, we were sisters; we were bound together like a knot until this investigation ended.

Shoulders slumping forward, I wanted to fall to the earth and curl into a ball, ashamed that I even felt this way. How could I be jealous? Maewol had been abandoned as a child, left parentless for five years. How dare I feel envy? "Do you still want to investigate with me?" My voice sounded drained of all ire and strength.

The knives in her eyes withdrew. "I do."

"You want to know the truth, no matter how horrible it might be?"

She gave me a firm nod.

"Let's go, then," I murmured. A few more raindrops

plopped down from the sky. Storm clouds were gathering. "Let's go before the rain makes it impossible for us to find our way back home."

We arrived at Shaman Nokyung's hut and secured our ponies in the stable; by then Maewol looked thoroughly beaten by the merciless lashing of wind and rain. Her robe hung from her slight figure like wet rags, her face looked sickly, and her lips were blue. I felt as thrashed as she appeared.

Without a word, we went our separate ways, staggering to our respective rooms. But as soon as Maewol disappeared behind her door, I paused. She wanted to investigate with me—and I'd agreed that we would—yet I had hidden from her the name that haunted the top of my suspect list: Shaman Nokyung.

I hesitated a moment, then turned and made my way down the veranda over to the shaman's room. There was a pair of straw sandals before the sliding doors, meaning she was in. I pounded my fist on the wooden frame of her door, loud enough that she'd hear it over the thundering rain. I waited, but not for too long. The door opened, and Shaman Nokyung froze at the sight of me. "You've returned. Where is Maewol?"

"In her room," and then I lied, "I think she's ill."

At once, Shaman Nokyung brushed by me and thudded down the veranda. She would likely fuss over my sister, help her change into a dry hanbok, and perhaps even prepare a hot herbal drink for her. That would give me enough time.

Gently, I shut the latticed door behind me, closing myself up in silence. I was dripping rainwater onto the floor, but there was no time to vacillate. My socks squelched as I roamed and sifted through the shaman's belongings, inspecting every item until I discovered a few tattered books.

I picked the first up and flipped through, skimming down the vertical drip of Chinese characters. It turned out to be the book of saju, used to foretell someone's future. I picked up another, then another, until I came across a book that turned out to be a ledger, a collection of names and an account of who owed what. My attention came to an abrupt halt before a single brushstroke that sliced through a familiar name:

Hyunok owes 3 mal and 9 dwe of rice

And next to it, she'd scribbled in the word: *dead*.

I flipped through the rest of the pages, and more crossed-out names appeared. I counted a total of thirteen female crossed-out names, with the word *missing* scribbled next to twelve of them. All the girls involved in Father's investigation were in Shaman Nokyung's ledger. She hadn't put only Hyunok's family in debt—but the families of every other missing victim.

And she had likely buried these families in debt without a single note of remorse. Why should she feel guilty for ruining the lives of those who had cast out her daughter,

Seohyun-Eunsuk? A mother's han, her grief-ridden and help-less rage, was the scariest.

I shook my head. There were other names written. Many, in fact. This ledger was so thick it likely contained the names of everyone in Nowon Village. And if that were the case, then it was a mere coincidence that the victims' families had ended up in this ledger. I needed to find more condemning evidence.

"What else?" I whispered, looking around.

There was a lacquered cabinet a few steps away from me, gleaming in the gray storm light. The one in which Shaman Nokyung had stored her coins. With a few long strides, I arrived before it, opened each drawer, and found them filled with thread and fabric, ribbons and trinkets, and other items I didn't bother examining twice. But there was a drawer at the center of the cabinet; it was the only one locked, secured by a brass-shaped butterfly. A key was required, but I remem-bered seeing it hung from a necklace the shaman wore. I glanced around, searching for another method, when I saw a heavy porcelain pot resting on top of another cabinet.

Taking it, I raised the pot high and paused only for a moment before smashing it against the lock. The brute force was visibly damaging the wood; Shaman Nokyung would find out, and likely chase me out of the hut. But it didn't matter. Father had been poisoned; I didn't care about any-thing anymore.

One final time, with all my strength I brought the pot

down. *Clank*. The lock broke open and clattered onto the ground.

My heart pounded against my chest as I opened the drawer and peered inside. There was a bag of coins, and next to it, a small porcelain pot. Inside was a powder of a light purple hue.

Bringing it to my nose, I sniffed. It was scentless. It would be wise to bring this substance to an apothecary to identify it . . . But what harm could a little lick do? And I wanted to know *now*. Hesitating a moment, I dipped my finger in, then stared down at the powder that thinly coated my fingertip. I gingerly touched it to the tip of my tongue; a bitter taste crept up my tongue.

Outside, footsteps creaked down the veranda.

I shook a bit of the powder into the pouch tied to my hanbok; the pouch was wet, but it would have to do. I needed to find someone who could tell me what this was—why did Shaman Nokyung feel the need to lock it away?

Suddenly, the bitter taste turned into a tingling numbness. I spat, but it was too late. Now I couldn't even feel the touch of my fingers pressing against my lips. I ought to have felt concerned, but instead my heart raced with relief. I'd found concrete evidence.

A burst of rain-laced wind filled the quarter, and I turned to see Shaman Nokyung glowering at me from the doorway. She didn't look like a killer, wrinkled and frail as she was. "What are you doing?" she whispered, her voice cold.

"I'm looking for answers," I slurred, unable to feel my tongue. "You've hidden too much from me."

"Such as *what*?"

I couldn't confront Shaman Nokyung just yet, not until I could confirm her guilt. "Seohyun is Eunsuk, your daughter. Why did you hide that?"

"So you came into my quarter," Shaman Nokyung said slowly, observing the broken lock, "to look for evidence that Seohyun was my daughter?"

"You were the last person seen with her, the last person fighting with her." She didn't look convinced and was staring at the pouch I gripped in my hand. "I thought maybe you would have a journal hidden in here, revealing what you spoke of that day."

The corner of her lips trembled, her eyes reddening. "And how does that have anything to do with your investigation?"

"Because I couldn't understand. Why would you hide being Seohyun's mother?" I rubbed my mouth again, the numbing tingles now spreading from my mouth all across my face. "Were you ashamed that sh-she was a tribute girl? Did she die because of y-you?" Trying to pronounce each word felt like pushing through a mire thick with mud. Sweat broke out on my brows. "And n-n-now, are you blaming the villagers for her d-death by ruining their lives? I saw how much the villagers owe y-you."

"I do not have time to deal with your overflowing imagination." She stalked into the room, passed me, and gathered up her blanket. "Your sister is sick and trembling from the cold. Go kindle the ondol furnace—"

"I s-swear," I whispered, "I'm going to take my sister away f-f-from you."

Her eyes grew redder along the rim. "Do what you wish. But take her away later if you don't want to *kill* her."

"Maewol is safe with m-m-me."

"Safe?" Anger burned in her voice, yet there was something else, something like fear that opened like a raw wound. "You should never have returned. You'll be the death of your little sister, Min Hwani. You nearly got her killed in the forest, and now— If you don't believe me, go look at her yourself."

The desperation in her voice slid a note of panic into me. And then I remembered Maewol's pale lips and her gait swaying with exhaustion. In that moment, I forgot about my dead father, I forgot about the poison in my pouch and in my mouth, I forgot about the suspect staring me in the face.

I rushed out of the room, hurried down the veranda, and arrived at the latticed entrance to Maewol's room. I opened the door, and my gaze fell onto my little sister, bundled in a blanket. Her body trembled violently, as though she lay bare in the middle of winter, and yet when I crouched next to her and touched her head, the heat emanating from it burned my palm.

"What's wrong with her?" I managed to slur.

"Your sister was never very strong," the shaman answered, coming in behind me. "Ever since your family left her, she stopped eating well. People here in Jeju die all the time from starvation, but I always feared Maewol would die from a broken heart."

"Burning up" was all I could say this time, no longer able to get more than a few words out of me. "Shiromi berries." That was what Mother would get whenever anyone in the family fell ill.

"You won't find them in the village."

Of course, they were difficult to obtain. One had to climb all the way up to the top of Mount Halla to find them.

"I could go g-g-get them," I said, wiping my forehead with the back of my sleeve. But sweat continued to dribble down my face. I didn't feel hot, yet I was perspiring as though I had traveled under the scorching sun for hours.

"You'd likely get lost—" Shaman Nokyung peered at me, her brows pressing together. "Are you ill?"

I could no longer move my mouth to say anything, my entire face numb, even though my mind was unaffected— that was still racing. How bad was Maewol's fever? What could I do?

The sound of muffled voices outside interrupted my thoughts. I waited, wondering if I was imagining the sound. Perhaps the purple substance caused hallucinations as well. Yet I heard it again, a male voice calling out something, but it was unclear. I was about to stand when hot fingers touched my wrist.

I glanced down to see Maewol staring weakly up. "Dusk and fog," she whispered.

The memory of the nine circles flashed through my mind. Boksun had told us, *Seohyun said only two words: Dusk and fog.* Holding Maewol's hand tight, I tried to ask her if she knew what those words meant, but I couldn't move my mouth.

Maewol read the question in my eyes though. She spoke in a voice so quiet I had to lean forward until I could feel her breath against my cheek. "You know what it means."

I squeezed her hand, gently. *What?*

"After the Forest Incident, you were drifting in and out of consciousness—" Maewol paused, gathering the strength to speak on. "You kept saying, 'Dusk and fog. Dusk and fog.'"

Confusion pounded in my head, sweat dripping faster down my face. Why had I uttered those words? I tried looking back to the Forest Incident, but the blankness of my memory was so glaringly bright that my mind ached.

Outside, a voice rang out, clearer now. "Is anyone in?"

I staggered to my feet, wanting to get away from Maewol's waiting gaze; she expected me to remember something. I did have the answers, buried so deep in my mind all I could do was skim my fingers along the edges. Thorny frustration filled my chest as I walked over to the door, which we'd left open.

Outside in the yard were two manservants who were carefully lowering a palanquin onto the muddy earth. One of them lifted the wooden door of the vehicle, and in the darkness within, I caught a glimpse of bloodred lips.

"Bring her in," a frighteningly familiar voice said.

I frowned, taking a retreating step back. But before I could slam the door shut, the two servants hurried up onto the veranda and grabbed me, their fingers digging into my skin. My mouth wouldn't move as they dragged me to the palanquin, but I managed to let out a hoarse cry as they shoved me into the shadows.

Rain drummed on the rooftop of the palanquin.

I sat cross-legged, staring at a pair of eyes that held all the annoyance of a guardian who'd had to cross a thousand li of seawater to track down her foolish niece. For the longest moment, Aunt Min said nothing, and I could no longer tell whether I was sweating from the purple substance or from the sheer distress of seeing her again. Then, to my horror, I felt the vehicle lift into the air. We were moving.

Eemo. I can't leave now! I wanted to scream those words at my aunt, but I couldn't. I turned at my waist, shoving my elbow desperately at the door. But it wouldn't budge. It was locked from the outside.

"The trouble you have caused me," Aunt Min whispered, her voice thin and cold. "We will be returning to the peninsula first thing tomorrow. And I'll make it impossible for you to run away again."

I shook my head and stared wide-eyed at my aunt. *No, no, no, no. Eemo, please!* My sister was dying. Father had been poisoned. I was also poisoned and on the brink of finding the truth. I needed to stay on Jeju Island. She couldn't take me back to the mainland now.

"I'm going to do what your father ought to have done long ago." Aunt Min raised her jade-ringed fingers and massaged her temple. "As soon as the princess selection ends and the ban against marriage lifts, I will see you find a husband."

My gaze darted around the palanquin, and never had I felt so trapped. The walls seemed to be closing in around me. Then I felt it, a disturbing crawling sensation—like an ant scuttling across my skin. I couldn't see a single one, but I could feel them, thousands of ants, their tiny legs moving across my bare legs, my bare arms.

"The young gentleman who asked for your hand has retracted; he learned that you'd run away. Everyone will see you as a loose woman when you return to Mokpo. Still, you are fortunate. Another gentleman has approached me. He is an old lecher, but who else will have you?" She arched a fine, dark brow as she glanced condescendingly my way. "You will marry him, Min Hwani. I promised your father that if anything happened to him, I would see to it that you married—"

I slapped a hand over the back of my neck, then looked at my palm. No ant. Nothing.

Aunt Min's sharp brows drew together; her eyes gleamed

like ice crystals. "What"—her voice dropped into a quiet, frosty tone—"is the matter with you?"

The palanquin swayed from side to side as the servants carried us down the rough road, up and down the rolling hills, and I rocked back and forth with all the movement, the repetitive motion burying me deeper and deeper in nausea. I wanted to claw my skin off; I wanted to vomit.

"Ants," I finally managed to say, as I pushed myself as far into the corner as I could. "There are a-a-ants in here. Th-thousands."

Aunt Min slowly shook her head and clucked her tongue. "Clearly, you have lost your mind, Min Hwani."

thirteen

SQUINTED AGAINST THE BRIGHT MORNING light. For a second, I thought I was back home in Mokpo; I would have to get ready to greet Father as I did every morning before he left for the police bureau.

But the sunlight lost its warmth, dimming into the flicker of candlelight in a shadowy room. It took a moment for the memories to roll in. The swaying palanquin filled with insects . . . my glaring aunt . . . then bursts of damp air as hands pulled me outside . . . then confusion, my confusion, seeing neither hills nor valleys but gray courtyards and stately pavilions . . . tiled-roof buildings upheld by red wooden beams.

The world had blurred. Voices had rushed toward me. And pitch darkness after that.

Had I passed out?

A glance around showed a spacious quarter, surrounded

by latticed hanji screens awash in rainwater. Thunder rumbled outside. I shifted on the sleeping mat, wondering where I was, but then I paused, feeling something strange. I ran my hand down along my arm and stopped at the touch of something long, thin, and cold.

I jolted up—and found myself covered in needles.

"It is acupuncture." A young woman around my age sat by my side with a brass bowl in her hands. "I attended to you while you were asleep. It ought to relieve the numbness you were mumbling about when you were half-conscious."

In a flurry of panic, I plucked all the needles out despite the woman's objection. "Who are you?"

She collected the scattered needles with her lips thinned, clearly trying to repress her irritation. "I'm an uinyeo."

Female physicians were rare to find, most of them situated within local pharmacies to serve wives and daughters, or the palace to serve the queens, princesses, and concubines who were forbidden from being touched by male physicians. "What happened?" I asked.

"How much do you remember?"

"I remember sitting in the palanquin with my aunt—a palanquin filled with invisible ants," I told her. "And then, later, I remember being pulled out into a courtyard. I tried standing up, but then I felt so feverish. So disoriented. And I don't remember what happened after that."

The physician nodded. "You passed out soon after. Your

aunt, Matron Min, was absolutely horrified by the time you were brought here."

"Where is here?"

"You are in the gwanheon, the government office of Jejumok Village. And this place"—she twirled her finger around—"this is Dongheonnae pavilion. It is the women's quarter belonging to the magistrate's concubines. But ever since he built them their own homes, it is now the building used by his relatives whenever they visit Jeju."

"Wait," I whispered. "This magistrate . . . which one?" From what I'd read in Father's library, I knew that two magistrates ruled Jeju: one south of Mount Halla, and the other north of the mountain.

"Are you speaking of Magistrate Hong?" I asked, and held myself back from adding, *the tyrant.*

"I am."

I supposed I ought not to have been surprised. Aunt Min was distantly related to Magistrate Hong, and of course she would have chosen to stay at Dongheonnae pavilion rather than at an inn at Nowon Village.

"Since I've finished tending to you, agasshi, if you need any further assistance, you will find me in the medical ward. It is in the eastern courtyard, next to the servants' quarter."

"And my aunt . . . ?" I asked, remembering her sharp gaze, as though I were the bane of her existence. "Where is she?"

"She is a few rooms down from your quarter, agasshi.

Your aunt retired early for the night, so you will meet her tomorrow and return to the peninsula with her."

So soon.

I pressed my palms against my eyes. I was so tired. My mind felt numb and clouded with dense fog. Every thought weighed heavy, as though rocks had been sewn to them—

A drop of water splattered onto the floor, right at the edge of my sleeping mat. Rainwater must have seeped through the black tiled roof.

"Ah, now I remember why I brought this," the physician said. She placed the brass bowl on the floor next to me, and it caught the dripping rain. *Plop—plop, plop—plop, plop, plop, plop.* The rain fell harder, likely sweeping through the courtyard and over all the pavilions in merciless gusts. "The roof still hasn't been fixed."

It was raining. My aunt was sleeping. Surely no one would be outside, prepared to catch me if I ran away. "If you are done tending to me," I said lightly, "then you may leave. It is late."

The physician bowed her head and, rising to her feet, turned to leave. But she paused and knelt down before me again. "Begging your pardon, agasshi, but if you are thinking of running away, it will not be easy. The soldiers guarding the gate were warned not to let you out."

I tapped my finger on the floor, trying to think of another way out. Then my thoughts slowed to a halt. I was in the government office of Magistrate Hong, a man who could be involved in Shaman Nokyung's conspiracy against the village daughters. He had sought out the shaman's assistance several times before. But this was mere speculation. I couldn't be too certain about anything except for the fact that Magistrate Hong was the only one who could convince my aunt to let me remain in Jeju. The question was, how was I to sway him to do so?

"Do you know if my father, Detective Min, ever visited the government office?" I asked.

"He did, agasshi. Several times."

"Do you know why?"

She fidgeted, her eyes shifting from one side to the other with indecision.

"Whatever you tell me will remain safe with me," I assured her.

"I do not know much, agasshi, but each time Detective Min visited, he left looking very upset and frustrated. There are others who told me that Magistrate Hong always refused to cooperate with the detective."

This sounded typical of Magistrate Hong, the man who had dismissed the case of the missing thirteen by saying that all the girls had run away of their own accord. How would he feel if he learned of Father's poisoning? Magistrate Hong's reaction would at least solidify one thing—whether he had a hand in Father's death.

"You're a physician." I scrambled for the pouch tied to my hanbok, and from it, I took a pinch of the purple powder I'd secreted from the tiny pot in Shaman Nokyung's room. "Do you know what this is?"

She opened her palm, and I placed the now clumpy powder onto it. The first thing she did was *not* put it in her mouth, as I had. She smelled it, then recoiled from the substance. I took a whiff of it myself and smelled nothing; I tried a few more times until I caught the faintest scent of something deep and old, like an ancient forest.

"Kyeong-po buja," she whispered.

"What is that?"

"Poison."

The word slammed into my chest, my suspicion confirmed. Shaman Nokyung, the woman tending to Maewol at the moment, the woman my sister trusted more than anyone else in the kingdom—*she* had poisoned my father.

"It is made from a purple flower. Poison exists in all parts of the plant, but especially in the root."

"What is it like to . . . to die from it?" My voice wavered as I asked.

"You would feel tingling and numbness of tongue and mouth, nausea, and vomiting with stomach pain, your pulse would grow irregular and weak . . ."

I saw my father so clearly before me, as if he were in this room. I watched him stagger by me, his breathing labored, confusion knotting his brows. His skin so deathly pale and clammy, washed in sweat that soaked his hair and streamed down his face. I watched him die.

"You shouldn't be carrying this, agasshi, not even a small amount like this," the physician said, shaking her head at the pinch of purple in her hand. "One-fiftieth grain of kyeong-po buja will kill a bird in a few seconds; one-tenth grain a rabbit in five minutes. A few pinches of this and not even a wolf, let alone a man, would be able to survive it. It is so powerful that if the powder touches an open wound, your whole body would go numb, and you might even feel like you are suffocating."

If the poison was that powerful and immediate, I wondered, how had Father made it all the way to Boksun while poisoned, and then all the way to Gotjawal Forest days later without being immediately debilitated as I had been? And I'd only taken a lick of the poison.

"What if . . . what if very small doses of the kyeong-po buja is administered to a man?"

A shadow flickered over her brows, and I knew what she was thinking: Why was a proper young lady asking all these questions?

"If very small, he might feel a little ill and not understand why, and over time he would have trouble breathing and feeling. It would be like taking tiny, seemingly harmless sips of a snake's venom until it finally kills you."

I stared back down at the purple powder and imagined Shaman Nokyung's wrinkly fingers pinching the substance and sprinkling it into Father's tea. Into his meals. She might have even blackmailed a patron of hers into slipping the poison into the food he was eating at Gaekju Inn.

"Are you still not feeling well?" the physician asked.

I realized I was breathing fast, sweat sheening my brows, and one glance at my reflection in the shiny brass bowl reflected a deathly pale girl with wide, frightened eyes. It had been one thing to suspect Shaman Nokyung, but for the suspicion to congeal before me was terrifying.

So you want to know the truth? I remembered asking my sister. *No matter how horrible that truth might be?*

She had given me a firm nod. But I knew that if I told her the truth about Shaman Nokyung, I would end up losing a sister. I opened my palm, watching the powder fall and crumble onto my skirt.

"Is the magistrate here?" I whispered.

"I believe he is, agasshi. He works in the building across from here."

So the magistrate I'd heard so much about was only a few paces away. "Will you send a servant to inform him that I request an audience?"

"This late?"

"It's urgent."

Her mouth opened in protest, but as though remembering her place, her lips shut and she rose to her feet. Hands gathered, she bowed and murmured, "Of course, agasshi."

She left, and I sank back into my thoughts. Shaman Nokyung was a woman who suffered from aching limbs, and she was old; she could *not* be the masked killer. But her connection to the magistrate . . . perhaps the answer to this puzzling question lay there.

As soon as I heard footsteps hurrying across the yard, I stood up.

The physician entered and bowed so low that I could not see her expression. "Agasshi, he has rejected your request."

I was so speechless it took a few moments to form a word. "Why?"

"I do not know," she whispered, and an odd, knowing glint flashed in her eyes. Eyes, I realized, that were hiding a secret. "The magistrate said he does not wish to see you, or anyone related to the case of Detective Min's disappearance."

Always respect your elders, Father had taught me. But he hadn't taught me what to do when all my elders were blocking the path to investigating his death.

Pacing my room, I turned through all the memories of Father's journals, but I could find no wisdom there for my predicament. I bit my nail, remembering Maewol, who somehow found all the answers and who somehow always found me when I ended up lost. What would she do?

When the rain finally stopped, I gripped the brass door handle and pushed, the wooden frame rumbling open. A blast of chilly night air greeted me. Remnants of rain dripped from the tiled eaves like a string of crystal beads, and beyond the veil, I saw the vast grounds of the government building. It was divided by black stone walls capped with black tiles, dividing the different courtyards and flared-roof buildings.

What would Maewol do?

As I slowly walked down the stone steps, I knew Maewol would have committed into action the very first outrageous thought to surface, and would not have stopped to worry or calculate the outcomes.

Magistrate Hong's office was indeed only a few paces away. Iron cauldrons were stationed around the vast courtyard, but the fire had been doused today, so all I saw of the building was the silhouette of a flared rooftop, upheld by towering pillars. Several latticed screen doors marched down the building, and two were glowing yellow, lanterns and candles lit within. Magistrate Hong was still in.

I pushed my shoulders back and whispered to the dread in me, "I have to do this."

Gathering my skirt, I lowered myself, and the moment my knees sank into the mud, I heard footsteps trudging quickly toward me. It was a fearful servant who hovered a few steps away from me, his eyes asking me, *May I assist you, agasshi?*

I fixed my gaze ahead, onto the glowing screened door, and spoke in the voice Aunt Min used on me when she'd made a decision that could not be altered. "Inform the magistrate that I will not move from this spot until he agrees to speak with me."

The servant bowed and hurried off.

I waited, and a part of me expected Magistrate Hong to summon me at once. *A young lady outside in the mud? Of course, of course I will speak with her, poor girl.* Instead, the deep silence of the night stretched on for too long, with too much indifference.

The pain in my folded legs and the damp chill bit deep into me until I no longer felt anything . . . except the crawling sensation of ants, traveling up and down my skin. A remnant of the poison, but it felt so real—I could *feel* their tiny legs. I twitched at the desire to scratch myself, but resisted. Should the magistrate glance out from his office, I wanted him to see a woman sitting straight, hands gathered in her lap; the display of sheer stubbornness. Then, perhaps, he would give in to my request.

Suddenly, the ghost of an ant crawled down my cheek and slipped beneath my collar. I squeezed my eyes shut and clenched my teeth. When would the damned ants leave me alone—?

My eyes shot open at a memory, remembering what Iseul had told me. Father had complained about insects infesting his room when there had been none. Itchiness that had tormented him all night.

I will not leave, I told myself, clutching my fingers so tight, my knuckles felt like they'd crack. *I will not leave.*

More time passed, and as the pitch-dark sky eased into a shade of gray, waiting became easier. I didn't know if it was the exhaustion or the lingering effects of the poison, but I no longer felt like I was in my own body; these legs and arms were no longer mine, the eyes that saw and the mouth that breathed were also not mine. I felt as though I'd transformed into something as still as an ancient nettle tree. I would wait for days if I had to. I had no other choice.

The doors slid open, lifting my gaze up from the mud. A male servant stepped out. "Come inside, he will speak with you."

I tried to stand, but couldn't at first, my knees frozen in place and my legs screaming in protest. But I managed to rise to my feet and stagger up the steps onto the terrace that wrapped around the long building.

Inside, the magistrate sat before a low-legged table that was covered with a ceramic wine bottle and a bowl, and from the heavy smell of liquor hanging in the room, it was clear that he had been drinking for a while. His eyes wouldn't meet mine. "Sit down."

I did so, my skirt blooming around me like a flower trampled into the mud. At last, I looked at the man I had seen on the vessel, whom I had heard the villagers complain about, whom my father had admired many years ago.

"What do you want from me?" he asked, and his gaze lifted to me. His mask of indifference had cracked, and I saw a ghost lurking beneath. "You have until this candle dies out to speak."

I hesitated, not knowing where to begin. There were so many things I wished to discuss. That Father had been poisoned. That I'd come because I wanted to know if Magistrate Hong could be trusted. That I wanted to know what I was up against. But instead I returned to the conversation we'd first had on the vessel. "You once said that girls disappear all the time. That they are not missing, but rather have run away. Do you still believe that?"

"So it was you on the vessel that day? Not a boy but a rosy-cheeked girl." He glanced at my braided hair, at my silk dress. "You ran away from home, Mistress Min. And just like yourself, I assure you, other girls have reasons to leave their family."

"Thirteen girls do not simply disappear, sir. They are *taken*."

He remained still. Unrepentant. Unmovable. "Well," he said softly, "what can I say? We have a difference of opinion."

"One girl, Hyunok, was found dead after trying to escape her captor."

"Dead from slipping down a mountainside. Perhaps looking for her lover."

"She was only *fourteen*."

"Peasants have no morals."

The candle flickered, growing dimmer.

I knelt before a man who simply did not care about the lives of lowborn girls. He didn't care, just as I hadn't cared. I had come to Jeju only looking for Father, looking at the case of the missing thirteen as a way to find him—but then I'd seen myself in Iseul's eyes. I had seen the grief I'd felt when

Commander Ki had first told me, *I fear your father will not return home, Min Hwani.*

"Have you ever lost a loved one, sir?" I asked.

A shadow shifted across his face, but his eyes remained blank. "Everyone at my age has lost someone dear. It is a part of life."

It was as though I were speaking to a wall. I dared to keep my eyes fixed on his face, at the dark pouches under his eyes, the paleness of his skin, the drooping corners of his lips. All signs of sleepless nights . . .

"What haunts you, sir?" I asked, remembering that Magistrate Hong had often summoned Shaman Nokyung to help him with his nightmares. But when the magistrate continued to remain still as a rock, I said, "Do the girls—the missing and the dead—visit you in your dreams? Asking you for help?"

A tremor shook his hand as he reached for his bowl of rice wine. He gulped it down and muttered, "You are bold, young mistress."

"They say that those who have nothing to lose are the boldest," I said. "I have no father. I have no mother. I have nothing, sir."

Maewol. The thought flickered across like a firefly at night. *I have her.* But it was a flash, and then gone. Maewol was my sister, but she didn't feel like family. I was sure she felt the same way.

"Well, the world is unfair and unjust," he said, his voice wavering. "We live in a world where hardship crushes those who are deserving of better, where obstacles line the path of those who try to do good. And all the while, the path clears easily for those that have evil in their heart. No matter how hard you strive to fight evil, nothing will change. Absolutely nothing at all. The sooner you learn to accept that, the easier your life will become."

"You are not wrong, sir," I said quietly. I had caught a glimpse of Magistrate Hong's reality on this penal island. "But my father always told me to be what I long for the world to be like—to be just, to be fair."

A humorless smile lifted the corners of his lips. "You remind me of myself. I, too, would have left everything behind to search for someone I loved. I would have given up my life to pursue truth and justice."

I waited, wondering, *What happened to you, then?*

"Do you know what happens when a man realizes that all he does makes no difference?" he asked.

He spoke of my worst nightmare. I imagined all of my efforts to find Father wasted; I imagined leaving Jeju with the investigation unfinished. The answers I'd risked my life trying to find, left abandoned. The girls still missing, with more yet to disappear.

"No," I confessed, "I don't know."

"A deadly sense of futility settles deep in his bones, an exhaustion that douses even the brightest flame. That is what I learned, Mistress Min. I found out that bad things happen to good people, that villagers will be ungrateful no matter what, and that the corrupt always win." He poured himself another bowl of wine, gulped it down, and laughed as a haunted look clouded his eyes. "They always win."

In his whispered words, I could almost see his years unfold before me, the years trying to do what was right. Perhaps he'd tried to guard villagers from Wokou pirates and the king's heavy demands for tribute, for horses, seafood, grains, fruits, meats. Perhaps in his fervor to be just and fair, he had lost too many allies. Perhaps the villagers still shook their fists at him in spite of all his efforts.

I untied the pouch and placed it on the table. "There is a witness who testified of my father's condition, and I found a suspect in possession of this. Kyeong-po buja. My father was poisoned with it."

Magistrate Hong's eyes flashed up. "Who is this suspect?"

I swallowed, and could feel the bareness of my throat—a throat that could be cut for what I was about to say. "There's no need for you to know, sir, for you've made it clear that you intend to do nothing." I laid the test before him, hoping that whatever good remained in him would angrily spark awake, and would rise in protest. "The world has been unjust and unfair to my father. And you will do nothing about it." I clenched my fingers tight, waiting.

Magistrate Hong's chest rose and fell, his breathing heavy.

Then he reached out. His fingers put out the candle, and the shadows swallowed him.

"Leave," he rasped. "I don't want to see you ever again."

* * *

I had wasted my time with Magistrate Hong; he was a coward, and there were no answers to be gotten from him. Glancing past the courtyards and pavilions, I wondered how I'd get out to escape Aunt Min. It was late; perhaps the guards had left . . .

I managed to get to the gate, but to my disappointment, two soldiers were stationed at the entrance. With as much calm as I could muster, I moved forward and tried to appear like someone who had the right to leave. But I had taken no more than a step past the entrance when the guards dropped their spears, blocking my path. The iron spearheads gleamed in the torchlight. They couldn't know who I was. They'd never seen me before.

"I am Mistress Min's sister," I said. "It is time I returned home."

The first soldier slipped out a scroll from his robe, opened it, and inspected my face. Rolling it back up, he said, "We were warned that you might attempt an escape. Soldier Dongsu, accompany Mistress Min back to her chamber."

"I need to get back home!" I said. "Please!"

Unaffected by my plea, the second soldier stalked me like a shadow back to Dongheonnae pavilion, his frown glowering each time I looked over my shoulder. He wasn't permitted to touch me, yet the way he gripped his spear, I knew that any attempt to run away would be foolish. I paused before the steps as defeat sank heavy in my chest.

"*Agasshi,*" the soldier said, a warning edge to his voice.

I finally stepped inside, slid the door shut, then ran my hand over my face. What was I to do now?

The thoughts pacing my mind slowly came to a halt, distracted by the prickling of my skin, the sensation of being watched. I swung around and saw the wide-eyed female physician.

And next to her was Maewol, sitting cross-legged, sipping something hot.

"She said she was your sister," the physician said, "and asked for something to keep her warm."

I looked at Maewol closely—at her bluish lips, at her damp hair and the wet patches on her hanbok dress, soaked from the rain that must have leaked through her straw hat and cloak.

"How did you get here?" I blurted. "I mean, how did you get here in this weather?"

Maewol looked at me, straight-faced. "I just rode here."

"Through the rain? Maewol-ah, it only *just* stopped."

Maewol silently sipped her drink again as a drop of rain trickled down the side of her face. She looked even sicker than when we'd returned from Jeongbang waterfall. She wiped her running nose with the back of her sleeve.

In that moment, I could understand why Father had returned to Jeju for Maewol. I could imagine—just a fragment of it—how deeply he must have cherished her. This headstrong, troublesome girl who lacked any sense of self-preservation, and who was loyal to a fault. A girl who was both vexing and endearing, all at once.

"Maewol-ah," I rasped. "Why are you here?"

She shrugged her small, delicate shoulder, as she always did. "I thought you might need some help."

fourteen

MAEWOL AND I SAT SHOULDER to shoulder, hunched over a low-legged table illuminated by the flickering of a candlelight. I always carried my small journal with me, and so I'd opened it before us, intending this time to tell my sister everything I knew. Well, *almost* everything. Paper whispered against my fingertips as I flipped to the page where I'd listed all the names tied to the two cases:

> *Seohyun*
> *Koh Iseul*
> *Convict Baek*
> *Shaman Nokyung*
> *Village Elder Moon*
> *Magistrate Hong*
> *Boksun*
> *Father*

My gaze drifted along the names and fixated upon the shaman's. "We need to find who poisoned Father," I said, "and who is hiding behind the mask. I'm almost certain that the culprits are listed here somewhere."

Maewol, her brows knotted and her nose wrinkled, asked, "Why did you add the shaman's name?"

"Because," I said slowly, "she is Seohyun's mother. And because she foretold the ominous future for all thirteen missing girls. Well, twelve now, since Hyunok is deceased."

Her expression chilled. "Since when was predicting the future a crime?"

"You said you wanted to know the truth, no matter how awful it might be." I held her narrow-eyed stare; I wished she could see into the depth of my own truth. Then she'd know I didn't want to hurt her; I didn't *want* to suspect Shaman Nokyung, yet the evidence was pointing to her. "Listen, Maewol-ah. To find the truth, you mustn't have feelings involved. You must look at each witness and suspect like they're strangers."

"That's easy for you—" Maewol coughed, phlegm rattling in her chest, and I winced at the pain twisting her expression. Her throat sounded swollen, throbbing and sore, but she managed to push the words out. "I can't see Shaman Nokyung as a stranger because she isn't one. She's family; she's all I have. You need to learn how to have some faith in a person, Older Sister. I'm not saying faith in the shaman, but in *me*. Believe me when I say: Shaman Nokyung can be trusted."

Hiding my hand under the table, I clenched my fingers tight. I wanted to tell her everything I knew, but clearly she was too nearsighted. No matter what I told her, she would always side with the shaman.

"I do believe you," I lied, then cautiously added, "but we often think that those who are good to us are also good people. It isn't always like that."

"You mean like Father," Maewol croaked. "He was always good to you, but not to me."

Her words were as sharp as blades, because they were true.

"Yes," I admitted; the word tasted like grime. "Like Father. Sometimes we love someone so much that we fail to notice their dark deeds." As I had. "But no one is perfect, and when one errs, one must bear the consequence. Father paid the cost for what occurred in the Forest Incident . . . by losing you."

Maewol's lashes lowered and slowly a flush darkened the panes of her cheeks. At length, she whispered, "Are you saying that you think Shaman Nokyung is the killer?"

My mind raced, calculating the outcomes. If I said yes, I'd lose my sister to her loyalty. She'd tell the shaman everything. But I could also hold on to my sister a while longer, in the hopes that the accumulating evidence would convince her of the truth. I knew my sister. She wouldn't listen to me; she needed to decide for herself.

"No," I lied again, "I'm only warning you. You must be open to all possibilities when investigating."

Her tense shoulders eased. "Then who do you think *is* the killer?"

My eyes, on their own accord, fell on Convict Baek's name, paused there, then drifted lower. "I think the magistrate is involved," I said.

Maewol made a face. "Truly? I don't think he is."

"He's suspicious . . . Someone is secretly sending girls as tribute to China. It has to be someone with the power to do so."

"Isn't it obvious—?" Maewol coughed again. "It's Convict Baek. He was searching for Boksun, and he stalked Hyunok the day before her disappearance."

"He's *too* obvious. I suspected him right away. But if he was the culprit, why didn't Father arrest him? Maybe someone is trying to make him *seem* like the culprit, to distract us."

"Or maybe Convict Baek is like the oreum hill—the visible marker of a gigantic lava tube system below the land."

If Convict Baek is involved, I thought, tapping my finger against the table, *perhaps he is working for Shaman Nokyung?* I moved the pieces of the case around in my mind, matching different scenarios. *Or maybe Shaman Nokyung is under Convict Baek's control? Perhaps he has ties to those in power from his past life before exile . . .*

I heaved out a sigh. Something gnawed at me—the feeling that I was missing something crucial.

I clicked my tongue. "We're wasting our time, creating stories that don't have supporting evidence . . ." I flipped through my journal, inspecting every testimony collected, and the longer I observed each, the more my head ached. The dead were trying to tell me something, but all I could see was a confusing jumble of possibilities. It took a few moments of wading through the chaos to notice Maewol's absolute silence. I glanced up to find her fidgeting with her fingers. "What is it?"

Maewol kept her eyes lowered. "I . . . I want to tell you something. But before I do, I want you to make me a promise."

"What?" I asked.

"Promise me that, no matter who you suspect, you'll tell me. Don't leave me in the dark."

I had already lost track of how many times I'd lied to Maewol. "I promise."

Maewol let out a shaky breath. "I haven't slept. Each time I close my eyes, I see Father. I didn't before, but I do now, ever since I began helping you with this investigation. And I get the feeling . . . his spirit is trying to tell me something."

He's warning you, I thought, *to watch out for the old woman you call family.*

"Everything about this case . . . it all points back to the Forest Incident."

I nodded. "Yes. So?"

"You told me a few days ago of what Iseul shared. That on the day before Father's disappearance, he said he was going somewhere to cleanse his conscience. A place with hostile eyes.

"I became a little delirious yesterday with the fever. And I found myself remembering the last time I saw Father, remembering that he'd used the same phrase with me. Well, he didn't *tell* me, but I overheard him tell Shaman Nokyung why he'd come. He said he'd come to Jeju to cleanse his conscience—to fix his sins and mend the rift in our family, between myself and him, between all of us. I didn't believe him then. I thought it was mere talk, as it has always been before. But I can't help but wonder now . . . do you think there's a connection? Between the place of hostile eyes and where he might have disappeared?"

I stared at the table, yet I also saw something else. Stretching across my vision, the forest yawned awake again, branches unfurling until it filled the cavern of my mind.

The forest watches me.

Hostile and still, with remembering eyes.

Where would the most hostile place in the forest be for Father, the place requiring the cleansing of his conscience?

I thought of the spot near the scene of Seohyun's death, where Maewol and I had reportedly been found, lying unconscious in the snow, passed out either from fear or from the cold. There was also the place that didn't exist in my memory, the past Maewol couldn't escape from—

Realization struck me so hard I couldn't breathe. I looked up, my gaze locking with Maewol's.

"Do you think . . ." Maewol spoke quietly, as though afraid

of disturbing the silence. "Do you think he went to the Grandmother Tree?"

The place where Father's one mistake had resulted in the unraveling of our entire family. *Of course* that was the place he had written about in his note. The place where he felt watched, the place of hostile eyes.

"But his bloody robe was found in Gotjawal forest," I said, and now I remembered why the obvious hadn't seemed so obvious before. "Gotjawal is in the Seonhul district. That is at least . . . a ten hours' or more walk away from the Grandmother Tree."

"Let's go see anyway," Maewol said. "You and me."

Everything in me lurched forward, ready to go, but reality pinned me down. "I can't."

"Why not?"

"Aunt Min ordered the soldiers guarding the gate to not let me out. I *tried* to sneak out, but they recognized me." My voice deflated. "It's a dead end."

"Older Sister," Maewol said, her tone so matter-of-fact. "Dead ends only exist in your mind. There is always another way out."

"I need your back," Maewol said.

I must have heard her wrong. "What?"

"I said, I need your back."

"You want me to go on my hands and knees."

"Yes."

We were standing in the shadows, in the backyard between the Dongheonnae pavilion and the black-tile-capped stone wall—a wall that rose a head higher than me. I knew what Maewol was thinking, but I did not intend to be stepped on. When Maewol continued to gesture hurriedly at me, I said sternly, "No."

"I'm short, but I'm stronger than you. So I need to get on top of this wall so I can help pull you over!"

I shook my head. "You said there's always another way out—"

The sound of male voices echoed on the other side of the pavilion.

"She's not here!"

"But I escorted her to this room earlier—"

"Check the other rooms!"

I dropped onto all fours, the wet dirt scratching my bare palms. "Quick! Get on!"

Maewol lifted her skirt, revealing her muddy straw shoes. She stepped onto me, her weight digging into my lower back, then she pushed herself upward with such force my elbows buckled. Maewol came toppling down.

"Are you trying to kill me?" she demanded.

"Try again." I locked my elbows this time, and when Maewol pushed her feet off my back again, I heard the satisfying *smack* of her hand grabbing hold over the tiles. Now I only felt the tip of one sandal grazing my back as she dangled, leveraging herself upward with her other foot.

"Stop!" came a male voice, so loud Maewol gasped and both her feet landed back down on me; her sudden weight nearly sent me sprawling. "I order you to stop!"

"Hurry," I cried, fear roaring in my ears.

"I'm trying—!"

Then Maewol fell still, so still I glanced forward to see what had petrified her. Two soldiers held their torches high, illuminating a third person. Aunt Min. Her hair was parted perfectly down the middle and tied back into a coiled bun, where a binyeo studded in jewels gleamed angrily. Her silk hanbok rustled as she strode forward, descending upon us like a vengeful queen regent.

"*Min Maewol*," Aunt Min snapped, uttering the name she hadn't spoken in several years. Her voice dripped with revulsion. "Get *off* your sister. *Now*."

Maewol seemed to shrink before our aunt, leaving a sickly girl who gripped her hands together and kept her head lowered. Her entire body flinched when Aunt Min sharply said, "*Stop* dragging your feet. Walk properly."

Maewol had flinched in the same way five years ago, and it dawned on me why Maewol appeared so hurt by a woman she hadn't seen in years: Aunt Min was Father's sister. They were siblings who mirrored each other in the sting of their wrath.

"I never agreed with your father's decision," Aunt Min said as we followed her. "He should have taken Maewol to the mainland, too. Yet he left her here to grow up wild and untethered. What a disgrace to the Yeoheung Min clan."

Aunt Min spoke on about our family, and as she did, bitterness coiled tight in my chest. She always spoke of our clan with such pride, for we were distantly connected through our ancestors to Queen Dowager Hudeok, the mother of our current king. But her talk about our clan echoed so shallow to my ears. She cared more about our reputation, about honor, than her own nieces.

"Both of you will inherit your father's estate, split equally among you," Aunt Min continued.

I'd already known of this, for I had read Kyŏngguk taejŏn, the Grand Code for State Administration. But my sister's eyes widened a little, though she quickly lowered them again when our aunt glanced her way.

"Min Maewol, you are an heiress now and ought to carry yourself as one. You will be returning with us to Mokpo."

Maewol stiffened, and I could hear her unspoken protest. I knew Maewol. She would give up an entire estate to stay here with Shaman Nokyung.

"We will have you married off as well. But first, a country bumpkin like you must learn proper conduct . . ."

Bitterness sharpened into anger, and I had to bite down on my tongue to keep myself composed. Father was dead, poisoned. Twelve girls were still missing, the thirteenth girl dead. And what was my aunt chattering on about? Inheritance? Marriage? *Proper conduct?*

"I will instruct you soon on how to serve your future husband and his parents, and how to treat your servants well. Otherwise I can assure you, Min Maewol, that you will be beaten for your stupidity—"

"*No one* is going to beat my sister," I said heatedly. I caught Maewol's wrist; she halted next to me, tension cording her arm. "And we are not going with you."

Aunt Min stopped and didn't even bother glancing our way. "What did you say?" Her voice sounded perfectly composed—and perfectly cold. At my continued silence, she turned to the soldiers. "Make sure they don't run. Drag them if you must—"

"You will have to guard us night and day for as long as we live." I raised my voice a notch, which I had never done before with her. "We *will* find a way to leave again." And with that, I gently tugged at Maewol's wrist, leading her up the stone steps into the pavilion. It would be impossible to run away tonight, not with so many eyes watching us. But tomorrow on our way to the port . . .

I reached the last stone step when I heard another familiar voice, tired and yet commanding: "You will not return to Jeju again."

I glanced over my shoulder, and when I saw who it was, my hand dropped from Maewol's wrist. Magistrate Hong stood in the yard, half his face cloaked in shadow and the other half drenched in orange torchlight. A torch held by Scholar Yu. Why was *he* here? But with my impending fate of being sent back to the mainland and sold into marriage before me, I didn't have time to wonder at the bizarreness of Scholar Yu's presence. I hurried down the steps and pushed past the dumbfounded soldiers and my speechless aunt.

"Magistrate Hong, please. I need to stay," I pled when I reached him. Aunt Min wouldn't listen to me, but she would listen to a man of authority. "I need to return to the forest. There is evidence Maewol and I must find."

"You will not return to Jeju again," Magistrate Hong repeated. "So finish your task before you leave Jeju for good. If you wish to find the killer, then do so."

For a split second I stopped breathing. Convincing him couldn't possibly be so easy . . .

"But," he added. Ah, there was always a *but*. "Know that in choosing the path of your father, you are choosing death. In the real world, that is what happens to those who choose to do what is right—they lose, if not their life, then someone they hold dear."

"I will not die, and I will not lose," I said. "I'll show you."

"Do so." He looked at me, examining every corner of my face, and something like grief sank into his eyes. "I should have helped your father when he asked."

Footsteps crunched, quick steps, and I didn't need to look back to know who they belonged to. My aunt's angry voice shot out, "Lord Hong! Do not encourage—"

"You will let her go," the magistrate said, his voice firm. "Your deceased husband owes me a favor. I will have him repay it now through you."

As Aunt Min expressed her outrage, I finally took the time to examine Scholar Yu. His robe was no longer dusty, but shone blue like the sea. His black gat was no longer crumpled and tilted to the side, but it sat straight and high on his head, with beads of nobility hanging around his chin. I shifted my weight from one foot to the other, uneasy. Thinking back, it ought to have alarmed me a little, the fact that a man who claimed to be a drunk gambler seemed more interested in the collection of information than anything else.

"How can you let me break my promise to my brother, to care for his daughters?" Aunt Min was still protesting. "Are you willing to bear the consequence of their life in your hands?"

"No one is going to die." Scholar Yu stepped forward. "I will make sure they are accompanied."

"And who are you?" Aunt Min snapped. She'd stolen the words from my own lips.

Scholar Yu slipped his hand into his sleeve and pulled out a bronze medallion shining in the torchlight, and a gasp escaped my mouth. It was a mapae, a horse requisition tablet. I knew how it looked, for I'd once asked a police clerk to draw it out for me, curious after encountering mentions of it in the detective books I'd read.

Putting the medallion away, the convict—who was not a convict at all—stared Aunt Min down, until she turned as pale as ash. She too knew who he was.

"I am known as the street performer to my brothers, for how well I can take on the mask of another life," he said, his voice light and melodic. "But to King Sejong I am Scholar Yu Yeong-bae."

Maewol, at some point, had joined my side, looking as disoriented as I felt.

Yu went on. "I traveled a long distance to come and inspect the reported corruption within this government office. And I have written out a report so extensive detailing the wrongs committed by Magistrate Hong that pine and bamboo would wither by the time one reads it all."

"So," Maewol quietly asked me, "who *is* he?"

The man who had deceived us gazed down at Maewol, overhearing her. His mustache twitched as the corner of his lips rose, a mischievous look gleaming in his eyes. "You may call me Secret Royal Investigator Yu. Or if that is too long, Inspector Yu will do."

The longest night of my life came to an end when first light struck the hanji-screened door and washed the floor in a pale orange. "Inspector Yu will change everything for us,"

I told Maewol as I quickly dressed myself. "I've read about amhaengosa, these secret investigators. They're appointed by the king and have the authority of a highest-ranking local official. That's why he was able to dismiss Magistrate Hong."

Hope bubbled in me. Until now, my entire investigation had hinged on the neglectful and corrupt magistrate; at the end of all my investigation, only he'd have the authority to pass judgment. But now we had Inspector Yu.

"The inspector has the power to preside over retrial of cases unjustly judged," I explained, trying not to sound so wistful. "Magistrate Hong ignored the cases of the missing girls, and Inspector Yu can redress that wrong committed—if we provide him with enough evidence. Maybe he will even be accompanying us to the forest today?"

At Maewol's silence, I looked to see her moving at the pace of a snail, looking haggard.

"Maewol-ah." I had been tying the ribbons of my jeogori jacket but now paused. "Perhaps we should visit the forest another time. You're still not recovered."

"No," Maewol replied, her voice so hoarse it was painful to hear. "If I don't go, I'll die from curiosity. Do you want me to die?"

I sighed. "Why must you always be so extreme with your exaggeration?"

"I know what you'll do. You'll sneak out and investigate on your own." She'd read my mind. "It is better that you keep me within your line of vision. You don't know what I'm capable of when left on my own."

"Maewol-ah . . . We're heading to Mount Halla. The journey will be long and the path arduous. Think about it. If you suddenly grow sicker, how am I supposed to find Father while also taking care of you?"

"You don't even know how to get to the Grandmother Tree."

I opened my mouth to protest, but she was right. "Give me the directions. I'll ask Scholar Yu—" I stopped and corrected myself. "Inspector Yu to help me find my way there."

"If you leave without me"—Maewol set her chin at a stubborn angle as she donned a straw cloak—"I will secretly follow and likely end up dead. It's safer if I go with you."

Reluctance tugged at me, but I had to say it. "What if I promise you that I won't go out on my own to investigate? Then will you rest?"

She met my gaze. "You know we don't have time. Once word gets out that we're searching for evidence in the forest, maybe the Mask will hurry there and hide whatever might have been waiting for us today."

After a few more futile attempts to dissuade her, I gave in. I didn't have the will to argue with her, not when she was right.

"Let's go," I whispered when we were both prepared.

I slid open the door and stepped out into the morning cold, the air crisp with dew and the scent of possibility. A shiver ran down my spine. Could today see the end of the investigation? Was today the day we finally brought Father home? The world remained still, such complete silence blanketing the courtyard, offering me not even a hint as to what lay ahead.

Maewol sniffled. "At least it's not windy today."

The sound of clopping horses echoed somewhere nearby, beckoning us. Likely the two horses that would carry us into the forest of Mount Halla. There was no more time to waste now. Maewol and I moved forward, but I paused in my steps, the memory of the masked man flashing through my mind. I had to make sure nothing happened to us again. I touched my jeogori jacket, my fingers searching for the norigae tassel I knew I'd been wearing the day before. It wasn't there.

"Wait here." I turned and quickly headed back up the stone steps. I slid open the hanji door and searched the quarter until I found the norigae neatly laid out atop a cabinet. The physician must have untied it from my hanbok while I was recovering. Attached to the tassel was a decorative knife, and if she'd unsheathed it, she would have noticed how unusually sharp the blade was. I'd made sure to sharpen it against a whetstone before coming to Jeju.

Snatching it up, I tied the norigae onto my hanbok, then made my way back out. Maewol didn't seem to notice anything different. We continued on our way from one orange-stained courtyard to the next, past massive tiled-roof pavilions, and through the connecting gates.

Once we arrived at the entrance, we found a stable boy waiting for us, holding two ponies by the reins. One belonged to the government building; the other belonged to Maewol. And there was a third horse, its coat stormy gray, and perched atop was the young female physician who had tended to me last night. I hadn't observed her too closely yesterday, thinking I would never see her again, but here she was watching us. Her black hair was divided at the middle, then braided into a bun and tied with a red ribbon. She wore a warm cotton-padded apron over her dark blue uniform.

"I am Physician Aera, and I'll be accompanying you today," the young woman said. "Inspector Yu would have joined himself if he were not busy sorting out Magistrate Hong's corruption, so he requested that I keep you two out of trouble."

Disappointment pinched at me. I had wanted to ask the inspector several questions, such as whether Father had known of his true identity.

Physician Aera's gaze strayed to Maewol, then returned to me. "Are you sure you want your sister to accompany—"

Before the physician could finish expressing her concern, Maewol climbed onto her saddle and urged her pony forward. Her answer was clear: She would lead the way.

"I've tried to dissuade her." I tucked my foot into the

stirrup and mounted the saddle. "But once her mind is set, it never changes."

Together we set off, and once I was close enough to Mae-wol, I cast worried glances her way. My little sister thought she was invincible. Her determination was as great as Mount Taebaek, yet her shoulders were so small, her arms so thin, and her face so hazy with exhaustion. Her life might buckle under the heavy weight of her own stubbornness. *Thank goodness a physician is accompanying us*, I thought, glancing behind me. My gaze met with Aera's.

"Begging your pardon, but," Physician Aera called out, "where are we going, agasshi?"

"To the forest around Mount Halla."

She nodded. "I have been there, agasshi, so perhaps I will be of help to you both. We uinyeos go there often to forage for medical herbs."

"Like shiromi berries?" I asked.

"Yes."

"Do they only grow on Mount Halla's peak?"

"Unfortunately, yes."

My heart sank. I would have liked to pick shiromi berries for Maewol; that is what Mother would have done for her. But journeying all the way to the mountain summit was out of the question.

"It will only be a short visit," I assured Aera, my own guilt pricking at me. "We will go, then return so my sister can rest."

Once we rode out of the coastal village, the scent of the surrounding sea followed us, the saltiness adrift in the wind. Soon, we were surrounded by waves of grass and oreum hills stained in purple as the sun dawned. It was still rising when we entered the gentle, forested area of Mount Halla. The remnants of last night's rainfall still clung to the foliage, dropping in a steady beat, tapping audibly against Maewol's straw cloaks as we rode deeper into the forest. We followed the trail that wound through, steadily climbing, speckled with the morning sunlight breaking through the trees. The trail continued on, running alongside a murmuring stream that vividly reflected the green trees surrounding us, then plunged through crowds of wildflowers, bursting with shades of blue, mauve, and purple.

Maewol had not spoken a word since we'd left Jejumok Village, only coughed, hacking so hard I remarked on how she would likely cough out her intestines before we reached our destination. Her coughing continued until she suddenly fell still, like she was holding her breath.

I dodged under an oncoming branch. "What is it?" I asked.

She glanced over her shoulder to look at us, and the sight of her struck my chest hard: Her face was clammy with sweat and so pale, as though every drop of blood had left her. She shouldn't have come. I should have tried harder to convince her.

"We're here," she whispered, and then she rode forward, disappearing through the thicket.

"Now," came Physician Aera's voice behind me, her voice also lowered, "we must all stay together—"

I urged my horse faster, weaving past the trunks and large rocks, following Maewol's trail, and soon, I saw it. The Grandmother Tree, its ancient bark covered in wartlike mushrooms and the trunk twisted into a crooked line, like the back of an old lady. Maewol had already climbed off her horse and was now before the tree. Her hand wandered, and I could hear the bark chafing under her palm. "It was here," she whispered. "This is where it happened."

The place where Father had abandoned her as a punishment. He'd only meant for it to be a moment; he'd meant to come back—but everything had gone wrong.

Maewol froze, her hand still on the bark.

"What is it?" My heart beat loud in my ears. I leaped off my horse and hurried over to the tree where Maewol was, and I too froze at the sight of a sword mark, an *X* carved into the bark. Below, there was a deep crevice in the trunk, and inside it was a folded piece of hanji.

"Take it out," I whispered.

Maewol didn't budge, her eyes glazed. So I reached out, hands tingling, and slipped the folded paper out—stiff from being rained on, then dried by the scorching sun. I cautiously opened it, corner by corner, catching glimpses of brownish ink. Finally, the page unfolded before me. I stared down at the writing, which was not written with a calligraphy brush but rather by a cruder method—a finger, perhaps. And the ink was not ink, but dried blood.

I have loved you both
from the very beginning
before you were even born.
Please, take care of each other.

fifteen

THE FOREST WAS THE SAME as moments ago, and yet it felt different. Something had shifted in the air, in the color and smell of things. I clung tighter to Father's note, my hands trembling. Only the desperate, the dying, would write a note written in blood.

Father was gone, truly gone. And I knew that no matter how long and how far I searched, there was nowhere I could go to hear his voice again.

"This is Father's writing, I'm sure of it." A burning lump formed in my throat, but I managed to speak around it. "He's not coming back."

Maewol stood still by the Grandmother Tree, looking even paler than before, if that was possible. And absolutely lost. "I didn't think . . ." Her voice was faint, on the brink of sinking into silence. "I didn't think he was truly dead."

I tried to steady my hands as I folded the paper. "Did you really believe that?" I said, and my voice sounded garish; too high, ringing too loud and bright. "You thought he truly was alive."

"I . . ."

Silence stretched. The only thing holding me together was my sense of duty. It was my responsibility as his elder daughter to find Father and give him a proper burial. I couldn't cry now; there would be no end to it then.

"I thought he was hiding." Maewol's voice was strained. "I—I thought . . . maybe . . . I thought he'd returned to the mainland. Secretly. To investigate something else. But I didn't think—"

"He was poisoned, Maewol-ah."

"I told you. You can survive poisoning. He made it all the way to Boksun, so I figured it couldn't have killed him . . . I had hoped it hadn't . . ."

I'd felt little hope, even before this letter. Any shred of belief that Father might still be alive had crumbled, little by little, when Boksun had told us of his condition. Now I held proof from Father himself. But was this all? I looked around at the trees, leaves gleaming greenish-yellow in the sunlight. Dead leaves covered the soggy forest floor. There were likely thousands of crevices here to pocket secrets in.

At a crime scene, one must always search the periphery, Father had written in his journal, *to uncover further details that will piece together to make a whole story. For no man can venture into a forest and leave it with only a single rock disturbed.*

"Where are you—" Maewol broke into a fit of coughing. Coughs that rattled with shards and spits of fire.

Physician Aera, whom I'd completely forgotten about, rushed over to her side to pat her back.

Once the coughing eased, Maewol lowered herself onto the ground with the physician's help, sweating and shaking. "Where are you going?"

I realized I had wandered a few paces deeper into the forest, drawn away by a sense of knowing: Father would have left other clues behind for us. Quickly, I returned to the Grandmother Tree, where Maewol sat against the trunk with her arms around her knees. There were dark shadows smudged beneath her skin, which appeared as thin and frail as hanji, and her eyes clung to me. Wide and vulnerable.

"Agasshi." Physician Aera knelt next to Maewol, but her eyes were on me. "We should return to the gwanheon. That would be the right thing to do."

"I know, but . . ." I hesitated a moment before crouching down to hold Maewol's icy hand. Her fingers in my grasp felt as delicate and small as they had many years ago. As children, no matter how her whining would snap my patience in half, and no matter how my arrogance would leave a sour expression on Maewol's face, we'd always hold hands again when traveling outside. There had been a feeling of comfort then in knowing that we were together. In knowing that we were not alone in a kingdom of disappearing daughters.

"I need to inspect our surroundings," I told my sister, trying to hold her wavering gaze. "I need to see if any other evidence can be found. But I won't go if you don't want me to."

Without answering, Maewol rested her chin on her knee, and for a while, she stayed still. She wanted to go back; I could tell. There was nothing I could do about that. I folded up my plan; I'd have to return to the forest another time.

"Evidence does not wait," Maewol rasped. "What is here today can be gone tomorrow. Go. Please, go find what happened to Father. We need to know."

A mixture of relief and remorse prickled through me. "I'll be back soon. You rest here for now," I said, and when Maewol didn't protest, I rose to my feet and took a few steps back, my gaze still fixed on her. "I *will* be back. I promise." And then I glanced at Physician Aera; she was a lowborn woman, and yet not even the difference in our status could dim the disapproval sharp in her gaze. "Please, take care of my sister. I will return before noon."

With reluctance dragging at my heart, I left them and stalked through the crowd of branches, branches as sharp as nails that left cuts on my cheeks and seemed bent on piercing my eyes. I wanted to slow down, to move past the perilous tangle of trees and roots with care, but I felt chained to an inhuman force that tugged me forward. Whatever this feeling was—conviction? Or something otherworldly?—it seemed to know. Father was close.

I finished walking a wide circle around the Grandmother Tree and looked up at the sky. It was not yet noon; not enough time had yet passed for Maewol to begin wondering where I had gone. I had plenty of time still. I tried exploring a larger ring of land that visibly circled the tree, but I grew disoriented. With my poor sense of direction, I'd likely circle the same area a thousand times thinking I was examining the entire forest floor.

"Think," I whispered to myself. I needed a better method by which to search the woods. A map of sorts. A way to indicate to myself the examined circle of trees. The memory of the X Father had left behind on the Grandmother Tree sparked into mind.

This time as I covered the land, I used my decorative dagger to leave small slashes on each tree, though the farther I got from the Grandmother Tree, the less sure I was that I was traveling in a circle. It didn't matter. I just needed to cover each point; north, west, south, east. I examined every trunk, probed the forest floor for things disturbed, for any signs of Father, of which way he'd gone after leaving the note.

Finding nothing, I continued to cover the surrounding area, one ring (or whatever shape I was making in my wandering) at a time, marking off each tree. It became almost rhythmic, this motion of sweeping the ground with my eyes, then slashing the bark with my dagger. Ninety-seventh tree, ninety-eighth, ninety-ninth—

I raised my dagger to dig into the hundredth tree trunk, then froze. A breeze rustled through the flickering leaves as I stared at another sword mark, another *X* carved into the bark. In a flurry, I searched the crevices of the tree. There were no notes, no evidence hidden. I inspected the tree three more times as confusion whirled in my mind. This was Father's *X*, it had to be. But it wasn't a mark to indicate that he'd left something here.

My breath hitched in my throat. Perhaps it was a clue pointing me in a certain direction. Perhaps to the next *X*. With renewed determination, I moved through the forest, no longer trying to circle around the Grandmother Tree but around this one. This new evidence that whispered in Father's deep and gentle voice: *I was here.*

Just as I had hoped—or perhaps, just as I had feared—I discovered another *X* carved into a trunk. Father had left a trail behind for me to find him with. I continued to find more *X*s, and whenever I saw a nearby cave, I peered into a nightmare filled with the possibility of discovering Father's body. But each time I found only an empty cavern, and relief washed through me and left my legs trembling, until I found the next *X*. And the fear was renewed. *Would I find my dead abeoji here?*

The air sharpened with a biting chill as the shadows in the forest deepened, but I didn't feel it, so consumed by the search was I. And each time I found Father's mark, I couldn't stop there, my eyes instantly roving around for the next one and the next. The passing of time did not occur to me until a raindrop plopped onto the blade of my dagger, gleaming there for me to see. What time was it now? I caught sight of my reflection in the trickling stream, my countenance stained blue in the setting sunlight, the tips of my nose and ears red from the evening cold.

It was late. Later than I had hoped.

I gazed up the slope of trees that now shivered against the light rainfall, and I wondered how many more dozens of *X*s were waiting to be found. I was so close to the truth my skin prickled. Even the air seemed to tingle and crack, eagerly waiting for me to find the secret hidden in the overgrowth. But already my feet were taking retreating steps; I was walking backward, farther and farther away from where the clues were directing me.

Tend to the living first, I thought. *The dead later.*

I picked up the hem of my skirt and ran down the gentle slope, following the marks I'd left behind. The eerie blue of the sky condemned me; I should have returned to Maewol sooner. What if my sister's condition had worsened while I was away?

My chest tightened as I labored to breathe through the tangle of anxiety and dread. Faster, I needed to run faster. My only consolation was in knowing that Maewol, at least, wasn't alone.

Rushing past the whipping of leaves and branches, I wiped the stream of sweat and raindrops from my brows and resisted the urge to rest. My ankles, my thighs, my lungs were on fire. Everything burned. And when I could run no longer, I forced myself to limp, to cling to trees to keep me from collapsing to the ground in exhaustion.

Not too long later, I found the familiar winding trail, and soon I caught a glimpse of the Grandmother Tree.

"Maewol-ah! Physician Aera!" I called out, delighted to have arrived at my destination without getting lost. But whatever relief I felt was short-lived. Under the covering of the tree, I saw Maewol lying alone on the ground; one pale arm peeked out from her straw cloak and lay across her chest, the other lay unfurled across the earth. Motionless.

Dread thickened into a cold surge of panic as I knelt before her and gathered her in my arms, only to see her head loll and her mouth fall open. "Maewol-ah, I'm here. I came back." I shook her shoulders, once, twice, thrice—nothing. For a moment, I couldn't breathe as I stared at her, everything in me frozen cold. Then Maewol's eyes opened, the slightest bit.

"Maewol-ah," I tried again, "I'm back. Where is the physician?"

"She . . ." Maewol swallowed, then winced, as though her throat were on fire, "went to . . . search for . . ." Her voice drifted away, her dark pupils rolling back as eyelids shut again.

Physician Aera must have gone to search for me, or to find herbs for Maewol. I had been gone for so long. Clutching

Maewol's trembling body against mine, I stared at the trees, begging for Aera's return. I waited and waited, but there were no sounds of footsteps crunching across the forest floor, no sound of her crystal-clear voice calling out my name. She could be anywhere in the forest. Waiting for her was the right thing to do, surely, yet the violent shaking of Maewol's body left me impatient.

It was raining, it was cold, and I'd seen a cave nearby.

Holding both of Maewol's arms, I lifted her up into a sitting position against the trunk, then taking my dagger, I carved a message onto the trunk for Physician Aera. Hopefully she'd see the words: *We went to find shelter.* Once that was done, I hurried over to our two horses tethered nearby. The third one was gone, likely with the physician.

I hesitated. Maewol's pony was rather wild, and the government's horse was a stranger to me; I didn't trust either of them not to fling Maewol off. Instead of untethering a horse, I inspected Maewol's pony and found a saddle blanket. I held it tight against my chest to keep it dry from the light rainfall as I hurried back to the Grandmother Tree.

I untied the straw clock from Maewol, wrapped the blanket around her icy body, then lifted the cloak over her again. Turning my back to her, I carefully drew her forward so that her arms draped over my shoulders. The cave wasn't too far, and there was one mode of transport I knew would get her to shelter safely—the method Father had often used when Maewol whined about being too tired to walk.

Looping my arms around her legs, I held my breath and used all my strength to struggle to my feet, making sure to lean forward so that my sister didn't fall backward.

The rainfall was still light, tapping against the straw cloak, pattering against my forehead and sliding down my collar. The rain released the scent of fertile soil and decaying autumnal leaves—a scent once pleasant to me, but now I knew it would forever haunt me. The muddied wildflowers and the moist black earth sank under my steps as I followed the marks I'd left, moving at the pace of a turtle.

I wanted to walk faster, but my legs trembled under the weight, ready to give in at any moment. *Please, don't be too far away.* I gazed up at the dizzying number of trees, at the land that sloped upward. The sense of impossibility began to sink into me, but before it could swallow me whole, I shook my head and tried to keep my mind occupied. I focused on the sensation of my sister's arms over my shoulder, swaying side to side. She was alive still, her breath wheezing near my ear, and now and then she mumbled something. My entire body felt ready to crumble, but at least we were together, and I'd never cherished this more than now.

I didn't want to lose her. I couldn't.

We were once inseparable, Maewol and I. How had I forgotten that? My tired mind weaved in and out between the blue-gray forest and my faded old memories, weaving in and out with a thread and needle until the Maewol once my childhood companion and the Maewol hanging over my back became one. Our late-night giggle-filled conversations and our secret sharing, our magical stories spun between us and our silly games, I remembered them now. Maewol had irritated me, even then. Always quite the opposite of me. Loud, brash, and without any sense of self-preservation. She would always fling herself into danger for me.

At last, the cave came into view. Maewol's weight bounced against my back as I tried running, rain now streaming into my eyes, blurring everything into a wash of green, gray, and shadow. At last, a cool and dry darkness greeted me, and I carefully lowered Maewol onto the ground. My arms burned with exhaustion, my legs wobbled, but instead of letting myself collapse, I adjusted the dry blanket close around my sister. Pulled off her straw cloak and shook out the rain, a sparkle of droplets in the skylight, before draping it over her again.

It wasn't enough.

Maewol was still shuddering, yet hot to the touch now. Beads of sweat dripped down her white face, and her hair clung to her cheeks like an ink stain. And each time she breathed, there came an awful rattling sound, like there was water in her lungs. My sister was right before me, her hands in my hands, yet she was sinking into the black waves of the sea, and I didn't know what to do. Take her back down the mountain? That would take two to three hours in the damp cold, and then what? Find a village? I hadn't seen one on our journey here. I'd likely have to drag Maewol for a few more hours to find help while wandering.

Shiromi.

The memory of Mother prodded at me.

Shiromi berries, she'd said, *they grow at the top of Mount Halla. Always there if you look closely enough.*

I gazed out of the cave, at the blue trees and the blue sky. I couldn't be too far from the summit. And perhaps on my journey there, I'd find Physician Aera.

I squeezed my sister's hand. "Maewol-ah." I called her name a few times before her eyes opened—just barely, revealing an unfocused gaze, the black waves gripping her so strong she only barely managed to surface. "I'm going to find shiromi berries for you. The ones Mother said help fevers and chills go away. Would that be all right? Blink your eyes once if you want me to go bring them for you. But if you want me to stay by your side, blink twice."

Maewol slowly closed her eyes, like she was about to fall back into unconsciousness, but then her eyelids opened again. It was a blink. Her hazy gaze clung to me. She wanted my help.

The rain had eased into a fine mist, the woodlands still plunged into a deep-sea blue. As I fetched my horse, and as I rode up the sloping mountain, I fell into the pattern of calling out for Physician Aera, glancing around at the forest for signs of her, then glancing up at the sky—hoping that tonight the clouds would clear and allow the full moon to light my path. But what if it didn't clear away? And what if the physician was lost, or even injured?

Fear rested heavy on my back as I continued on up the slope thick with trees on all sides, until the path grew too steep and rocky. Gods, how far was it to the summit? I tried calculating. From what I'd heard, it took a total of five hours or so to climb from the bottom to the peak of Mount Halla, and we'd already traveled a good way up to reach the Grandmother Tree. Perhaps I was only two or at most three hours from the peak.

Tethering my horse again, I traveled by foot, continuing to mark my path through the trees as I went. My palm and fingers felt calloused, but I gripped my dagger's hilt tight, carving deeper and longer marks into the bark. Now and then, I even cut off strips of skirt to tie around branches, a silk marker of vivid purple and silver floral embroidery.

I couldn't risk getting lost.

I couldn't risk losing my way back to Maewol.

The slope grew steeper yet. My steady and slow breathing turned into short bursts. Dread pounded in my chest, curses flew from my lips, and I wondered if there was indeed a *wrong* path upward. Perhaps not all paths led to the summit. Soon I was almost climbing vertical over the sharp slabs of rock, and I dared not glance down. I knew what I'd see: the tops of trees and a frightening drop.

Still, I continued up the slope as the sky darkened into black, and to my relief, the moon shone bright, outlining the rocks and jutting roots of trees. And not long later, the trees were the ones that told me my destination was near, for they were twisted and stunted, sculpted by the wild winds that reigned on mountain peaks.

By the time I secured my feet on level ground, I crouched and placed a hand over my aching side. I tried to catch my breath, but before I could, it was stolen by the scenery around me, at once majestic and terrifying. The forest had thinned out. A delicate layer of snow had settled everywhere, whitening the wide plain, the scattered small rocks and shrubs. And everywhere else was simply moonlit clouds and pitch darkness. It almost felt like I'd climbed into a new world parallel to my own.

I snapped out of the daze. I needed to find the berries and hurry back.

I wrapped my arms around myself, to keep warm in the freezing cold, as I searched the ground for the berries. Those thick, juicy black berries Mother would bring down with her, some of them still attached to branches covered in needle-like green leaves. But all I saw was one berryless shrub after another. I walked higher up the summit, the slopes here gentle yet still treacherous, for the path was narrow and icy.

Nothing, nothing, nothing.

I couldn't find a single shiromi bush—

I came to an abrupt halt at the sight of berries that glowed round against needlelike green leaves.

I'd found it.

Grabbing my dagger, with a jerk, I sliced off a long piece of my hem. I spread the fabric open on my lap, and with fingers stiff with cold, I awkwardly plucked the shiromi and dropped them into the slice of silk. They were like droplets of hope. Hope that my sister would recover, hope that I could prove to her that I would never abandon her. And I made sure to try one, to ensure that these weren't death in the guise of life, for better I be poisoned than my sister. I was greeted by a familiar burst of flavors, and with it came no pain. No numbing sensation. "Thank the gods," I whispered.

All the berries picked off the shrub, I tied the silk into a closed pouch and traced my steps backward, the shiromi a nice weight that swung with my every step. The journey downhill was brutal on my knees, but much easier. I had the berries, the fear was gone, and the marks on the trees and the silk ribbons tied to the branches guided me back to the cave where my sister was.

She was curled in the same position I'd left her several hours ago. The straw cloak draping her shuddered as Maewol let out a rattling cough. My eyes burned wet, my nose tingled, and an emotion I thought I'd never feel again flooded across my mind. Unadulterated joy.

Maewol was still alive, and the berries were going to keep her alive.

Quickly lowering onto my aching knees, I drew out my dagger again. It was the Joseon way, to voluntarily cut your own finger and have the patient drink your blood when it seemed that they would succumb to a grave illness. With my blood dripping, I squeezed the shiromi until black juice filled my palm, and then I watched the two create a dark stream that dribbled into Maewol's mouth.

Now—now all I could do was wait.

The next morning came like a sigh of relief. I must have fallen asleep; when I opened my eyes and glanced at my sister, still sleeping on my lap, she looked transformed. The color had returned to her cheeks and her lips. She was still coughing, but she no longer felt like a girl drowning in a stormy sea.

"You're better," I whispered to myself, and Maewol opened her eyes at the sound of my voice. "Let's head back to the nearest village. Or is Shaman Nokyung's hut the closest—? We also need to notify the inspector of Physician Aera's disappearance—"

"No," Maewol's voice croaked. She weakly sat up and rubbed her eyes.

"What do you mean, *no*?"

"You were talking to me all night. I don't remember everything, but you mentioned marks Father left behind.

Let's follow them. And if it leads to nowhere by midmorning, then we'll leave. I know the way back to Shaman Nokyung. It's not too far."

I shook my head, determined this time. "I regret bringing you here. I don't want to regret my decision again. We're heading back." The terror of last night, when I'd almost lost Maewol, still lingered in me like a cold. "And there is Physician Aera to worry about. She's likely lost, possibly injured—"

"The physician knows the forest well; she told me herself while we were waiting for you. She didn't get lost; she probably returned to the Grandmother Tree soon after we'd left. She must have seen our horses still tethered there."

"And I left her a message on the tree trunk," I added.

"Then she must have known we were together, gone to find shelter. She would have left to find one herself. She is probably either searching for us, or—if she is smart—then she would have returned to the gwanheon to request assistance."

"And that," I pointed out, "is why we should return. Everyone will be worried about us."

"How about this," Maewol rasped. "The moment I feel even the slightest bit strange, or if you feel the slightest concern for the progression of my health, we will leave. For now, let's venture into the forest a little bit more. A tiny little bit." When I shook my head again, she rushed to add in a few wheezes, "I'll stay on the horse the whole time. No walking, no getting off the saddle. I'll stay warm in this cloak and blanket. And I'll eat plenty of these berries you picked for me. *And* if the physician is indeed searching for us, we might bump into her."

I nibbled on my lower lip, the memory of Father's *X*s returning to me, the beckoning tug of evidence that he had to be somewhere nearby.

"Don't you want to know?" Maewol dropped her voice into a haggard whisper. "Don't you want to find out what happened to Father before the masked man discovers what we're up to? Before he does something to hide Father's trail?"

I hesitated as Maewol locked her eyes on mine, her gaze determined and filled with curiosity. I was curious myself. "I won't leave you this time," I promised. "But first we should eat something."

I'd packed a simple meal for us, a meal that was supposed to last us only until noon yesterday, but was still waiting for us in my traveling sack. Maewol had been too sick to eat yesterday, and I too anxious and exhausted. We nibbled on it now, a few rice balls that had dried up overnight. A pity, for rice was precious in Jeju, though clearly plentiful in Magistrate Hong's storage.

Maewol stopped after a few bites. "It's too coarse," she said. "My throat is too sore to swallow it."

"It's not all coarse, jjinga-jjinga." I peeled off the hardest layer on each of the rice balls, eating it as I would nooroongji—scorched rice—while Maewol ate the soft, inner clumps of rice. I savored this moment of quiet peacefulness between us, watching the way the morning light softened my little sister's features.

Cherish this time together, a cold voice whispered, *for it will come to an end soon.*

"Are you finished eating?" I asked my sister, trying to beat the sorrow away. There was no point to my grief; feelings could change nothing. Whether I handed Shaman Nokyung over to Inspector Yu, or Aunt Min took me back to the mainland, I was going to lose my sister. "If you are, then let's go."

We set out through the golden morning mist, the trees and leaves burnished in sunlit yellow. I took Maewol to the last *X* I'd discovered, and the search for the next one kept my mind occupied, restraining my thoughts from drifting back to the lonely reality that I'd soon face.

It didn't take long before we found the next *X*, and my lingering sadness was replaced by a question. "I wonder where Father was leading us," I murmured.

"These marks," Maewol said, pausing to cough. "They certainly are not leading us in the direction of Gotjawal forest. It's going in the complete opposite direction. Southward."

Her observation was so unexpected, I almost dropped hold of the reins. *She is right.*

"So Father entered the forest to find the Grandmother Tree, to leave us the note." I spoke aloud my line of thoughts as I tried piecing threads together. "And from there, he traveled southward . . . Away from Gotjawal, away from where his bloodied robe was found ... But how can you tell we are going southward?"

"I know this forest like I know Shaman Nokyung's yard."

My brows crinkled. "The bloodied robe would suggest he died in Gotjawal. That is what the police believe. But Iseul's testimony points to Father as having visited this forest just before his disappearance. And the note we found tells us he was indeed near the Grandmother Tree ..." I tilted my head to the side, unable to account for the wide stretch of land that separated the two places. "What do you know about Gotjawal?"

Maewol shrugged. "I don't know—" Her head jerked. "Oh."

"Oh?"

"Maybe ..."

I waited. And waited. Then gently prompted her, "Maybe ... ?"

She shook her head. "Or maybe not."

"What are you thinking?"

"Around the time Father was here, there were rumors of a wild animal being sighted nearby. A bear. Everyone was talking about it. Everyone was saying to never walk through Gotjawal alone ... Perhaps he was never there at all."

"What?" I said.

"Perhaps the police were searching the wrong place for his disappearance," Maewol explained. "Someone could have easily planted his robe there, splashed it with blood, to make it look like he'd been attacked by the bear. An accident. And it worked, didn't it? The troop of police withdrew, and your Commander Ki closed the case, just like that."

I let her speculation sink in. It didn't seem entirely impossible.

"Whoever was responsible for Father's poisoning," Maewol continued, "they could have wanted to distract the authorities. It also means this person knew Father was in the forest, and had access to his robe. Access enough to rip off a piece to plant elsewhere."

I cast an uneasy glance at Maewol. Someone had poisoned Father, and that someone was likely Shaman Nokyung. But how could Shaman Nokyung have done all this? She was a frail old woman. But then again, poison had weakened Father, perhaps for this very purpose. To debilitate him enough that she could stalk him through the forest with a knife. To end his life and then to cut off a piece of his military robe.

"Something—or someone—was chasing him," Maewol concluded.

And as she did, my gaze fell down a gentle slope and landed on a crooked tree, where an unmistakable *X* stared out at me. Next to it were slabs of rocks that formed an entrance into a cave. I leaped off my horse, landing silently on the wet leaves, then skidded down the slope toward the cave. "I'm going to check inside," I called over my shoulder.

"And if you don't come out," Maewol said, dread in her voice, "I'll know you found something."

I walked into the shadows and kept my eyes fixed on the cavern floor, too afraid to look ahead. It had been a year since Father's disappearance. From what I'd gathered from his journals, I knew that if I found Father's body, I'd find him in a condition of such decomposition . . .

Whatever I found wouldn't look like Father anymore.

The daylight was thinning. Soon I'd be too deep in the cave to see anything. So far I'd found nothing. Perhaps there was nothing—

I froze.

There on the ground. A braiding of yellow, blue, and green strings—a bracelet I'd made when I was a child. It was tied around a wrist—Father's wrist.

He was lying still on the ground, like he had slept through an entire year.

Time slowed, weighing down my every step as I walked closer to him. He was supposed to be all bones. He was supposed to be unrecognizable. Was he really just asleep? Yet as I got closer, a blade sank into my chest and carved out a hole. Horror filled it. Father looked dried, a waxy substance layering his skin.

My heart heaved and tears burned my eyes. I was standing not before a slumbering Father, but a dead one.

I turned and stumbled out, running from the suffocating cavern. When I could no longer contain myself, I fell to my knees. My stomach lurched, and with each convulsion, vomit surged up my throat before spilling to the ground.

Thoughts reeled in my mind. Father was in the cave. After all these months, I'd found him. Once my stomach completely emptied itself, I felt numb and so drained of strength I collapsed to the ground, leaning against a rock.

"Abeoji," I rasped. But calling for Father beckoned the image of the waxy stranger lying in the cave. I squeezed my eyes shut, wanting to erase what I had seen, but it wouldn't go away. And the awful silence that had filled the cave pressed into my ears, filling my mind with its numbing tunes:

> *Mother, gone.*
> *Father, gone.*
> *Shaman, a traitor.*
> *And once you betray her . . .*
> *You will lose Maewol, too.*
> *No one to love you.*
> *No one to love.*
> *There's nothing left.*

Nearby, twigs cracked under footsteps. I snapped my gaze up. Through the wetness that blurred my eyes, the colors fused until I blinked fast enough to see Maewol wandering into the cave, her eyes large with fear and curiosity. She must have seen how I'd darted out.

All thoughts of my own grief vanished.

"No." I scrambled back onto my feet and chased after Maewol. My shoes scraped against the cavern floor as I raced toward my little sister, her straw-cloaked figure disappearing into the shadows.

"*Maewol-ah*," I called, "stop! Don't look—"

A hair-raising scream exploded from the dark. A thousand shrill blades that rang against the rock walls. Puncturing me. Ripping through my heart.

I grabbed Maewol's wrist and swung her around, away from the corpse. Her face smacked against my chest; her scream muffled, then turned into violent sobs. Sobs that cut into me, jagged and brittle.

sixteen

OUR SHOULDERS HUNG FORWARD AS we slumped, strengthless, over our horses' backs, swaying as we traveled down the mountain with the unspoken decision to return to the shaman's hut. We did not utter a single word along the way. There was nothing to say. Nothing at all. Our minds were numb, our hearts hollowed out.

Then the sound of another pair of horse hooves lifted me out from the haze. I looked up; at first, I saw nothing but trees, until I caught sight of shadows shifting behind the leaves. My grip on the reins tightened—then loosened at the sight of Inspector Yu and Physician Aera, who pointed our way. "There they are!"

Yes, here we were. The Min sisters who had traveled into the forest yesterday, but were we the same two girls today? I felt translucent, drained by grief.

Inspector Yu sat tall on his horse, shaking his head. "I had hoped I wouldn't regret my decision to let you both travel to the forest. I should have listened to your aunt—" His voice dropped away at a closer sight of us. He looked at us as though he were looking at a pair of ghosts. Slowly, he asked, "What happened?"

"Maewol fell ill." I paused. "And we found Father."

He didn't nod. He didn't respond at all, just stared.

I continued, my voice distant and empty. "Would Physician Aera guide my little sister back to the shaman's hut? She is too ill to stay out any longer. I'll take you to where we found him, sir."

Inspector Yu bowed his head, then with a gesture of his hand, Physician Aera rode forward and ushered Maewol away with her. The usual Maewol would have protested. She would have demanded to follow us, but it was as though someone had shot down the wild pony in her. Without uttering a word, she simply followed the physician away.

"You are certain it is your father?" Inspector Yu asked solemnly.

"Yes, sir," I replied.

"A year of decomposition would have left a corpse difficult to recognize . . ."

I tried not to remember what I'd witnessed. "It is my father, sir. I am sure of it."

"Lead the way, then."

I rode toward the place that had become Father's grave, the inspector following quietly behind. Once we arrived, I stayed outside the cave while the inspector disappeared inside. I stood staring at the forest floor, my mind—usually racing with thoughts—now utterly blank. Quite some time must have passed, for I heard footsteps again, the inspector striding out of the cave.

My chest tightened, and hope—that very last remnant of it—waited for him to say, *That was not a corpse. It was merely a heap of leaves. Exhaustion must be playing with your mind.*

Instead, Inspector Yu shook his head, his brows knotted, as he murmured, "I have never before seen a phenomenon like this. A corpse that has resisted decomposition, despite the passing of an entire year?" At last he arrived before me, and I wondered if he could hear it, grief splitting through my bones. "My instinct tells me that he was poisoned."

I dug my nails deep into my palm, deeper than I'd ever pressed, until the pain was so sharp that the ache in my heart lifted for a moment. Long enough for me to speak. "He was poisoned," I told him, my voice tight. "It was kyeong-po buja."

"But it was not poison that killed your father."

I finally looked up. "It wasn't?"

"I examined Detective Min's body," he said, his eyes watching me closely. "And I discovered a wound. He was stabbed."

I flinched, something flickering fast across my mind, like a moth in the night. A face—not Father's, but a young woman's. A scar running down one eyebrow, making it look like she had three brows. And under it, red-rimmed, desperate eyes. Her lips moved, but there was only silence. It had to be Seohyun I was remembering.

"Stabbed where?" I barely managed to say, shaking off the memory.

"Through his stomach. A skilled swordsman like your father, as I'd heard him to be, would have been able to fend off a thrust to the stomach. But I think he was too weakened by the poison. Too weak to even use his sword, for I found no blood on his blade."

I thought I would cry again. I waited for it. But I felt nothing but a gaping hole in my chest.

"Here," he said. "I found it deeper in the cave."

Inspector Yu placed into my grasp Father's jukjangdo; it was so heavy I had to hold it with two hands. It looked like a mere bamboo walking stick, but as I pulled at the handle, a blade drew out and rang sharp in my ears, gleaming in the daylight. Someone had poisoned Father in order to have a chance at stabbing him. And only one type of person would have done such a thing: a person aware of her debilitating weakness, and the overpowering strength of her victim.

"Wait." Inspector Yu turned back to me. "You mentioned kyeong-po buja. Why do you think it was this that poisoned him?"

I told him about Boksun's statement about Father's condition, about Seohyun's connection to Shaman Nokyung, about the witness who had seen the shaman arguing with Seohyun before her death—and how everything kept connecting back to the shaman.

"So I searched the shaman's quarter," I said as bitterness rose to my voice, "and found kyeong-po buja locked away. You must have heard of it before, sir."

"I have. Potent, it is. But why would an old shaman want to kill your father—Maewol's father?"

I had no idea. This was the question that kept catching me at the ankle, tripping me. "I know she cares for my sister deeply," I said. "I don't doubt that. But perhaps he got too close to some truth, and she felt so cornered that she—" I gritted my teeth. "She retaliated."

"Hm." Inspector Yu tilted up the brim of his black hat, revealing the sharp features of his face deep in thought. "You mentioned the masked man attempted to send Boksun to the Ming kingdom as a tribute girl. Acts of this nature aren't unheard of. Everyone knows that tribute girls are officially trafficked through the Joseon government."

I dared to stare him right in the eyes, too angry to care. *He* was a government official.

As though sensing my accusation, he added, "Many government officials have petitioned to our kings against this practice since nearly two hundred years ago. Even I myself have done so. But you know our history, Mistress Min. What can we do, a mere vassal state? They demand, and we must provide. It is vile."

"It is indeed vile," I mumbled as I frowned down at the jukjangdo still heavy in my hands. Father's disappearance revolved around these tribute girls somehow, but it was not the Joseon government who had kidnapped the thirteen girls. The government had no need to do so secretly—they were the supreme law of our kingdom. "Who else besides the government would want tribute girls?"

"I have heard that the actual number of women taken to the Ming Kingdom is much higher, as envoys and nobles privately take them there. Yet it seems unlikely that such a crime would take place in a small village like Nowon."

"So you're saying Boksun lied?"

"No . . . but perhaps she misunderstood her captor's motive. Yet, if what she says is true, then I have an even harder time believing that Shaman Nokyung is involved."

"She is acquainted with Magistrate Hong," I pointed out.

"I know that."

"You do?"

"I have gone through his expenditures, and a large portion of it was paying Shaman Nokyung for her rituals over the past several years. Perhaps Magistrate Hong was using her to reach the thirteen girls . . ." He pursed his lips, looking unconvinced of his own theory. "If you were a shaman behind the illegal capturing of girls to send as tributes, you would likely be earning great fortunes from this trade.

"Would you then choose to remain living in a small hut

at the base of Mount Halla? Why stay near Nowon Village and continue assisting starving villagers when you could go anywhere and rise in power by serving aristocrats?"

"Because Seohyun was her daughter," I told him. "Seohyun—the tribute girl who ended up dead in the Forest Incident, who was cast out and made miserable by the villagers."

"Ah" was all he said, sinking into his thoughts. "Now, that is interesting. Not greed, but revenge as the motive . . ." His voice trickled into silence, then abruptly, he said, "Come. I will bring you back to Shaman Nokyung for now. Keep an eye on her."

"But what about my father?"

"I need to go to Nowon Village to find the village elder. I'll need help transporting the remains."

My back stiffened. *Remains*. It sounded like he was talking about scraps of meat, the remnants of a pig or chicken left outside a kitchen. Not those of a man, once a living, breathing man. A man who had raised me all on his own after Mother had passed away.

"Will you be back?" I asked, but what I really wished to ask still hung on the tip of my tongue: *When will you arrest Shaman Nokyung?*

He glanced up at the sky. "By nightfall. And when I return, it will be to summon Shaman Nokyung to the gwanheon for an interrogation."

So it was happening. A mixture of relief and uneasiness

settled around me, and then it quickly tightened into a terrible sensation as Inspector Yu asked:

"Does your sister know of this?"

I squeezed my fingers around the jukjangdo. "No. I don't want to hurt her."

Silence beat between us.

"Good," he said, taking me off guard. "It is better this way. If she knows, she'll likely inform Shaman Nokyung, and who knows what will happen then. She may try running away to hide her guilt."

Inspector Yu left, riding away until he was no more than a smudge against the vast sky. I held Father's jukjangdo between my arm and side as I dismounted slowly, and trudging across the yard, I led the government horse into the shaman's stable. A temporary shelter for the creature until the inspector returned—at nightfall.

That was only a few hours away.

My hands sank, the sword grazing the ground, as I pressed my forehead against the wooden frame of the stable's entrance. I imagined Maewol's shock at the return of Inspector Yu, her confusion at the sound of his voice summoning Shaman Nokyung out. I imagined her mind racing, wondering who had accused the shaman. Then she would look at me. Hurt and betrayal would burn in her eyes.

"You're back."

My pulse leaped as I whirled around, staring at Maewol, as though my thoughts had summoned her.

"So?" Her voice wheezed as she frowned at Father's juk-jangdo. "Did the inspector discover anything else?"

I took in the sight of my sister, a sister I was on the brink of losing. Her hair was brushed, her small face washed of all dirt and mud, and she had changed into a clean white han-bok. Her eyes were still fogged with grief, yet a glimmer of curiosity peeked through the veil.

"The inspector told me . . ." I had to swallow hard, else my voice would tremble. "Father was stabbed to death."

A pause. "I thought so."

"You did?"

"I've been thinking while you were gone . . . Someone was chasing him in the forest. That is why he left so many marks on the trees—he was running and knew he might not leave the forest alive."

"Who do you think the killer is?"

"Convict Baek," Maewol said, and then frowned. "Why are you shaking your head?"

I hadn't realized the movement of my head. I stopped.

"Whom do *you* think it is?" she demanded.

I glanced at the hut, then at her. "Father was poisoned with—" I hesitated. I wanted to think over this matter for a while longer, to make the right decision, but Maewol stared at me with questioning eyes, and time was running out.

Hope bubbled in me. *Perhaps if I tell her now, she will be more forgiving than if Inspector Yu informs her.*

"It was kyeong-po buja," I finally said.

Maewol's stare remained on me, unwavering, and for a moment, I thought perhaps she would listen to me. I opened my mouth to explain the connection between the poison and the shaman when Maewol suddenly said:

"You *searched* her room?"

My muscles tensed with disbelief. "You knew about it?"

"I knew about it, because she uses it to help with aching limbs! She *told* me."

"You believe everything she says, yet you don't know her deepest secrets." Concern surged into my voice, and as gently as I could, I said, "You didn't even know Seohyun was her daughter."

"I don't need to know all her secrets. I trust her," Maewol said, "I know she wouldn't kill Father. She wouldn't dare harm him."

"And do you trust me?"

"I do."

"Then trust me." *Please*, I held myself back from adding.

"Shaman Nokyung raised me. She made me food every day for the past five years. She clothed me and gave me a place to call home. She has seen the worst side of me, the meanest side—and she has never once turned her back on me. She has been the truest person—truer than my own family. There isn't a time that I shed a tear that she didn't go out of her way to cheer me up." Maewol's mind was scrambling for a way to convince me. "She loves me like a daughter."

I stared at my sister as a cold stream of despair trickled through me. She wasn't going to change her mind. "I don't have to tell you this," I said quietly, "but I will, because I don't want you to feel betrayed when it happens."

"When what happens." Her voice dropped low.

"Inspector Yu will come to—to escort Shaman Nokyung to the government building, for an interrogation. She knows something, Maewol-ah. Stop letting your feelings cloud your vision."

"Well, it is too late telling me this, isn't it?" Maewol said, panic filling her eyes to the brim. "You've given me no time to find a way to defend the shaman."

"There's nothing to defend—"

"It's Convict Baek. You also suspected him at the start, but now he hardly even crosses your mind, does he?" she snapped, and when I kept quiet, she whirled around and headed straight for the hut.

I knew she was going to tell Shaman Nokyung. Perhaps they would run away together, and, to my shame, a part of me hoped they would. This way, Maewol wouldn't have to watch the shaman being tortured; police interrogations were infamous for torturing confessions out of people, even to death.

I stared down at the jukjangdo, my forehead covered with

a sheen of sweat. Then the dirt yard crunched. I lowered my hands to see Maewol urging Shaman Nokyung out, tugging at the old woman's long sleeve.

"Don't just suspect," Maewol said, waving an angry hand in the air. Her voice was nearly shrill with desperation. She was terrified, utterly terrified of losing someone she loved. "*Ask* her yourself. Ask her." She flung her stare at Shaman Nokyung. "Did you poison our father?"

Several emotions flitted across the shaman's face. Bewilderment, shock, disbelief, then a calm look of understanding hardened the lines of her face. "So that time you broke into my cabinet, you were trying to find evidence that I was your father's killer? Maewol already told me that you found him dead."

"Scholar Yu is a secret royal inspector. Did Maewol tell you this too?" I asked, trying to sharpen my voice, but I couldn't. Not with Maewol's stare boring into me. "I told him about you. About your lie. You said you hadn't seen Seohyun, but you had. A witness claimed to have seen you arguing with her. It is recorded in Village Elder's report."

Shaman Nokyung kept silent.

"Your daughter came to Nowon to escape the shame of living among her neighbors who knew she'd been taken away as tribute. But the villagers of Nowon found out and made her an outcast. They made her miserable. Why did she still continue living here for two entire years?"

Still silent.

"Please tell her," Maewol said. "Make her understand before they come to take you away. Perhaps you can convince Hwani to tell the inspector to stop this ridiculousness."

I gritted my teeth against the sting. "What I suspect is not ridiculous—"

"Very well, I'll tell you," Shaman Nokyung said.

I shut my mouth, ready to listen. Ready to not be swayed.

"Eunsuk, my daughter, she told me . . ." The shaman spoke slowly, as though so much dust had collected over the years that she had to wipe off each layer, reluctantly, until the memory stared clearly back at her. "She told me that on the vessel taking her to Ming, a drunk envoy revealed to her what had happened: A father in Nowon Village, in his attempt to protect his own daughter from being taken, had promised to find him another beautiful girl—one even more beautiful than his."

I flinched. Convict Baek's riddle echoed into memory. *What bribe is large enough that a beautiful maiden will be set aside?* I had dismissed his words before, thinking he was simply trying to taunt me. But now I saw that his riddle and Shaman Nokyung's testimony bore an eerie parallel.

"Eunsuk was chosen as the replacement for another man's daughter. That is what Eunsuk told me. Once a bribe is accepted by an emissary, no matter how handsome the sum, the emissary must find another girl to replace the one spared. For when the government sends virgin girls to Ming, meticulous records of them are kept."

I pulled at the collar of my hanbok, feeling trapped in the radiating heat of my uncertainty. I didn't want to believe her, I wanted to keep blaming her, yet I couldn't ignore the facts. I had read in a history book about the former Ming emperor, Yongle, who had initially demanded a thousand Joseon women. If only nine hundred and ninety-nine women had arrived in his court, the Joseon government would have had to answer for it. An emissary couldn't simply accept a bribe, allow a father to keep his daughter, without finding another girl to fill the allotment.

"The emissary needed to obtain another beautiful maiden." Shaman Nokyung's voice rasped, as though she were dragging the words out of herself, on the brink of collapsing under the weight of this memory. "Hundreds of houses in Nowon were searched again."

Hide your daughters, a servant had come running in to tell Mother. *You must hide them well!*

On that day, seven years ago, soldiers had crowded our yard. Quickly, Mother had lifted the lid of a large chest. *Hide in here*, she'd whispered to my sister and me. *And don't leave it until I tell you to do so.*

We—Maewol and I—had crouched inside the compartment, deep inside the pitch darkness. It had been a game of hide-and-seek to us then, and whoever was the quietest would win. And quiet we had been, muffling our giggles, while footsteps scurried around the house. And I'd heard Father's heavy voice: *Bring me my sword.* Our stomachs had begun to growl with hunger by the time Mother opened the lid and whispered, almost to herself, "Thank the gods. Someone came to tell the emissary to come inspect another girl. She must be quite beautiful." We'd come out, and all I remembered thinking was that my sister and I had both won the game. No one had found us.

"Yes." My voice cracked. "I remember that day."

"Yet it was my daughter who was taken, taken from all the way on the other side of Mount Halla. And when I found her again two years later in Nowon?"

My hands grew clammy as I waited, seeing the pain twist Shaman Nokyung's face.

"There was murder in my daughter's eyes. She told me in riddles what had happened. She and many other girls had been given to Emperor Xuande for his imperial harem. She also told me she was going to kill the person responsible, that she'd found out who it was, but she wouldn't give me a name. I told her to stop, of course. What mother wants blood on their child's hands? I told her to keep her head down, to just forget about everything that had happened. And that is when we argued. She called me a coward."

"And then . . . the Forest Incident happened," I whispered.

Shaman Nokyung shook her head. "She didn't kill herself, Hwani-yah. Your father told me so. Before he found you and Maewol near the crime scene, he found Eunsuk first. She had fallen off the cliff, or perhaps someone had pushed her—then that someone returned to stab her in the back."

Convict Baek had claimed a similar story, that Seohyun-Eunsuk had been murdered. How did he know of this?

Silence crackled between us, my mind reeling. Shaman Nokyung surely would not have told me this fact if she was involved. Had I wasted my entire time in Jeju pursuing a woman innocent of Father's death? My clammy hands twisted around the jukjangdo, and I winced, the disorientation sharpening into a painful throb.

"You say I will be interrogated . . . ," Shaman Nokyung whispered, a tremor lacing through it. "Please, tell the inspector to spare me. I know I will say things I do not mean."

My hands froze. "Why would you say things you do not mean?"

"I have *seen* how those inquisitions are carried out," she said. "People are tortured, witnesses and suspects alike; some even die from the beating. And my daughter was right. I am a coward. And I will absolutely say anything to make the torture stop."

Maewol remained standing next to Shaman Nokyung, staring at me as though I were an outsider, a frightening plague she wanted distance from. A soft, pleading voice in me wanted to say, *I never wanted the shaman to be the suspect. I only followed the trail of clues, though maybe I made a wrong turn somewhere.*

But instead, I remembered why I had come to Jeju: to solve a crime. Not to reunite with my sister and live happily ever after.

"Whether you are guilty or not, ajimang," I said, "it is up to the inspector to find out. Not just you but all witnesses will have to take part in the trial once he reopens the case—"

"I used to look up to you, but now I see the truth of who you are," Maewol whispered. The distant look in her eyes grew, as though she had stepped onto a vessel and was now watching me grow smaller and smaller on the shore. Soon I'd be erased entirely.

"Maewol-ah," I whispered.

"You can't see beyond your own conclusions. That's how the Forest Incident happened, because Father wouldn't listen to me. Now?" Maewol shook her head. "Older Sister, you're not listening to me, and perhaps you never have."

She took a step back, and linking her arm with Shaman Nokyung's, she turned her back to me. "Don't worry," she whispered to the old con woman, "I'll find the real truth for you."

seventeen

By nightfall, Inspector Yu would return. He would arrest Shaman Nokyung and take her in for an interrogation. I'd told him I was certain it was her, yet doubt now lurked in me, stirred by Maewol's words. *Father didn't listen to me. That's how the Forest Incident happened.*

I paced the room, and no matter how deeply I breathed, the suffocating sensation wouldn't leave. The walls were drawing close in around me. My muscles wound so tight, ready to snap apart. In three long strides, I crossed the room and flung open the latticed door.

The sun was setting. *Older Sister*, Maewol's voice echoed in my ears, *you're not listening to me.*

If Father were here, I knew he would have risked his life to listen to his younger daughter if need be. I ran both hands over my face, and left them there, fingers over my eyes. In the darkness, I forced all the suspicions crowding my mind to fall away, until there was only one question: What was it my sister had tried to tell me?

Convict Baek. His name rose to mind at once. Maewol was convinced it was him. The most obvious suspect of all. But Father could *not* have died over an answer so easy to find.

I squeezed my eyes shut and focused, returning my thoughts to Convict Baek and his riddle. *What bribe is large enough that a beautiful maiden will be set aside?*

Shaman Nokyung had offered her answer to it. Another beautiful maiden. The shaman had said that seven years ago her daughter had been stolen from the Seogwipo district to replace the original daughter meant to be taken as a tribute. There were two things I found odd about this. First, that the shaman's account of her daughter's kidnapping fit so well into Convict Baek's riddle. And second, if this were so, then why had Baek told me this riddle at all? Did he want me to find the truth, or was he playing a game?

I needed to know. I had to speak with Convict Baek again. Dread weighed my steps as I moved across my room, snatched up my small journal, pulled my jangot over my head, and collected the jukjangdo sword. I couldn't risk visiting Baek without some form of self-defense.

Tucking the cane-sword under my silk covering, I stepped out onto the veranda. I was about to hurry down the stone steps when the thought of Maewol grabbed me, bruisingly tight. I turned, glancing down the veranda to my sister's room.

I didn't blame myself for having suspected Shaman Nokyung. She was still a suspect. But I had done wrong in hiding my thoughts from Maewol, in lying to her, in always treating the investigation as my own. I wished I could bravely knock on her door now and tell her everything, but our falling-out was still too raw.

I hurried down the steps, then paused again to glance at Maewol's room. It was nearly nightfall; I had no time to hesitate.

The black stone village lay swamped in a reddish-orange mist, the same color as the sky above. Mud squelched as I rode down the miry path until I arrived at the tree from which Maewol and I had surveyed Convict Baek's house before. Tethering my pony to a branch, I counted the wooden logs raised on the jeongnang gate. Two: Convict Baek had left and did not intend to return for a long time. Yet there was light glowing in one of the rooms.

Right then, the door creaked open. Gahee stepped out with a basket filled with what looked like laundry. She hoisted it onto her head, clinging to it with one hand while with the other she held the sort of paddle used to pound the wet clothing.

My gaze swept over Gahee's face, rippling with scars. I had only seen the scars before and had noticed nothing else. But today—perhaps it was the color of sunset that poured over her—I noticed the symmetry and elegance of her features.

What bribe is large enough that a beautiful maiden will be set aside?

"Another beautiful maiden," I whispered, and then a sudden possibility sparked in my mind, so bright that I flinched. Seven years ago, the shaman's daughter, Seohyun-Eunsuk, was kidnapped, and on the other side of Mount Halla, Convict Baek had decided to slice his daughter's face. He had wanted to ensure that Gahee would never be beautiful again, never beautiful enough for an emissary to steal away.

Seven years ago, Gahee would have been twelve.

Most tribute girls were between the ages of eleven and eighteen.

The spark burned like a racing fire. I hurried toward her, the jangot billowing behind me, the cane-sword swaying under the grip of my arm, and when I stepped into her periphery, she cast me a cutting glance.

"What do you want." It was not a question, but an order.

"You're doing your laundry this late in the day?" I asked.

She paused, her stony expression wavering. "It is the only time when I can be alone."

It took me a moment to understand what she meant. In the daytime, other women would be doing their laundry by the brook. Surely the daughter of Convict Baek would not be welcomed among them.

"If you are here to speak with my father," Gahee said, "he

is not here. I don't know where he left to, but until he returns, I am instructed not to interact with anyone. Especially you."

For some time, I quietly walked alongside her until we were outside the village, near the small brook. There, she unloaded her laundry and dunked the clothing into the trickling water.

"Your father was searching for Boksun." I eased the jangot off my head and neatly hung it over my arm, the cane-sword now in my hand. "I found her. It turns out she was a kidnapping victim who managed to escape. Her captor was a man who wore a white mask."

Gahee gripped the paddle, pounding the clothing on smooth stone. Water splashed. "I don't *want* to know."

"There is also a new magistrate in Nowon. He will preside over the retrial of cases." He was actually a secret royal inspector, but I didn't want to bother explaining the situation to her. "And I have spoken with villagers. Everyone suspects your father. The magistrate will, to be sure, have your father investigated, especially now that—" Cold crept up my spine. I tried again. "Especially now that my father's corpse was found."

Her grip on the paddle weakened. Gahee looked up at me, and in the pool of her dark eyes, I saw the scales of something dart by. Fear? Remorse? "Your father . . . was found?"

"He was poisoned," I whispered. "Then stabbed to death."

Gahee continued to stare, as though she couldn't quite understand me. She then blinked and lowered her gaze.

"Your father, even knowing whose daughter I was, treated me with so much . . . kindness." Then softly, "It has been a long time since anyone showed me such kindness."

"You spoke with him?"

"Yes. I told him . . . I told him . . ." Gahee shook her head and returned to her work.

Kindness. *That* was what had lured words out of Gahee, not threats. Not fear. Father must have known—when investigating, he was neither kind nor mean without reason. He had two sides of him: the interviewer who treated his suspects like they were birds with a broken wing, and an interrogator who was as ruthless as a sharpened ax.

"So, what did you tell my father?" I asked. "He is dead now, but maybe you could speak for him? Please, tell me what he knew before he died."

Gahee squeezed the beaten garment, twisting out the water. "You said a new magistrate is in power."

"Yes." *Or soon to be.* "And I have a feeling that we'll find answers. My father used to say that no matter how deep the lies, truth will always surface. For truth is unyielding; it will strive for the light year after year after year."

Gahee paused, her eyes fixed blankly at the burbling water, her fingertips red from the icy brook.

"I grew up thinking that no one could stop my father," she finally said. "No one stopped him from letting Mother die of a broken heart. No one stopped him from . . . from slicing my face." She grabbed the wet garments, visibly fighting away a memory. A muscle worked in her jaw as she lay the clothing out on the grass to dry. "He held me by the throat in broad daylight. I screamed for help. The villagers . . . they stopped by the gate and just watched as Father ruined my face, telling me that I mustn't stand out or I would become a tribute girl."

My gaze traced with new horror the scars on Gahee's face, my suspicion confirmed. Three dark lines grooved through her cheeks, and the puckered ridges extended the corners of her lips. Her father had wounded her face in the way that young women on the mainland were known to do. I'd read of cases in Father's journal of girls who'd scratch or burn their face with ignited moxa cones, desperate to escape the tribute system. They had risked everything by ruining their faces, for the punishment of trying to escape was severe: all family assets would be taken away, and any father's government position would be stripped.

Gahee crouched before the wet clothing laid out before her. "My father told me that if I kept my pretty face, I would be taken like Lady Moon."

An inarticulate sound escaped my mouth, my tongue turned to stone.

"He told me her beauty was a curse," Gahee went on. "For he had just witnessed the village elder desperately trying to bribe the emissary." She let out a breath, a puff of cloud in the cold air, as she rose to her feet. "Then later that day, I looked out at the backyard of our home and saw the village elder speaking with my father. I don't know what they talked about—"

Village Elder Moon couldn't be involved in any of this. Yet my imagination unfolded in my mind, the village elder's voice whispering, *I have work for you, if you want it.* He had everything Baek would have wanted, and it would be Baek's in return for finding him a replacement girl.

"When Father returned," Gahee continued, "he told me we were going to be very wealthy, that I would never have to go a day without food again. And the next day, Father was gone. Gone for weeks. And I heard whispers from the villagers that he'd been seen in different parts of Jeju, looking for a beautiful maiden. I think it was Seohyun he found, for when Seohyun wandered into Nowon a few months later—the most beautiful woman I'd ever seen—Father looked utterly terrified, like he'd seen a ghost. And he murmured something about how he wished he'd never assisted Village Elder Moon in the first place."

I stood still in numb terror for what felt like an eternity, gripping on to Father's jukjangdo, the bumps of the bamboo handle melding into my palm.

"When the trial begins, promise me something." Gahee finally tore her gaze away from the laundry and glanced over her shoulder at me, her eyes steady and unapologetic. "Promise that my father will never come back home. If he knows what I told you and returns, I won't survive it. And then my blood will be on your hands."

We stared in silence. The weight of her request settled heavy over me.

"If he is the culprit, then he won't come back." I was trembling too hard, shocked to the bone. My grip tightened around the bamboo. "That, I can promise you."

Gahee had just revealed two critical pieces of information: Her father was likely involved in Seohyun's kidnapping, and Village Elder Moon might have bribed him into doing so.

I stood shivering alone by the brook, Gahee long gone. The weight of disorienting questions anchored me. Whom was I to turn to with this new intelligence? Should I run to Inspector Yu? Only this afternoon I had accused Shaman Nokyung. What would the inspector think if I approached him with a new prime suspect already?

First tell me, Father's voice prompted, as though we were studying the case together. *How does this all connect to the Forest Incident and my murder?*

I prodded at the earth with the jukjangdo as my mind paced. Gahee's testimony had sent my suspicion spinning toward her father; he had to be behind Seohyun's kidnapping. And most likely not just that. My instincts told me that Convict Baek was responsible for far more atrocities.

Think, Father encouraged me. *Pay attention to the details. Find a pattern.*

As I sank into my thoughts, I crouched and lowered my

hand into the dewy, lush grass, plucking out handfuls of it as I tried unpacking my suspicion, thought by thought.

If Convict Baek was involved in Seohyun's kidnapping, could he have also been involved in her death? Perhaps Baek feared that Seohyun's arrival in Nowon had been his fault. And perhaps he'd feared what Village Elder Moon would do if he discovered Seohyun's identity: the replacement daughter returned to avenge her fate as a tribute girl. So maybe Baek had killed Seohyun to cover up his blunder.

That was how the Forest Incident might have occurred.

On the day of that incident, Maewol had witnessed a masked man holding a sword. If Convict Baek had indeed killed Seohyun, then perhaps he was the wearer of the white mask. A mask that had been witnessed over and over again in the cases of the missing thirteen. I had no idea why Convict Baek would have wanted to steal more girls, but the thread connecting him to the Mask, and thus to the disappearing girls, seemed too clear to ignore.

I released the plucked grass from my hand, watching strands of green fall.

The question now was: *What should I do next?*

I rose to my feet and clapped the shreds of grass from my palms and skirt, then picked up my overcoat and the juk-jangdo. Father was gone, yet I knew what he would have said if he were here with me.

Learn everything you can. Collect every testimony, every rumor, every suspicion.

My legs moved of their own accord, at first long strides, and then a rush of steps. Gahee's testimony had wide gaps in it; the seemingly condemning connection between Convict Baek and Seohyun was based on pure speculation. I needed something more, something as solid as the earth under my feet.

I needed Village Elder Moon's testimony.

I barely knew where I was going, but when I blinked, I found myself staggering back into the village and down the path that would lead to Mehwadang, the residence of Village Elder Moon. He was supposed to be like my father, the one solving the case, but now I wondered if he had ever been on my side at all. I recalled the vague remarks he'd made before that brimmed with new meaning.

My daughter was nearly kidnapped once, he had told me. He'd left out that she'd nearly been kidnapped by the tribute system. *Yeonhadang. I built it in the hopes that she would recover.*

Had he built a second home for her to bury her deep in the wilderness, where no emissary would ever lay eyes on her again? Where she'd be so isolated that everyone would forget her beauty?

I glanced at the sky. The streak of orange light now lay low over the horizon. Inspector Yu would arrive at any moment for Shaman Nokyung, and I needed to be there to tell him what I'd learned—and of the new doubts I had. But more than anything, I needed to speak with Village Elder Moon.

My heart was pounding and my mouth dry by the time I arrived before Mehwadang. I'd heard of this estate before, a humble one made of volcanic rock and thatch, passed down from generation after generation in the Moon lineage. The jeongnang had one wooden log in it, indicating that the village elder was away but nearby.

I slid my azalea-purple jangot over me, letting the overcoat drape around my face and over the jukjangdo as I paused before the pillars. I wanted to call out for a servant to direct me to the elder, wherever he was—but I paused. A sudden flush burned my cheeks. It was evening, and here I was, an unmarried woman, come to demand an audience with a man. It seemed my aunt had left enough scars on my calves that my instinct was to recoil from impropriety. I should have brought Maewol along with me.

I waited for a while in indecision.

"How long will you linger outside?" The voice startled me around, and I found myself standing before the shadowy figure of Village Elder Moon. "If you have come to speak with me, come in."

I held my hands together and bowed my head. "Sir, I wished to speak with you, but it is late. I'll come again in the morning."

He lowered his head, then glanced behind him. "Chaewon-ah."

From the deep darkness cast by a tree, a young woman stepped out, her face hidden under a jangot of pure green silk, two red collar strips tied together at her chin. We remained frozen in this position, two young women with jangots held over their heads, like we were taking cover from the rain. And I knew she was watching me from within the shadow of her veil.

Village Elder Moon broke the stillness between us. "I brought my daughter out for a stroll; it helps her fall asleep some nights. Perhaps you would like to come in and have tea with us? We were just talking about you."

"You . . . you were?" I asked.

"Come," he insisted as he removed the wooden log from the jeongnang.

I glanced at Lady Moon Chaewon, but the shadow cast by the jangot made her expression impossible to see. Was she aware of what her father had done years ago? As I followed the two across a vast dirt yard, surrounded by three long huts, more questions iced my heart. Had Convict Baek killed Seohyun and my father, or had Village Elder Moon instructed Baek to carry out the killings?

I shook my head; I didn't want to even entertain this possibility.

Up the stone steps we went and onto the veranda, where we took our shoes off, then down the shadowy main quarter until we arrived before a screened door. A servant appeared out of nowhere, sliding the door aside and entering first; after a shuffling moment, the dark room brightened with the lighting of a lantern. It was a spacious library, filled with floor-to-ceiling bookcases, and on each shelf were stacks of books with five-stitched spines. At the far end of the room was a low-legged table and two silk floor mats.

"My daughter and I like to spend our evenings in this library, built over generations." Village Elder Moon paused before a shelf and picked up a book. "Chaewon reads poetry here while I go over the investigative records. I remember you asked about the report I took during the Forest Incident." He handed me the book. "Here. You may read it yourself, if you wish."

I accepted the book, but nearly dropped it as Chaewon slid off her jangot. Staring at me was the face of the moon itself—round and glowing. Her arrow-nipped chin and straight nose, her delicate brows and perfect red lips. She was the most exquisite young woman I'd ever laid eyes on, and now I understood why the emissary had rushed out of our yard seven years ago. He must have heard that in Nowon existed "the Pearl of Joseon," the village elder's daughter. Yet what I noticed the most were the deep purple shadows under her eyes. The mark of a girl haunted by ghosts.

"You are here for a reason," he said. "Speak."

I mentally slapped sense into myself. "What I wish to talk about . . ." I glanced at Lady Moon again. "It might not be fit for your daughter's ears."

"If it is about the investigation, then there is no need for caution. Whatever I know, she knows. She has assisted me in the administration of Nowon Village since she was young. You will not find a more intelligent and toughened girl."

With one hand, I slid my jangot farther over my face so as to examine him more closely from its shadow. I needed to read his every expression, his every passing emotion. None could be missed. "I was made aware that . . ." I cleared my throat. "That you bribed an emissary to not take your daughter, and that you hired Convict Baek to find a replacement girl. Seohyun ended up taking your daughter's place seven years ago."

The village elder's and his daughter's faces remained blank. Perhaps they were shocked? They were difficult to read.

"I did what a father had to do." His voice was so quiet it barely disturbed the silence between us. "I paid a large bribe, thinking it would appease the emissary's greed. But he wanted more." His brows lowered, and the remorse he felt was clear—finally, an emotion. "He had promised the emperor the most beautiful woman in Joseon, so he said. If I paid him some more, he would give me a month to find a replacement girl. And I would need to deliver her before the end of his tributary mission."

"So . . . you hired Convict Baek?"

"I had heard of his ruthless ways, and that he cared for nothing—except for his daughter, whom he was always struggling to provide for. She was a scrap of a girl: all bones and often seen begging for food. He accepted my task without hesitation and returned with a name: Eunsuk of Seogwipo.

That is the name I gave the emissary. I . . . I have regretted what I've done since."

I shook my head, lost in the maelstrom of leads that seemed to go nowhere. Village Elder Moon had hired Convict Baek to scavenge Jeju for a beautiful girl, but that in itself couldn't be a crime; it was the emissary who had taken Seohyun-Eunsuk in the end.

"Eunsuk—the tribute girl who replaced your daughter—somehow escaped Ming that same year, made her way to Nowon, and died in the forest two years later. Apparently she was murdered." I looked down at the investigative record clutched in my hand, and on the cover a date was written in black ink: 1421. "A masked man was also seen that day, and again throughout the case of the missing thirteen—"

"Perhaps Convict Baek acted without my knowledge," Village Elder Moon said, concern weighing his voice. "The suspicion did occur to me, now and then. I don't know what he, or anyone, would want with thirteen girls."

Yes, but still. I couldn't get past a thought that newly emerged in my mind: Seohyun's death would have benefited no one more than Village Elder Moon. If Seohyun had discovered the secret of the village elder's bribery, she would have exposed it and he would have lost his respectability, perhaps even his position.

I nodded nevertheless, playing along. "My thoughts as well. I can't figure out the connection." I glanced at Lady

Moon, so silent, her gaze lowered. She hadn't uttered a word. "You must be tired, my lady."

She smoothed her hand over the green jangot, glowing in the candlelight, and said nothing. She was like her father's shadow, standing by him so silent and without any will of her own, it seemed.

"It is late," I whispered. "I should go now. Inspector Yu said he would arrive at the shaman's hut by nightfall."

"Ah, I assisted him earlier today. He left a few moments ago, before my short stroll with Chaewon." Village Elder Moon glanced toward the door. "Night has already fallen."

I shot a glance to the left, at the latticed hanji window on the other side of the library. The white screen was no longer orange with the dimming skylight, but pitch black. Dread sank into my chest.

"If you wish, I will send a servant right now. I will ask Inspector Yu to come to my residence." He glanced at his daughter, an apologetic look in his eyes. "And I will explain everything to him. I am tired of hiding this truth for so long."

"There is more . . . ?"

"Yes. There is more." Village Elder Moon placed a protective hand on his daughter's shoulder. "And you will learn of it soon too, when Inspector Yu is here."

Something like relief blossomed in my chest. Perhaps it would explain everything. "Then I will read these records until Inspector Yu arrives."

"As you wish." The village elder turned to leave, then paused. "I am sorry about your father."

The relief withered; pain jabbed me at the memory.

"I saw the condition of his remains." He shook his head, bewilderment knotting his brows. "No corpse could be in such a condition, not with the humidity of Jeju. It has to be witchcraft. For now . . ." He waved his hand at the low-legged table. "Read the report. The parts where Shaman Nokyung is mentioned. *She* is the woman you must be most wary about."

eighteen

ONCE I WAS ALONE IN the library of Mehwadang, I took
off my overcoat, leaned the jukjangdo against the wall,
and sat cross-legged before the table, the investigative record
opened next to my journal. I compared notes. Everything that
Gahee and Village Elder Moon had shared with me matched
the subdistrict administrator's report. Shaman Nokyung had
been the last person to see Seohyun, and the witness had
overheard Seohyun say, *I am not Eunsuk anymore. Eunsuk
died in the kingdom across the sea, where her dignity was
taken.*

Now I understood what she'd meant, and I shivered, trying not to imagine too much. I flipped through the pages,
then paused. On the day Village Elder Moon had shared his
memory of this report, he had told me something else. I held
the page still in midair, slowly turned it over, turning the next
page and the next, waiting for the memory to sink in.

What else had we talked about?

His daughter.

And witchcraft.

He had said that his wife had consulted shamans to help their daughter with her sleeplessness, though he himself didn't believe in witchcraft. And yet . . . just a few moments ago, he had told me the opposite. Witchcraft, he'd told me, was the reason behind the preserved state of Father's remains.

Inconsistencies and contradictions, I'd read in Father's third journal, *should always be questioned.*

"Agasshi." There was a silhouette outside the latticed door. "I have brought a warm drink for you."

I told the servant to come in, and as the lanky girl set the tray down and laid out the bowl and pot for me, I continued to stare down at my journal. I pretended to be reading as I let my thoughts trail back in time, until my mind paused before another incident. Village Elder Moon had told me that Convict Baek couldn't be the culprit, that he was too obvious for my father to have not figured out. I had stopped focusing on Baek for that very reason. Yet Convict Baek had been involved in finding Seohyun, and perhaps even killing her. The village elder had known this all along.

Once the servant left, I picked up the willow-green ceramic bowl, filled with a warm herbal drink. I took a sip and stared blankly ahead. Was Village Elder Moon trying to confuse me? Was he trying to lead me astray? Perhaps when

Inspector Yu arrived, the village elder would finally tell me everything. I *wanted* to trust him.

I sank so deep into my thoughts I forgot the time, then surfaced again, wondering when Inspector Yu would arrive. Perhaps soon. I rose to my feet and returned the investigative record onto the shelf, which was stacked with more records. But the other bookcases were on other subjects: history, politics, medicine—I paused at this, and slipped out the medical book.

Father had been poisoned, most likely by kyeong-po buja. I was still convinced of this. Flipping through the chapters, I searched for information on this poison. There were detailed prescriptions for a variety of diseases, and even remedies for poisoning, but there was no mention of kyeong-po buja so far. I paused, turning pages back. I'd caught a glimpse of something. No, it was an illustration of a different herbal plant. I wiped my brow; it was getting hot in this library. The ondol floor beneath me burned my soles. I continued to flip. Stopped again before a page with a folded corner. I looked over the curious content, wondering why *this* page in particular had been marked as important—

The book dropped from my hand. Pain as sharp as a blade ruptured through my stomach and I shriveled to the floor. I remained as still as I could. *It's my monthly pain*, I assured myself, *it has to be.* The next wave struck harder, now with the strength of a sword's hilt smashing into my chest, fracturing my ribs. Mouth agape, an inarticulate sound escaped me.

I wrapped my arms tight around me as I hunched forward. And before me was the medical book. My hands shook violently as I reached out and turned back to the page with the folded corner.

Symptoms of arsenic poisoning, it read. *Stomach pain, chest pain, nausea, vomiting, irritation, occasional itchiness*, and it went on. *Most victims die in a day or less, though some unfortunate few stay alive for a fortnight.*

I stumbled up to my feet and grabbed ahold of my overcoat and jukjangdo, and, while clutching my stomach, swayed toward the latticed door. I swayed instead into a table, knocking down a porcelain jar that shattered, and the shards dug into my feet as I made my way to the door. Throwing the overcoat over my arm, I tugged at the brass handle with my free hand, only to be plunged into a nightmare: The door wouldn't budge. Sweat poured down my face in buckets; I was on fire. The entire library felt like a furnace.

Heat.

Understanding clicked. Political convicts were fed sayak, a mixture of arsenic and sulfur, in heated rooms, for heat expediated its deadly effect. My grip loosened, then my hand dropped to my side, hanging there.

Village Elder Moon, who'd felt like a reincarnation of Father, wanted me dead. I thought I would feel fear. Or rage. Instead, I felt deep sadness.

My knees buckled and I sank to the burning floor. My

hanbok clung to my skin and my drenched strands of hair plastered onto my forehead. *So this is how it feels to die.*

I thought of Father, and I knew he must have been dying from the same poison. I felt less alone. I'd go to him soon. It wasn't as scary as I thought, death. It was just leaving one place to go to another.

The floor scalded my cheek. I turned and found myself staring at my arm stretched out on the floor, surrounded by scattered porcelain shards. My palm lay open, fingers slightly curled in. It took a few moments before I noticed it. The small scab running down my thumb. The spot I'd sliced open to drip blood into Maewol's mouth, along with the shiromi juice.

Father had left her behind once.

He had lost his life trying to turn back time.

Maewol, I couldn't leave her behind.

Not again.

I slowly looked around, my thoughts sluggish in the heat. I didn't know what to do. I couldn't escape through a locked door. It was a dead end.

Dead ends only exist in your mind. I could almost hear my sister's voice, paired with the shrug of a delicate shoulder. *There is always another way out.*

It occurred to me then that my other hand was clinging to my necklace—and the wooden whistle hanging from it. With all my remaining strength, I forced it to my lips and blew.

Its shrill noise pierced the silence at the same time nausea punched me hard, and I coiled into a ball. I swallowed down the urge to puke. I blew on the whistle again. *Pierce the night,* I begged of it. *Reach someone's ear.* If I was going to die, I would at least make sure that everyone would remember the noise coming from Village Elder Moon's hut.

Footsteps creaked, and this time, terror thrummed in my chest. I didn't want to die anymore. I rose onto my elbow, trying to rise to my feet, but at the sudden movement, nausea swelled and I heaved, though nothing came out.

"Take the whistle from her," came a woman's bored voice outside.

Lady Moon. The shock was enough to strike me like a splash of cold water. Enough to drag me up onto my feet, to jolt a wave of alertness through the thick haze in my mind.

"B-but, mistress." It was the servant girl who'd served the tea. "She might hurt me."

"It's been an hour. And with the heat, she's as good as dead now. Hurry, before someone hears."

I heard the sound of jangling metal—a key in a lock. Almost instinctively, I grabbed the nearest shard of porcelain and quickly surveyed the room. Nearest to the door was the area most swamped in darkness—I'd moved the lamp close to the desk at the far end of the library. I staggered across, nearly crumpling to the ground in agony, but I used Father's cane to keep me on my feet. I finally managed to hide in between two tall bookcases, the stacks of books casting deeper shadows onto me.

At last, the latticed door slid open. The lanky girl walked in, slowly, her steps full of caution. I hated what I was about to do, but I couldn't let the Moons get away with Father's death. I gripped the jukjangdo with one hand, and with the other, I held the porcelain fragment so hard that I could feel my own skin burst and bleed.

When the servant girl was right in front of me, looking in the other direction, I swung out. A scream burst from her as I placed the shard against her throat, and I pinned her against me. In three quick strides, I was out the door, pushing her forward like a shield. All the while, I feared I'd already cut the girl, that blood was streaming down her throat, for she was frantically sobbing.

"P-p-p-please!" the girl begged. "P-p-please don't h-hurt me. Oh, p-please!"

Lady Moon stood before us, her calmness such an eerie contrast to the servant. She had her hands gathered inside her sleeves. Her face was as expressionless as the eyes of the dead, staring and blank.

"Move." I tried to sound as threatening as possible. "Or I'll kill her—"

"Talk any louder," Lady Moon said, "and they will hear. The house is full of servants."

She stepped to the side, revealing before me the opened entrance door, not too far away. She was letting me go? Or was this a trap?

One, two, three.

I shoved the servant aside and ran, bursting out of the hut. Cold air exploded onto my face. I didn't know where that speed and energy had come from, for as soon as I ran onto the road, I felt the pain—in my stomach, in my chest, on the shard-embedded soles of my bloody feet. I hobbled forward, using the cane-sword to steady me as I threw glances over my shoulder. No one was following. Yet.

Lady Moon was likely searching for her father to tell him of my escape.

Nausea seized me again, worse than the first time. I held my stomach, hurrying my steps through the village; if I vomited now, I'd be on my knees, retching so loud that I would be caught by whoever the Moons sent to silence me.

They would likely send the man in the white mask.

Almost there, I kept reminding myself. I'd left my pony tethered to the tree near Convict Baek's house. If I could reach the creature, I'd be able to ride to safety. But as I passed the convict's hut, my steps slowed until I was dragging my feet, sheer agony ripping me apart, bone by bone. Unable to go any farther, I crumpled to the ground and coiled tight, clutching at my stomach.

"Mistress Min?" A familiar voice came from above. Gahee. She was holding a wood-and-hanji lamp while staring down at me with a look of curiosity and concern. "I'd thought you'd left."

"Not yet," I whispered.

She remained still, then looked around. "You shouldn't be here. My father might return at any moment."

I struggled to mouth the words. "Help me to that tree."

It was then that a flicker of concern crossed her face. She crouched next to me and pulled my arm around her shoulder. Leaning my weight into her, I rose slowly to my feet, and step by step we made our way to the shadows, speckled with starlight.

"What's . . . what's wrong with you?"

"Poison." I untangled myself from Gahee, whose muscles tensed with shock, and I staggered over to my pony, clutching the reins. "Just leave me here. I'll ride back to—" I doubled over as another wave of pain slammed into my stomach. A moan escaped me as I sank to the ground.

"Should . . . should I get your sister? I saw her earlier."

"Wh-where?"

"She came to ask me questions, and I told her you'd come as well to ask. She saw your horse here and told me if I saw you, to tell you she'd wait for you at the inn."

Village Elder Moon had tried to kill me. Or perhaps he *had* killed me. I'd come too close to the truth, which meant Maewol was in danger as well.

"I have to find my sister." Hands pressed into my stomach, I tried rising back to my feet. "If I don't, the Moons will find her first."

Gahee set her lamp down and touched my sleeve. "I don't think that is a good idea. You look too ill; you'll likely faint off your pony and crack your head—"

The thundering of horse hooves broke the nighttime silence. My hand flew to the handle of Father's jukjangdo, afraid that I'd see a white-masked man. But relief swooped in in the form of my sister, leaping off her horse and dashing to my side, her eyes frantic.

"A villager just told me they saw you heading this way—" She knelt before me, half shadow, half lamplight. "What's wrong with you? You're trembling."

I opened my mouth to speak, but the poison clutched me with a merciless grip, making it impossible to form words.

Gahee replied for me, "She was poisoned."

Maewol's eyes widened as emotions converged in her gaze—shock, fear, outrage, and the spark of a quickly turning mind. "I'm not going to let you die," she said, then called out over her shoulder to Gahee. "Prepare three scoops of warm water and a fistful of salt dissolved into it."

Gahee nodded and ran off.

"Why"—I squeezed the word past the twisting of pain— "why water and salt?"

"When I saw Shaman Nokyung using kyeong-po buja for her pains, I was afraid she might take too much by accident, so I once asked a medical woman what I could do if someone got poisoned. She told me the best thing I could do was to help induce vomiting."

Gahee soon arrived with a bowl of salt water. Maewol tried to pour the contents down my throat, but with the wave of pain that violently shook me, she only managed to get half down. Agony distorted my face as I swallowed, and immediately afterward, I puked onto the grass and felt even more ill than before.

Gahee wrung her hands as she watched. "I hope this was a good idea."

"It is," Maewol snapped, her face stricken with fear. With more hesitance, she said, "It has to work . . ."

"I'll get more."

Once Gahee was gone, I struggled to sit back up, leaning against the trunk. I tilted my head up and stared at the starry sky through the canopy. I slowed my breathing, trying to conserve as much of my strength as possible; I needed to tell Maewol everything. "If this doesn't work, we won't have much time then—"

"Don't say that!"

"*Listen* to me."

Maewol fell silent, her face ashen, and she grew even paler as I described what had happened in Mehwadang. I told her about Village Elder Moon's contradictions, the herbal drink, and Lady Moon. "She sent her servant in to collect my whistle, then ended up letting me go."

Maewol's brows knotted. "But why would she do that?"

"I don't know."

"Maybe . . . maybe that was her plan. She sent the servant

in to unlock the door for you, without seeming like she'd disobeyed her father."

At first, protest rose in me, but then as the thought settled, it didn't seem impossible. Perhaps Chaewon was as frightened of her father as Gahee was of hers—both girls exhausted by the weight of their fathers' sins.

"The real question is," Maewol continued, "why would the village elder want you killed?"

"He must somehow be connected to the missing girls."

"Do you know what kind of poison he used?"

"I don't know, but in the medical book I was reading at Mehwadang—" I paused, letting the surge of pain rip through me. My voice was weaker now. "I noticed a page folded. It was about arsenic. And all my symptoms matched it."

"Arsenic!" Maewol reached out and held my sleeve. "That's the same poison used to kill Father."

I turned a questioning look at her.

"I always go to the inn when I have questions," Maewol explained. "There is such an assortment of people, an assortment of knowledge. And I realized that the answer to his strange condition was no great mystery."

"What . . . do you mean?"

Maewol waved her hand around. "This is the island of political convicts, and you know how convicts are executed here."

"Sayak. There is arsenic in it."

"Yes. And the people at the inn told me of a few cases

of poisoned bodies exhumed a few years later, only for the corpses to be found in a remarkable state of preservation. It seems there is something in arsenic that resists decay."

I fell silent as the information sank in. "So that might explain the state of Father's remains . . ."

Maewol nodded. "Precisely."

"Sometimes arsenic takes a fortnight to kill a man . . . ," I whispered. "That's why Father made it all the way to Boksun's hut and back."

"And who knows," Maewol added darkly. "The Moons might have even tried poisoning Father to death on the first few days of his investigation. If he'd died then, everyone might have thought he'd died from a natural illness."

"But he lived on . . ."

"They must have realized the poison wasn't working fast enough, so they sent someone to end Father's life."

"Because Father must have found the truth," I pieced together under my breath. "The Moons must somehow be connected to the missing girls. But how?" I paused, squeezing my eyes shut as I willed the nausea to subside, but it wouldn't. "Hyunok was . . . found dead in the forest." Sweat dripped down my brows as I desperately gripped onto composure. "And the other twelve missing girls . . . were seen near the forest . . . before their disappearance."

Maewol leaned forward, wiping the dampness from my face. "The hut we found in the woodland must have been a temporary shelter, before the masked man meant to take the girls somewhere else." She placed a hand over mine. "Older Sister, you need to rest."

But my mind continued to race.

Seohyun, too, had been found in the same forest. She'd known something. That's why, upon looking at the paper stolen from the masked man, she'd immediately recognized the nine circles. *Dusk and fog*, Seohyun had whispered.

What did that *mean*?

I looked at Maewol, remembering the familiarity that had sparked in her eyes at those two words. "After the Forest Incident," I whispered through my clenched teeth, "you said I'd mentioned two words: *dusk* and *fog*. Do you remember anything else?"

Maewol shook her head. "We told Village Elder Moon what you'd said, and when he questioned you, you replied you couldn't even remember why you'd said those words."

"How did the village elder look when . . . when he was questioning me?"

"He looked . . ." Maewol remained still, staring fixedly at the grass. A look of intense concertation burned in her eyes. "Eager . . . and a little scared. I had thought he'd appeared that way because he was bent on finding the truth. But now I wonder . . . maybe the words *dusk* and *fog* are evidence that points to him, somehow?"

"We need to find out." I grunted as I leaned forward, grabbing the jukjangdo.

"What are you doing?"

"Writing the words down." There was a patch of lamp-lit soil. Brushing aside the leaves and twigs, I used Father's cane-sword to write *dusk* out in the only alphabet we had in Joseon: Hanja, classical Chinese. "You don't have any other evidence to work with, Maewol-ah. You *need* to find out how the Moons are connected to these words—"

"*Stop* that." Maewol's eyes gleamed. "Stop speaking like I'll be investigating on my own. You'll be here."

"But I might not. You're the only family I have, Maewol-ah, the only human being in this kingdom I care about. I need you to—" My voice wavered. "I need you to survive. You'll be in danger otherwise."

Maewol sniffled.

I blinked the burning out of my eyes. Tears were useless right now.

We sat like this for a while, the silence wrapping around the stabbing agony that had spread to every corner of my body. I pulled the necklace up over my head, the wooden whistle dangling from it. "Here, this belonged to Father. It has helped me out of difficult situations."

Maewol took it, and after a hesitant moment, she hung it around her neck. "We're going to solve this case together." There was a stubbornness to her voice, a stubbornness that dared me to challenge her. But the look suddenly wavered, replaced by a different expression—one of a surprised alertness. She took the jukjangdo and wrote the Hanja character for *fog* next to the character I'd written.

Staring at us from the earth were the two words Seohyun had whispered to Boksun, and must have whispered to me as well. *Yeon*, for dusk. And *ha*, for fog.

"Yeonha," Maewol said. "Yeonha . . ."

Our gazes locked. "Yeonhadang," we both said, our voices quiet and tense.

The second home of the Moon family. The one Village Elder Moon had built for his daughter.

nineteen

"Rest your eyes for a little while," Maewol told me.

My eyelids did feel heavy, like they were thick blankets. So I closed them. I meant to rest for a bit, but when I opened my eyes again, disorientation consumed me, for the sky was no longer pitch-dark; it was colored pink and purple with the rising sun. And I was not under the tree, I was in the storage room of Convict Baek's home, wrapped in my jangot, wearing someone else's straw sandals, slightly too big for me. Nearby was a cloth covered with bloody shards of porcelain, likely plucked out from the soles of my feet. And next to me was Father's sword.

"You're awake."

I turned to see Gahee crouching before me. There were shadows under her eyes.

"I kept watch," she said. "But my father didn't return. So we thought you would be warmer in here than under a tree."

"Where is my sister?" I asked.

Gahee paused, avoiding my gaze. "Your sister told me about Scholar Yu's identity, and left to find him. She will return soon."

"Where is my sister?" I whispered again, dread awaking in me.

"I told you, she went to get Inspector Yu—"

"You're lying to me."

The scars that slashed Gahee's face seemed to redden as her cheeks drained. "I . . ." Her frightened eyes bored into me. "I told her it was a bad idea, but she wouldn't listen."

A cold ball of dread sank into my chest. I couldn't breathe. I couldn't think.

"She said she would send a note to Inspector Yu." Gahee's lashes remained lowered, her voice knotted with tension. "We are to wait here until he arrives with a physician."

My body began to shake. I crossed my arms, trying to make it stop, but the tremors only intensified. I knew my sister—headstrong, rash, and loyal to a fault. "She left, didn't she? She left for Yeonhadang."

Gahee reached into her hanbok and placed a folded note into my hands, like the ones Maewol and I had slipped back and forth to each other between the doors. In quick, inky characters, she had written:

Stay alive, Older Sister. I'll return soon with the evidence we need.

I closed my eyes against the swell of fury and horror.

Foolish, *foolish* girl. I flung my silk jangot around me for warmth, picked up Father's sword, and struggled to my feet. When a wave of pain knocked into me, I held the wall for support, then stalked out of the storage room while Gahee followed after me.

"If you're trying to go after her," she said, "you might die before you even reach the place."

I shook my head, strands of loose hair falling over my face. "Maewol doesn't know what she's getting herself into. This man outwitted Father. She needs me." I stopped, suddenly aware of Gahee's desperate gaze clinging to my back. Slowly, I glanced over my shoulder at her, and a bitter appreciation welled in me. "You helped us, Gahee. Thank you. But, you know . . . your father might be involved in this."

Gahee's lips were pale and cracked. "I know," she rasped. "I became sure of it when Maewol told me about the evidence pointing to Yeonhadang. I've secretly followed Father there before."

I pulled out the sheet of hanji, which Boksun had given to me. I'd kept it on my person, not sure of its importance, but now I knew it was a map. "Does this make sense to you?"

Gahee looked at it. "The nine circles are the nine-peaked oreum hills. These lines must be rivers. And these dots must be villages. That should be Seonhul Village." She pointed to the dot closest to the ring of nine circles. "And that is where Maewol is heading to, and finding her way to Yeonhadang from there."

"How would she know where it is?"

"The Seonhul villagers know. I asked them questions about the mansion, and they all knew of its existence."

I nodded, slowly digesting every word she said. "Did they mention anything suspicious?"

"Nothing. They said it was an ordinary giwajip mansion. Isolated, though." Gahee folded the map and gave it back to me. "But this map is too vague. Your sister mentioned you were prone to losing your way. I will guide you there, but only up to the forest that looks out onto the mansion. I won't go any farther than that. If . . . if my father is there, I don't want him to see me."

"Yes, yes, of course," I said. "But why are you still helping me?"

"Because of your father." A muscle worked in her jaw, and when she spoke, her voice strained into an aching whisper. "There's something your father told me, which I've thought of every day since his disappearance."

"And what is that?"

"He was the only one to truly see me. He saw my desire to help him, and he saw my fear. I didn't help him in the end. Still, he called me brave. He said it was brave of me to be the daughter of such a father. He left me with a question, though: *You can choose to keep silent*, he said, *but if you do, would you be pleased with that decision in the years to come?*"

For a moment, I saw Gahee as Father must have seen her: Not a stepping-stone in his investigation, but a girl who had the potential to be so much, yet had grown confined within the terror wrought by the hands of her own father. Detective Min Jewoo had cared for Gahee, for Seohyun, for the missing thirteen.

Perhaps he had seen glimpses of his own daughters in them.

"The moment I chose to help you, I realized something." Gahee finally lifted her gaze up to mine, and it was like seeing the faintest flicker of light in the darkness of night. "Doing what is right, it is so utterly terrifying. And yet so freeing."

We traveled for three hours through small villages, vast fields of swaying grass and scattered lava rocks, and finally rode into a forest swamped in blue mist. It was cold and damp here. The path we followed sloped upward, and I wondered when the steep incline would end, when, at last, the slope descended into a forest that stretched across flatland.

"We're near," Gahee said quietly.

There was an eerie silence to this place. Neither the birds nor any sign of animal life could be heard. It almost felt as though a clear bowl had been placed over us, blocking out all sound.

I felt I had to whisper as well. "Where are we?"

"At the crater, and above us is the volcanic rim that circles around this basin."

Clutching the reins with one hand, I craned my head

back, staring past the canopy. Pine trees rustled across the nine peaks, which soared up for at least a thousand paces. It was like staring at a stormy wave about to swallow me into its deep green depth.

"Hurry," Gahee said. "This way."

I followed behind, and the deeper we ventured in, the colder the air became. Clouds formed before my lips. "You said you trailed your father here?"

"Yes."

"Why?"

"I was curious as to where he was always disappearing. He always left with a cotton sack."

"What was in it?" *A mask, perhaps.*

"I tried to look once, and when he caught me, he said—" Gahee kept her gaze fixed ahead, and I knew that if I could see her face, it would have been as a blank as the cold sky. "He said he'd break all my fingers if he ever caught me again."

I bit my lip, not knowing what to say to this.

"It is strange," she went on. "Sometimes what fathers think is for our good, is not something we desire at all." She paused. "I never *asked* Father to sell his soul for my future, but he did. He did it 'for my sake.'"

I bowed my head, understanding. There were many things Father had done for Maewol and me that I wished he hadn't— like risking his life to solve this case. For once, I wished he had been a selfish coward.

"Do you love your father?" It took a moment to realize

that it was I who'd asked the question. I quickly added, "You don't need to answer that." Whether Gahee loved her father or not had nothing to do with the investigation, and everything to do with how guilty I would feel once Convict Baek was locked up in the prison block.

Gahee had not uttered a single word; I thought she wouldn't answer. Then she replied in a small voice, "I used to believe I loved him. And then I grew up." She pushed aside a branch. "My father did all he could to provide for me, and whenever I think of this, I feel gratitude—and beat myself for it, for I also remember all his dark deeds. But when I think of him as a criminal . . . I can't help but remember that he skipped his meals so that I could have a full belly."

The weight of her answer hung heavy around me as we continued through the quiet forest. Father had once written in his journal that no one was completely good, just as no one was completely bad. I hadn't fully understood his words until Convict Baek.

Finally, I saw an opening beyond the thicket of leaves, a glimpse of a treeless flatland. And at the far center of this field was a giwajip mansion, like the ones I'd seen on the mainland, only the black tiled roof looked blacker than any I'd ever seen. And the tile-capped stone walls stretched on and on for hundreds of paces, walling in the flared-roof houses.

Maewol-ah. I wished my sister could hear my thought. *Are you in there?*

Gahee and I arrived before the edge of the forest, and the

silence felt heavier, pressing down on my chest. I wanted to vomit again, and I wasn't sure if it was poison still lingering in me. I clutched the collar strip of my jangot tight, bringing the veil closer around my face. Beads of dew clinging to the purple silk dropped and slid down my face.

"Agasshi." Gahee watched me, her eyes wet and the tip of her nose red. "This is where I bid you farewell. Please . . . please don't make me regret my decision."

My fingers were so stiff, it took several attempts before I finally managed to tether my pony, somewhere deep in the forest where the creature wouldn't be seen. I slid the silk overcoat off my head and hung it over a branch. The leaves rustled as I pushed them aside with Father's jukjangdo, making my way back to the edge of the forest, which gazed out at Yeonhadang.

I'd lost Father to the secrets contained within this house.

I couldn't lose my little sister as well.

I readied myself to dash out into the clearing, but it looked so far to reach the mansion. And the crater was so flat, I'd be easily seen. I waited and waited, my mind racing for answers. Gradually, it dawned on me that with every passing moment, I was finding more and more excuses to remain hidden among the trees. *Now*, a voice in my head urged me, *go now*.

Terror hummed in my bones as I ran out. My legs and arms turned to water; I went stumbling onto the grass a few times, staining my skirt in mud and grass marks. No matter how fast I ran, the distance seemed to remain the same. Still a hundred paces away, the mansion was as small as my thumb on the horizon. Faster, I needed to run faster.

What felt like a half hour later, I found myself before the stone walls that circled the house. Maewol would have climbed over this wall. I took a few steps back, ran forward, and leaped, grabbing ahold of the tiled top. But after a night spent vomiting, I had little strength. Down I went, collapsing to the ground.

I tried a few more times, but in vain. There had to be another way in. I hurried along the wall, looking for something to step on. I found nothing, but I did notice the small gate, the one used by servants. It was slightly ajar. Common sense told me not to enter the house through a gate—I'd likely walk straight into someone this way, but I couldn't think of another option.

I peered into the yard first. I caught a glimpse of steam rising from somewhere, yet I could hear no sounds of life. I clung to the jukjangdo, the bamboo slippery in my clammy hands, and stepped in. The steam was drifting out from an empty kitchen. But there was a pot on a clay stove, and when I glanced inside, the white eyes of a gray scaled fish stared out at me, frothing and boiling in a spicy paste stew of tangled vegetables.

There was something disturbing about this place.

Back outside, there was a raised platform covered in

baskets full of garlic, carrots, fruits, and a mountain of corn-cobs wrapped in bright green husks. Then along the wall, there were large brown pots. I snatched off the lid for each, and all the pots were filled to the brim with pickled vegetables and plum wine. There was enough food here to prepare a feast, but where were the guests?

Leaving the servants' courtyard behind, I traveled through a connecting gate into the next courtyard, for Yeonhadang was divided into several courtyards that contained flared-roof buildings, separated by low stone walls, like all other mansions. And the deeper I ventured into the compound, the eerier it got.

The place seemed deserted, like an abandoned village, yet the grounds were immaculately kept. All the yards and verandas were well swept. The hanji paper screening the latticed doors was intact, not punctured by the notorious rain and wind of Jeju. One of the doors, in fact, was slightly open. I glanced in to see light glowing against porcelain pots, lacquered furniture, and floor mats of golden silk, with lotuses embroidered into it. Then I realized the chamber wasn't entirely empty.

Panic sharpened in me as I stood frozen, staring at the figure of Lady Moon, sitting on the ground before a low-legged table. If Lady Moon was here, it meant her father was also present. He must have traveled to this house right after my disappearance. I needed to find Maewol, quick.

I took a slow, retreating step back. My jukjangdo sword clacked into a pillar. *Damnation.*

Lady Moon cast a sidelong glance my way, then stilled when our stares locked. Tension prickled around us.

I licked my dry lips and whispered, "The soldiers are coming."

The color on her cheeks turned a shade paler. "You're lying. Only you are here."

"Do you think I would have risked my life coming here without informing them? They know about Yeonhadang. They know your father poisoned me. My sister didn't come here without notifying Inspector Yu first." I quickly glanced around, making sure that I was still alone. "Tell me where my sister is. If you cooperate, I will tell the inspector to show you mercy."

She shook her head slowly. "I don't believe you."

"May my father be cursed in his next life if I am lying to you," I said, and my own oath frightened me. Yet I was convinced that Maewol must have notified Inspector Yu. She was reckless, but she wasn't a fool. "The authorities will come for your father."

Lady Moon's lips now looked as white as her cheeks.

"You helped me escape once, didn't you?" I said, and when she didn't object, my courage grew. "Help me find my little sister. I promise I'll tell the inspector everything you did for me—"

"It wasn't intentional. I meant to take the whistle from you."

"And then you decided to let me go."

She continued to stare at me, looking disoriented, as though confused by her own emotions. "What will happen when the soldiers come?"

"They will take your father, of course, and he will be executed." I was certain of that, and I wanted to be there, to see her father drinking from a bowl of sayak. "No one survives killing a military official. And that is what your father did. He killed Detective Min, *my* father, with the same sort of arsenic that I was given yesterday."

"No." Her brows crinkled. "Father said it wasn't him—"

"You may examine my father's corpse for yourself. After an entire year, his corpse remained in a state of preservation. It did not decompose as it ought to have. It was because of arsenic."

For a long moment, Lady Moon remained at a loss for words, staring down at the table. There was a steaming pot and, next to it, a bowl. "It's cold," she whispered.

I blinked. "What?"

"If you heat up the ondol furnace for me, I will let you go and not tell Father." She paused. "I'll even tell you where your sister is."

She was either a scheming monster, or she was a reluctant accomplice of her father's. I didn't have a choice, either way.

I quickly darted around the building until I found a little

furnace room below the structure. There was a weak fire already burning. I'd learned how to heat the ondol at Shaman Nokyung's hut, so in no time, I fanned the fire to life and kept fanning so the smoke would spread beneath the ondol floor. Once I finished, I hurried out, almost expecting to find Village Elder Moon standing in the courtyard. But it was still empty, still quiet.

"I'm done." I panted, having rushed through everything. "You promised to tell me where my sister is."

"Don't you hear it?"

Wings fluttered.

I whirled around, heart pounding. It was only a bird, descending from the sky and perching itself on the black-tile-capped wall. It whistled.

I gritted my teeth. What was she *talking* about?

The bird continued to whistle, a faint, piercing noise.

Whistling? Since when did birds—

My blood turned to ice. Birds did *not* whistle, not like this. But I knew what *did* make such a shrill noise.

"Where is it coming from?" I demanded.

No reply came. I turned to Lady Moon, who seemed lost in thought. "I said, where is the sound coming from?" She stared blankly down as she poured tea into a bowl, a bowl already overflowing with liquid and streaming across the table.

I didn't have time for this.

The next moment I heard the whistling, I chased after it, a sound that would stop, then start again, as though Maewol was taking in deep breaths before blowing on Father's police whistle. Beads of cold sweat washed my forehead as I scrambled around, trying to find the source.

A few times, I crossed the shadowy backyard of a pavilion, passing by a large, thick circle made of wooden slats and weighed down by a stone slab. It looked like the covering of a well—only it was too big to be a well. But when I returned to the spot for a third time, dread plunged into my stomach.

Surely she couldn't be down there . . .

Then I heard it—a faint, faraway whistle.

I laid the jukjangdo down and crouched, and with all my remaining strength, I pushed at the wooden covering. I pushed and pushed, and with each attempt, the covering moved by a bare fingertip. Soon my dress was clinging to my sweaty back. Strands of hair dangled wet before my eyes. The stabbing sensation from last night's poisoning hadn't left me, and worsened as I strained myself. But I had to keep trying.

"Maewol-ah, I'll find you," I hissed through my teeth, gritted together as I leaned my weight into each shove. "I'll find you and bring you home."

My arms were trembling by the time the covering budged a quarter of the way open. A cold draft breathed against me, and I found myself staring wide-eyed into the mouth of a stairway made of large rocks. Picking up the jukjangdo, I crawled into the opening, where the stream of daylight illuminated the damp steps and the moss-covered stone walls.

"Maewol-ah?" I quietly called.

Silence.

I held my breath and descended, step by fearful step, into the pitch darkness below. Each time a flight of stairs ended, another began. My muscles tensed; I was ready to turn and bolt should the painted-white mask appear.

"Maewol—"

I nearly screamed when my sandal bumped into something. It was only a wood-and-paper lantern. Next to it was a flint box. My hands were shaking so violently, it took a few tries before I finally managed to light the lantern, its warm light glowing through the rice paper screens and illuminating a second gaping hole far below the staircase, staring at me like the mouth of a tiger.

A whistle rippled in the silence. Louder than before, but still echoing from somewhere far away, so faint this time I almost wondered if I'd imagined the sound.

Maewol-ah, I'm coming! I rushed down the remaining steps, ice-cold dread pumping through me. The air itself seemed to freeze into icicles. And when I passed through the rocky entrance, it was like stepping into the middle of winter.

Where was I?

Something wet dropped from above me in a steady beat. *Drip—drip—drip.* And the echo of each splatter resounded against the floor, the walls, and a ceiling that sounded too high up.

I slowly raised the lantern by its long handle. I could feel my breath vanishing from me as I craned my head far back.

The darkness bared glimpses of fang-sharp limestone, and a cavernous tunnel carved out by lava from the ancient times. Yet the lava tube was so immensely high that I couldn't even see its ceiling.

Shivering, I carefully trod across the slippery, uneven floor, using Father's cane to keep me from stumbling. The cavern seemed to go on and on, seemingly endless and eternal, as though I had died and had woken up in the underworld. But *someone* had blown that whistle. My sister was here somewhere. Or the masked man might be hiding in the darkness, holding on to Father's whistle. Perhaps he was watching me now.

Fear made me impatient. I breathed in deep, then yelled, "*Maewol-ah!*"

My voice echoed, rippling through the deep cave, only to be met with indifference.

"Maewol-ah!" This time my voice faltered. "Mae—" I couldn't finish her name this time as burning shards filled my throat.

Had I only imagined the whistle?

Just as I had imagined Father's return while living with Aunt Min . . .

So many times I'd jolted off my sleeping mat, thinking I'd heard the gate creak, thinking I'd heard quiet footsteps, only to run out into a shadowy hall filled with a stillness as impenetrable as death itself.

I crumpled to the cavern floor, and when I closed my

eyes, it was to see Maewol lost in the woods, waiting for Father. *One, two, three . . .* She had believed then that family would never leave her behind. They would come for her if she counted to a hundred three times. *Ninety-eight, ninety-nine . . .*

I thought of the other girls, the missing girls, who had been counting away for a year, waiting for family to come find them. But no one was going to find them, were they, for everyone who knew the truth was dead or dying. Seohyun. Father. Hyunok.

Perhaps even me.

Helplessness settled into my bones, as heavy as metal. I couldn't rise back to my feet; I couldn't. Everything felt futile. Magistrate Hong had been right all along. The wicked thrived, yet those who strived for good, they were trampled over like flowers—

A sound came. Faint, yet not too far.

The whistling noise.

I hadn't imagined it.

It pulled me to my feet, breathing strength back into my limbs. In steady and long strides, I pushed my way through the darkness. Maewol could be waiting at the end of that sound, or maybe not, but someone was calling for help.

I continued until the lantern light, and my own reflection, stared back at me. It was a deep, crystal-clear lake in the middle of a cave. And there was a boat too, with an oar resting over it. I'd never seen anything like this before. If I had come here on an excursion, I would have looked around in awe, but instead it was a knife's tip that had led me here, and the sight of the dark waters only filled me with dread.

Swallowing down the nausea, I got in and began paddling. The water rippled with each stroke, the only sound that could be heard. I tried not to look down. There was something terrifying in not knowing how far I'd sink, if I fell. I didn't know how to swim. I paused, lifting the lantern; on either side of me were the cave walls, narrow enough for the lantern light to reach both sides.

I kept on going until I saw a large, shadowy object on the other side of the cavern floor. With all my strength, I pulled the oar through the water, and even when burning exhaustion stabbed at my arms and shoulders, I didn't slow down until the boat would go no farther. At once, I was on my feet, hurrying across the hardened lava floor until I saw it.

A wooden cage holding the silhouette of four girls.

Whispers emerged.

"It's . . . it's not her!"

"It's not?"

"I thought it was her voice."

"It's not Lady Moon." An achingly familiar voice. I raised my lantern, and the light illuminated the bruised face of the girl whose eyes gleamed with the fierceness of a military general. "It's my sister."

Relief rushed through me at the sight of Maewol, but came out as anger. "How did you end up in here?" I demanded, almost on the brink of crying. "Why would you come here on your *own*?"

"What else was I supposed to do?"

I shook my head, both incredibly upset and incredibly proud of my sister. "You should have waited for me!"

"I didn't want to come on my own." For once, there was a real sense of remorse in Maewol's voice. "But I came here for *you*."

I ran a hand over my face and the roaring in me eased. "Well, I've found you. Now I have to find a way to get you out."

twenty

THE THREE FOUND GIRLS GLOWED like pearls hidden in the depth of the sea, even though they'd been trapped in a cave for over a year. With wide eyes they watched me as I searched the far side of the cave, where they swore the key was, left there for the servants to use whenever they'd come to clean out their chamber pots or bring them their meals. I found it hanging from a nail hammered into the wall—not just one key, but many, hanging all together from a knotted string.

I hastily returned to the cage, the keys jangling. "Which one is it?"

"We don't know." Bohui, fourteen winters old and the oldest of the three, had round cheeks and a complexion as smooth as milk. "There's a key for every cage here."

I swung the lamp farther into the cave, shocked. The darkness lifted like a veil, revealing rows of empty wooden cages, marching farther into the cave, too far for the reach of my lamplight. A heavy weight sank deep into my chest. How many girls had slept and cried and screamed in these enclosures?

"There were others here before us," Kyoungja, the second girl, whispered. "At least two more cages filled with the likes of us." She pointed into the darkness somewhere. "Eunwoo and Gayun were in that cage, and remained with us the longest."

The third girl, twelve-year-old Mari, hadn't uttered a word since I'd arrived, but now she spoke in a small voice. "They told us a secret."

"And what was that?" I asked encouragingly.

"They told us what the girls before them had shared. Apparently, many years ago, a girl named Seohyun found this cave. It was before any of us were trapped down here, but I suppose she guessed what the cages would be used for."

A breath hitched in my throat as the loose threads connected.

"She managed to escape before she could get caught. That is what the girls before us overheard the servants here talking about."

Seohyun had escaped—but in the end, Convict Baek had caught up with her. And he had killed her for having discovered Village Elder Moon's secret.

"Now it is just us," Mari continued. "Eunwoo and Gayun disappeared like the others, and when I asked the village elder where they had gone, he told us they were taken back home."

"He was lying," Maewol whispered, holding on to the wooden bars like she wanted to break them open. "They are still missing."

We needed to get out of here. I returned to the cage in three quick strides and grabbed ahold of the brass lock, which was shaped like a fish larger than my hand, with eyes that stared warningly at me. I'd used locks like these before, to secure household possessions. *Only*, I thought with horror, as I selected a random key and tried opening the lock, *these girls aren't the jade rings, silver hairpins, and rolls of silk I keep locked in my cabinet.* Yet here they were, Bohui, Kyoungja, and Mari, locked within a cage as though they were.

"How did you end up here?" I asked as I tried another key.

"The three of us went to collect wood in the forest, for kindling," Bohui explained. "Our parents sent us to go together. But while we were searching, a masked man appeared."

I shook my head. "What did he say to you three?"

"He ordered us to follow," Kyoungja whispered. "We saw he carried a sword, so of course we obeyed."

I tried yet another key. "And then what happened?"

"He took us to a hut in the forest." Mari's fawn-like eyes watched my hands. I'd slipped the key in and tried shaking the lock, hoping it would open. It didn't. "He told us to sit still and tied our wrists. I got so scared I tried to leave, but he warned that if I disobeyed, or even made a sound, he would throw me off a cliff, where another girl had once been thrown off. He left us in the hut until night, when he returned and took us to Village Elder Moon's second home."

"Has Village Elder Moon hurt any of you since?" I asked.

"No," Kyoungja replied. "He promised us that if we ate our meals and complied with his orders, he would take us back to our parents."

I couldn't figure the village elder out. *If you were my daughter*, he'd told me, his voice so genuine, *I would be proud of you*. How could one man seem like two different people? One, who reminded me of my kind father, and the other, a blackhearted killer—

Click.

To all our surprise, we stared down at the sixth key I'd slid into the fish lock, now hanging open.

"There isn't time to gape." Maewol shouldered the door open and gestured at the other three. "Quick."

The girls hurried out, following Maewol and me to the boat. It was only when we arrived that I realized it was long and wide enough to carry only three people. I tried to think of what to do, but my sister was quicker.

"I'll take Bohui and Mari first, since Bohui is the eldest and can keep Mari calm and hidden," Maewol said, reminding me of the wild pony that she was, always so surefooted no matter how rough the hills and violent the gales. "Then I'll take my sister and Kyoungja."

We nodded. I passed the lantern off to her, and as Maewol rowed across the clear lake, she took the light with her.

Soon, Kyoungja and I were left in such a deep darkness that I couldn't even see my hands or feet. I felt like a spirit floating in oblivion.

"They'll be coming soon." Kyoungja's voice loomed in the darkness somewhere, a bare whisper. "The servants."

"What do you mean?"

"They always come around this time . . . when my stomach is growling. They bring an entire feast for us."

I remembered the smell of food filling the kitchen courtyard. An empty courtyard, and something about it unsettled me.

"We were fed so well," Kyoungja continued. "Usually, the servants never speak to us. But one of them once told us to eat everything, that our meals would promote fertility and youthfulness. I didn't know what she'd meant, and I still think about it now and then."

I grimaced, feeling sick to my stomach. These girls were being fattened like pigs before a feast . . . *For whom?* I wondered, tapping my finger against the sword handle. Then understanding slid into me.

A feast that would take place in the kingdom of Ming.

Shrill noises rang in my head, the sound of pieces connecting into a terrible truth. Boksun, the victim who'd escaped, had shared that her captor intended to take her to Ming. Kyoungja, Mari, Bohui, and the other girls before them had all been kept to be used as tributes. Lady Moon had managed to escape this fate, but how had her escape led to this—to her father capturing and sending even more stolen tribute girls? For what end? Was it the greed for money that drove him?

Before I could ask Kyoungja more questions, I saw a glow of yellow—a speck at first, then a stretch of light that shimmered across the lake and against the cavern walls. Maewol had returned.

Even though we were floating on the middle of a lake deep under the earth, I knew we were so close to safety I could taste the fresh air and the honey-sweet sunlight.

Kyoungja, however, did not seem as hopeful.

"There is a terrifying legend about a cave nearby. It's haunted me since my arrival here." A tremor had snuck into her voice. "A long-ago magistrate once battled a giant human-devouring serpent." She glanced up at the looming darkness and shuddered, as though she'd see snake scales stretching above her. "I fear the giant serpent awaits us."

"We will be all right," I said, my voice firm. "Once we cross the lake, we'll only have to travel a little bit more down the cave, up a staircase, then out the opening. We are very close to freedom, Kyoungja-ya."

After escaping the cave, we could run into the dense forest and let the thousands of trees hide us. All these thoughts strengthened my arms as I plunged the oar through the waters—I'd offered to row Kyoungja and my exhausted sister to the other side.

"We should travel to Jejumok, where Inspector Yu is." I wiped the sweat from my brows with a forearm. "It will be the safest there."

When we finally reached the other side, I carried Father's jukjangdo while Maewol raised the lamp high enough for the light to circle around the three of us. We kept close as we rushed to where my sister had left Bohui and Mari. They were still there, huddled in a shadowy corner, yet they looked ill and their eyes were too round.

"What is it?" Maewol asked. "What's the—"

Bohui's hand snatched my sister's wrist. With the other hand, she placed a finger over her lips. *Shh.*

We remained still, the five of us, and all I could hear was the dripping of water and our shallow breaths. I could even hear—or perhaps I was imagining it—our hearts pounding hard against our rib cages.

Time passed by and I wondered if the two girls had imagined the sound.

Then we heard it. Footsteps.

Mari crumpled against the wall, nearly letting out a whimper if not for Maewol's hand clamped over her lips. Bohui and Kyoungja linked arms, standing shoulder to shoulder. I turned to them, and under my breath, so quiet that I was mouthing the words more than I was speaking them, I said, "Everyone hold hands and do not make a sound. If he passes us by, I'll tug, and we'll find our way to the entrance without light." I quickly leaned forward and blew out the lantern.

The footsteps neared, heels scratching over the grimy floor. I squeezed my eyes shut as panic trickled into me like cold water, rising and rising until it filled the hilt of my throat. The footsteps drew even closer. With one hand, I gripped the jukjangdo handle so hard my knuckles ached, and with the other, I clung to whoever's hand I was holding, and her fingers dug into mine, cold and shaking.

Please, please, please pass us by.

The darkness behind my eyelids illuminated yellow. I opened my eyes slowly, praying that it was Inspector Yu. I blinked against the bright torchlight, and when my eyes adjusted on a face, panic choked me.

In the torchlight, a familiar face stared at me. Chiseled cheekbones and dark, intense eyes. Black hair tied into a topknot, a silver pin gleaming through it. The fatherly warmth I remembered was gone, like paint wiped away, revealing an emotionless and stony slate. His lips were set in a straight line, without a hint of either pleasure or displeasure curving the corners. His eyes, too, were impossible to read—staring and blank.

Village Elder Moon stood tall, one hand on the hilt of his sword, hanging from a sash belt. The other hand held the torch, its light dancing across his shadowy face.

Evil.

Now I realized why I'd so struggled to understand this man. It was because I'd imagined evil as being made of horns, spikes, and sharp teeth, not glowing with the appearance of goodness and respectability. *Sometimes*, Father's words whispered into my left ear, *good things turn out to be counterfeit*. Village Elder Moon's kindness, as genuine as it might have been, was as cheap as brass painted gold.

"You walk the path of your father," he said, his voice as empty as his expression. "You have chosen to die."

"You p-poisoned him," I stammered.

"Because I hoped to give him a kinder end. But the arsenic wouldn't work fast enough."

Tears burned in my eyes as Father died all over again in my mind. Pain ripping his spine apart, stabbing at his chest, the poison soaking into his blood so that even in death his body had failed to disintegrate peacefully into the earth.

"So you had your minion Convict Baek stab him."

He expelled a breath. "The only thing Convict Baek did was lead the girls to Yeonhadang."

I felt the air sucked out of me.

"You stabbed my father?" Maewol demanded.

I blinked at his admission by silence, my mind spinning.

"And Seohyun," Maewol continued, "she was murdered . . . by you?"

My head shook. "No . . . no, that cannot be. Convict Baek was seen. The masked man was seen in the forest—"

"I lend Convict Baek the mask when he is tasked with bringing the girls to me. But other times . . ." Village Elder Moon reached behind his head and pulled the mask over his face, held in place by a string. I took a step back, tripped over a protruding surface, and ended up sitting on the floor as Father's jukjangdo clattered down next to me. The bamboo gleamed orange in the torchlight, catching the village elder's gaze, but after a moment of staring at it, he looked away. To him, it was only a cane.

"Seohyun found her way to this cave," he continued in a dead and cold voice. "She meant to come for my life but ended up leaving with my secret. I had to silence her. And so I wore the mask. With a mask, you can be and do anything you desire, even send police investigations into chaos. That is why your father took so long. He thought the Mask was one man, but it was two."

The masked man in the forest five years ago, and the one behind Father's death . . . It had always been none other than Village Elder Moon.

"It's not right," I rasped. "It's not right, what you did."

His onyx-black robe rustled as he crouched. The white mask loomed before me, smiling with its eyes closed. I opened my mouth, wanting to scream, but I couldn't. It seemed none of us could, choked with terror, for not a word was uttered.

I flinched as he reached out. With a finger, he tilted my chin up. "What is right to you, Hwani-yah," he whispered from behind the smiling red lips, "is not right for all."

I shuddered under the awful gentleness of his touch.

"The day the emissary came, I told him who I was, that I belonged to the Nampyeong Moon clan, that I was the village elder. He and his soldiers laughed at me." His touch withdrew, and resting his hands on his knees, he fell still—so still it was as though a real face did not exist behind the mask. Then the flicker of torchlight illuminated just a bit, the eyehole carved into the mask, dark pupils watched the girls behind me. The slightest note of distaste soaked his voice. "They dared to call me a country bumpkin. I never felt so powerless. And I never forget a slight."

"So the girls that are now missing . . . ," Maewol said quietly. "The other ten girls . . . No, Hyunok was found dead, so that leaves nine girls remaining . . . they're gone?"

"I made a deal with another envoy, Emissary Lee: Should he receive a bribe from a high-ranking father and require a replacement girl, I would provide one. I would keep the exchange secret, on one condition—that the officials show favor should my daughter be selected as a candidate."

"Why are you telling us this?" I whispered.

"Because I owe you and your sister a confession, and I know you will carry it to your graves." He rose to his feet, then unhooked the sword from the scabbard. A glimpse of the blade glowed bright like the embers of a burning fire. "My daughter and I have too much to lose for anything to go wrong."

Fear prickled through me as I slowly rose to my feet. The end of our lives flashed through my mind: five bloody corpses buried in the cave, and with us, the entire truth. I flinched as someone's hand touched mine, but it was only my sister.

Maewol. My heart twisted into an aching knot as her fingers entwined with mine. I held her tight, palm pressed against palm. She was my sister, my little sister.

Maewol raised her chin at an angle that said, *I am not afraid.* Yet her voice shook as she said, "You would kill us to take what you w-want . . . But is wh-what you desire worth that much blood on your hands?"

"Is it worth it, you ask?" the village elder said softly. "My daughter has made it to the last round of the princess-selection process. Our family leaves for the capital this month to start a new life, and Chaewon will live in a pavilion outside the palace, to be tutored by palace maidens . . ."

His words barely registered as cold sweat dripped into my eye. I blinked it away as I looked around. The torchlight only illuminated so much. A portion of the cavern wall. The lumpy black floor. The tips of stalactites dripping down from the ceiling. The shimmering surface of the black lake, four paces away. The bamboo walking cane lying innocently next to my feet. I'd forgotten all about it in my terror.

". . . the high officials who owe me favors, they put in a good word for my daughter." His blade rushed out in a high-pitched ring. The girls huddled closer to the cavern wall. I stood still, my grip over Maewol's hand loosening until it was empty. "I will soon become the father of a crown princess. And without you five, there will be no one to talk of my crime." He turned the blade, as though observing the way our frightened faces reflected on it.

"Y-you will have ended the lives of not only five," Maewol said, "but s-sixteen girls."

"What is that sixteen compared to the number of girls taken by the Joseon government? Every three years they capture girls to send as tribute to the Ming court. Hundreds of them. Girls disappear every day. They are sacrificed for a greater good."

I moved my feet by a hairsbreadth until I could feel Father's jukjangdo. But I knew that any attempts to wield this sword would likely end in me skewered by Village Elder Moon's blade. I returned my gaze to the lake, watching it from the corner of my eye. Perhaps we could make it back to the boat and cross to the other side, where he couldn't reach us . . .

"Who determines wh-who should and should not be sacrificed?" Maewol said, while taking in shallow gulps of air. "It's monsters like y-you who make it a curse to be born a w-w-woman."

"You have spoken enough." Village Elder Moon must have noticed my eyes on the lake, for he took a few steps around us, blocking our way to it. He held the torch high, its light flickering across the faces of all five of us, sending another flash through my mind of our impending doom.

Blood pooling the cavern floor. Wounds gaping open. Lifeless, staring eyes.

"Do not look so frightened," he whispered as his gaze settled on Maewol, the strongest among us all.

No, no, no. The word pounded in my ears as he angled

his sword, as my little sister slowly crossed her wrists before her, knowing that death was imminent. "Dying is what each person must endure once."

The blade drew back, ready to strike.

I darted to the ground, grabbed the jukjangdo handle and the blade came flashing out. Village Elder Moon's eyes widened, caught off guard, as our blades clashed. His sword went flying out of his unprepared grip, clattering and skidding into the shadows.

I tried wielding the jukjangdo again, but he whirled away, and my blade struck a rock, the impact of it wrenching the hilt out of my grip. I didn't have time to scramble for my sword, not while Village Elder Moon was striding over to his blade, which gleamed in the light of his torch.

I knew we would all die if he reached it.

"The jukjangdo," I gasped at Maewol. "Find it and use it if you must!"

With that, I charged forward and crashed into the village elder's back. We both lost our balance. The torchlight hissed into the water as I stumbled with him. We pitched forward, my feet leaving the ground, my hair dancing over my face—

I don't want to die anymore.

I closed my eyes, tightening my grip on the village elder. I'd once made a will, wanting nothing to do with a life so desolate without Father.

Now what I wanted more than anything was to see the faces of family reuniting with the three found girls.

I want to stay.

Water exploded around me.

The shock of its icy embrace shot straight into my heart. I couldn't breathe, overwhelmed by the salty cold, overwhelmed by the absolute darkness. I couldn't see the surface or the bottom, I couldn't see anything, but I could feel the village elder's hands. They pulled and dug into me, trying to pry himself free.

With all my strength, I continued to cling to the village elder's robe as we thrashed in a blackness that seemed to leak through my eyes, surging fear into my soul. The village elder's hands, too, turned desperate. Fingers grappling for anything, grabbing strands of my hair, wrapping tight around my throat as I struggled to hold on. My limbs felt numb and frozen, about to shatter as the cold deepened.

I cannot die.

I will not die.

A dizzying lightness clouded my head, and exhaustion sank into me, into the tips of my fingers. My grip slackened. The village elder's violent touch withdrew, the sensation of his robe billowing against me vanishing. Water rippled as he pushed away. Then there was stillness as I floated in the black void.

I cannot die.

I will *not die.*

I reached out, but my arms wouldn't move, wouldn't strike outward to push me up from the depths. They remained motionless, floating in the still water, long strands of my hair curling around them. My head grew so light that I imagined a circle of glowing light above. The circle moved from side to side.

My eyes felt heavy as a calmness settled over me.

There had to be a bottom to this lake.

Perhaps once I reached it, I could curl up and fall asleep.

I blinked against the tiredness, watching as the circle suddenly stopped and remained, like it was staring down at me. Orange bubbles erupted. Slowly, a shadowy outline appeared, nearing me. The blur of white fabric unfurled, and the flash of hands filled my vision. Then I felt myself being lifted upward, gliding through the water.

A heave, and I was on my back. On dry land. At once my lungs grabbed for air, through the pain tearing at my chest, through the sharp shards of water rattling in my lungs. A firm hand sat me up and struck my back, once, twice, until breathing became easier. It was only then that I noticed Maewol, who was soaking wet, her long hair dripping and her eyes wide. Bohui, Kyoungja, and Mari hovered behind my sister, wringing their hands. And there were others.

My mind jolted awake.

Others?

There were three men uniformed in black robes, and the sight of the fourth washed me with relief: Inspector Yu. We were safe at last. Yet, even as I thought this, I found myself surveying each face, each dark corner. Where had Village Elder Moon gone?

My mind continued to drown in this question as the people around me spoke in low murmurs. Their voices sounded like garbles underwater, but then Maewol touched my hand, and the sensation of her small fingers unclogged my ears.

"We ran here as soon as we heard screaming," Inspector Yu said, his voice crisp.

"It was me. I was screaming," Mari said. "When you fell into the water."

It felt like the black water of the lake was still trickling into my lungs, filling me with cold. "You did not see the village elder?"

We all stared at the lake.

"I'll have my men search this cave for him. But perhaps he drowned."

Perhaps . . . I pushed my wet hair away from my face. "How did you get here?"

"Gahee rode over to me, informing me where I might find you. She told me Maewol had sent a note but I never received it. And then there was Lady Moon, she directed us here." He let out a breath of disbelief. "My men are searching through the rest of the compound right now."

Shivering, we all made our way down the cave, following Inspector Yu, who was holding the torch. The other torch-bearing soldiers stayed to search for the village elder, and I glanced over my shoulder, watching the flicker of their fire-light growing smaller and smaller in the distance. Something felt wrong.

"I don't think he drowned," I whispered. "What if he managed to escape—"

A guttural cry echoed.

We froze.

"Gods," Maewol whispered. "What was *that*?"

Inspector Yu glanced up, frowning. "It came from outside."

Dread plummeted down into my stomach. I immediately thought of the girl who could not sleep at night, haunted by the ghosts of her father's victims, the girl who had let me escape the furnace-hot library.

Before I knew it, I was running.

Footsteps followed behind, and soon Inspector Yu and Maewol were hurrying alongside me. We ran up the moss-covered stone steps and crawled past the covering out into the open sky. The sheer brightness of the day stunned me to a halt. Raising a hand over my eyes, I squinted around, and slowly my vision adjusted.

There was a trail of water staining the courtyard ground, deepening the light dirt into dark brown. Strength drained from me as we followed the trail into the next courtyard and up the terrace toward the chamber where I'd last seen Lady Moon.

My steps slowed, almost as though something in me wanted to turn and leave. To never have to witness what lay beyond; I had seen too much for one lifetime.

I stopped before the double doors of the room. They had been slightly parted when I'd first glanced in earlier today, but someone had slid them wide open. I looked up, with the same slowness that had dragged at my steps, and followed the watery footprints.

Past the silk floor mat. Past a teabowl flipped on the ground. Past the low-legged table . . . where a white powdery substance lay scattered like salt.

Village Elder Moon sat on the ground, hunched over, water dripping from the strands of his loosened hair and beard down onto his daughter, who lay on his lap. Her arm was stretched across the floor, palm out, fingers still and unmoving.

His mask must have fallen off in the lake, baring now the emotions engraved into the lines of his face. He touched her cheek. "Wake up, Chaewon-ah." He shook her shoulder. "Chaewon-ah. Do not be angry with me. I did this all for you."

In a daze, I wandered in and lowered my stare to the floor; it was scorching hot. A few steps more, and I reached the teabowl. I didn't even need to draw it to my nose to pick up on a strong herbal scent.

Like the warm herbal drink, mixed with arsenic, that I had been served in the library.

I glanced back up at Lady Moon, lying motionless, a sheen of blood coating her mouth. The truth struck me so hard the bowl slipped from my hand.

Lady Moon had poisoned herself.

Everything was a blur after that. Of soldiers rushing in, ropes being tossed, arms being twisted back and tied in rough motions. Of silk, of blood, of Lady Moon's staring eyes. And of her father's fragile voice, still calling her name, as though expecting her to wake up. But she was gone. Her father's own darkness had taken the very life he'd cherished.

"*Chaewon-ah.*" His voice reached out for her and stroked her pale cheeks, for his hands could not, tied as they were. "Abeoji came back for you. *Chaewon-ah.*"

Was this justice?

The daze clouding my head wouldn't leave as I sat on the burning floor, sweat and lake water streaming down my face. I pressed the base of my palm against my chest, massaging the ache pounding under my ribs. Everything still ached. The cracks still gaped wide, cold wind blowing through. The lost were still lost. The dead, unrestored.

I didn't realize how much time had passed until Mae-wol touched my shoulder. She offered her arm, helping me to my feet. We stood still, watching as the soldiers hoisted Lady Moon's body onto a wooden stretcher. A straw mat was pulled over her. All that was left to see were her fingernails, stained a faint orange color.

"Bongseonhwa," Maewol whispered.

I stared closer at the stained nails. Maewol was right. Lady Moon must have collected bongseonhwa flowers, to pound and turn into the paste children would use to dye their nails, and hope the stain would last until winter—for if it did, it was said that one's true love would arrive with the first snow.

My shoulders slumped forward, feeling beaten to the ground. Lady Moon—Chaewon—she had just been a girl, like the rest of us. Maewol, too, looked defeated. When a single tear dribbled down her cheek, she quickly wiped it with the back of her sleeve. "Why does it feel like this?" her voice rasped. "Like we've lost?"

A shadow stretched out next to us. Inspector Yu stood there, the wide brim of his black hat casting a shadow over his face as he stared at the straw-covered corpse. "We lose every day. That is part of this line of work." He glanced down at us. "The work of fulfilling our obligations to others. We save some, but we lose most. This is not a novel situation."

I shook my head, not feeling any better. Now I understood Magistrate Hong. It was this, the sheer exhaustion and horror of failing to save lives—it dimmed our eyes, drained us of our strength, hollowed out our bones.

"But there are two types of people," Inspector Yu added, his voice quiet. "Those that retreat and huddle together like frightened birds, overwhelmed by the darkness of this kingdom, and those that grasp their freedom to struggle on the behalf of others, their eyes fixed on a great light that will always shine for those who seek it." He flipped back his robe and crouched on the floor. Picking up Chaewon's teabowl, he slipped it into a sack—collecting evidence.

"Pull yourselves together, Min Hwani, Min Maewol," he said, not unkindly. "We need to bring the girls you've found back to their homes. Family is waiting for them."

twenty-one

OUT IN THE OPEN, THE three found girls rode side by side, each of them alert and tense. They jumped at noises, startled by the clamorous village we passed through, by the rattling of a horse-pulled wagon, and even by the barking of a small dog. Inspector Yu made sure to place them at the front of the line of soldiers, far away from the wagon that carried Chaewon's body and her shell of a father, whose wrists were tied with rope. He had been forced to walk while everyone else rode; Inspector Yu had provided each girl with a horse from Yeonhadang.

"It's been so long," Bohui whispered, holding tight to her saddle.

In the daylight, I noticed how pasty white Bohui's skin was. All three found girls looked as though they'd forgotten the warmth of the sun, forgotten what the world looked like. Their heads were craned back, like newborns taking in the sights around them, pointing at things in nature.

An entire year, I thought, *is a long time to be trapped in such darkness.*

I followed their gaze. Dewdrops clung to needle-sharp pines, gleaming like gems. The open field undulated gently, like a grassy blanket laid out over the waters, molding to every wave. We were lost in the middle of the sea, only the sea was a shimmering green. Shadows as large as whales moved over us, clouds swept away by the wind. In the distance, huge hills rippled in the horizon, layer after fading layer.

"What is going to happen now, sir?" came Maewol's voice. She was riding alongside me and the other girls.

Inspector Yu glanced over his shoulder. "As soon as I can, I will return to the capital with a report of all that has occurred. The name of the emissary, the high officials, the servants; I will list all accomplices in my report once I interrogate Village Elder Moon. I do not doubt that he will drag everyone down with him."

I resisted the temptation to glance far back, down the line at the man responsible for all this. I could feel his stare boring into my back though. I wondered if he thought it was my fault that his daughter was dead.

"And you, Mistress Min?" Inspector Yu asked, facing ahead again. "Will you be returning to Mokpo?"

Startled by the question, I glanced at my sister, then quickly looked away. "I don't know."

A beat passed.

"You *should* go," Maewol blurted. There was hurt in her

voice. "You don't belong here anyway. It's too wild and uncivilized for you."

I didn't belong anywhere now. No father, no mother anchored me to a place.

Maewol continued, her voice overly sweet. "She has a grand life awaiting her. She is betrothed to a man twice her age, and once she marries him, she'll move across the kingdom to live in his home and serve his in-laws like a slave."

My ears burned. This was the fate for all women. Yet the way Maewol spat it out made it sound like something outrageous.

"Hm. You've solved a dead-end case with your sister," Inspector Yu pointed out, slowing his horse. The smirk returned to his lips, the smile I had last seen when he'd pretended to be a drunk ex-scholar. "With a mind like yours, you could try entering the palace to become a lady investigator for the court."

I dropped my gaze and stared at the pony's mane brushing against my arm. I didn't want any of those things. All my life had been spent trying to please Father. Now he was gone.

We traveled through two more villages, then more open fields; the remainder of the journey passed by in a blur of green and a scattering of stone. I hardly blinked throughout, just staring ahead in a fog that had crept into my mind since seeing Chaewon's death.

But when we arrived at the stone fence that walled in

Nowon Village, surprise pierced through the haze in my mind. I blinked at the sight of a crowd of villagers, old and young, gathered at the gate. Their eyes were red, and deep lines were carved into their tanned faces.

"Eomani! Abaji!" Bohui's voice burst out, followed by Mari's, then Kyoungja's. Each climbed off their horse and shouldered their way through the crowd and into the embrace of their family. Mothers, fathers, siblings, grandparents, all held them tight, rocked them back and forth, breaking the embrace now and then to touch their hands, their arms, their hair, like they couldn't believe their long-lost daughters had returned home.

I could almost feel the warmth of the embraces myself. Almost.

As the three girls reunited with their families, I returned my attention to the crowd. The strangeness of this moment explained itself in little snatches of conversation.

"We heard!" one villager cried. "A servant from the government office told us!"

"We didn't believe it at first," another said. "We thought the servant was lying, telling us the Min sisters had found the killer. So did everyone else at first."

Inspector Yu reined his horse to a halt as more people gathered around him, around us. "Soldier Choi," he called out over the clamor. "Arrest Convict Baek before he hears of our return and tries to escape."

The soldier bowed his head and rode off.

"And Solder Shin—" Inspector Yu nodded toward us. "Escort the Mins to their home."

I cast a last glance at the inspector, wanting to thank him, but he had already disappeared in the crowd angrily swarming around Village Elder Moon. Their rage was filled with anguish and helplessness, fueled perhaps by the realization that the other missing girls were not returning home.

Soldier Shin rode toward me. "Agasshi, I will accompany you and your sister safely to where you need to go."

"To Shaman Nokyung," Maewol said. "We are going there."

In silence, we rode through the village and out into the open, Mount Halla watching us as we neared the isolated wilderness where the wind swept through without any obstruction. The closer we approached the fortune-telling hut, the more a realization solidified in me like a heavy weight: Shaman Nokyung had lost her daughter twice, and I had unburied the agony of her loss.

When we arrived, we tiredly led our ponies—the ones a soldier had run off to collect, after we'd pointed out where we'd left ours—toward the stable. Once secured, we approached the hut.

The shaman stood outside waiting for us, her white hanbok loose in the wind. The news must have reached her as well.

I tried avoiding her gaze, but when our eyes met, she nodded at me—as though in silent forgiveness.

"You both must be tired, Maewol-ah." She paused. "Hwani-yah."

The veranda creaked as Maewol and I walked across it, both to our separate rooms. Shaman Nokyung followed.

"While you were both gone, I heard how your father had . . . passed. And I remembered something," she told us. "A year ago, I was worried for your father, seeing him so ill. I thought it was illness then, not poison. I told him to go home.

"I asked your father what he thought was best for his daughters—a father who put his own needs first and lived, or a father who died over an investigation and orphaned his two girls?"

Maewol pulled open her door and murmured, sounding like she was about to fall asleep, "Of course Father chose death."

I too could feel a black wave of exhaustion about to crash over me. I opened my own door, about to step in, but halted at the sight of Father's burnt journal. The old bracelet I'd made for him was curled atop it.

I walked into my room and knelt before the pile, a pile of what had once been evidence but was now the remnants of a father who was gone and would never return.

I gathered the items and, too tired to think anymore, curled onto a sleeping mat with the memories clutched against my chest. Tears leaked down my face, and when I was too tired for even that, sleep finally came.

It was the deepest rest I'd had since the day Commander Ki had knelt before my aunt, his face pale and sullen, and said, *Detective Min will not be returning home.*

epilogue

Three months later

THE FIRST SNOW FELL IN fluffy white flakes, drifting slowly down onto the secluded hill that overlooked the distant sea. Mother had been buried here, so my sister and I decided that Father, too, would be buried on this hill.

There were many more decisions we ended up having to make in the period leading up to the funeral, for I was the mat-sangju, the chief mourner, and Maewol was the sangju, the principal mourner. Father had followed the ways of the former era, leaving his entire estate to his daughters, rather than being bound by the new male-oriented heir system. In doing so, he had made it our duty to carry out the pre-burial and funeral rites, and every year on the midnight of his death, we would have to perform a jesa ceremony.

The preparation for Father's funeral had, fortunately, kept

my mind occupied. And as soon as the funeral came to an end, Maewol and I were swept into the inquest investigation, spearheaded by Inspector Yu. As he'd suspected, Village Elder Moon dragged everyone down with him in a grief-stricken rage: Convict Baek, Emissary Lee, his eighteen servants, and the name of every high-ranking father who had begged him to find a replacement girl for their daughters.

Weeks later, when the verdict was made in accordance to the Great Ming Code, Village Elder Moon accepted his fate with a stare as blank as that of the dead. He was to be decapitated for having committed murder. Convict Baek, his accomplice, was to be punished by strangulation. As for the emissary and the high officials who had solicited his assistance, Inspector Yu promised the king would deal with the culprits accordingly.

"It's over now," Inspector Yu said, as the main courtyard emptied of all the spectators who had come to view the sentencing. "You should move on and learn to live again. Have you thought of what I told you?"

I gazed at the chair where the village elder had been sitting moments ago. His white hanbok stained in blood. Strands of his black hair hanging over his gaunt and empty face. His torso tied to the back of the chair. "What is that, sir?"

"About putting your mind to use in the palace. I'm leaving for the capital tomorrow and, if you wish it, I can try to win the king's favor for you. There is no guarantee, but perhaps he might find a place for you in the palace. There is always a need for bright-minded young women like yourself."

I bowed my head. "Thank you, sir, but it is not what I want." The path into the palace was a treacherous one, filled with men like the village elder who would sacrifice many lives in pursuit of selfish ambition. And it was far away from Maewol.

"Then what do you want?" he asked.

I shook my head, unsure. "For all my life, my only desire was to please Father."

The corner of his lips rose, his eyes gleaming with amusement. A flicker of annoyance crossed through me. He was looking at me like I was an ignorant child.

"You are not so conventional as you think you are," he said softly. "Conventional girls do not run away from their aunts to cross a thousand li of seawater, nor do they charge into dark caves and wrestle killers into lakes." He paused as he examined my face, then the bemused look eased away. "You have a knack for solving mysteries. I'm sure you can solve this one on your own. Perhaps you'll find the answer here in Jeju."

I wasn't sure what Inspector Yu had meant until, one morning, a villager ran into Shaman Nokyung's yard. Not to seek good fortune, but to seek *my* advice.

353

I was only eighteen—no, nineteen now. I couldn't understand how I could possibly help until the villager whispered, "It is a mystery I cannot solve."

My mind creaked awake, and a tingling sensation hummed in me.

"Someone stormed into my home and broke all the jars, and I think it was out of revenge. I had an argument with one of the villagers . . . ," she whispered as my heartbeat quickened. "I didn't know who to bring this incident to but you, mistress."

In that moment, I'd realized what I wanted: to be like my father, not because he was my father, but because I had grown up reading his journals and had discovered, here in Jeju, that I had a knack for untangling knots. And with each knot I untangled, it felt like I was making a bit more sense of this world and all its seemingly arbitrary heartaches.

I brought out my own journal, laid it open on a low-legged table, and raised my ink-dipped calligraphy brush over the hanji paper.

"Tell me," I said, "what time of day was it when you returned home?"

Winter in Jeju remained gray and mild. It seldom snowed, and while the wind was chilly, I didn't feel the need to bundle myself as I'd had to do on the peninsula. Then spring arrived—not quietly, but with an explosion of sweet-scented canola. Brilliant yellow flowers carpeted the roads, the fields, the high hills, layer after yellow layer. They lit up the island and lit my mind with memories of home.

"Do you want to visit them?" I asked over our morning meal of seaweed soup. "Mother and Father?"

Maewol shrugged her small shoulders. I thought that was an indifferent no, and so later in the day I garbed myself in my best mourning hanbok and made my way to the kitchen. There I prepared a bottle of makgeolli and a drinking bowl, for rice wine was Father's favorite drink after a long day of investigation.

"I'm ready."

I looked outside the kitchen to see Maewol, dressed in white, though her hair was loose and tangled.

I sighed, taking her by the wrist. "Let me."

Inside my room, I sat cross-legged behind my sister as I untied her sloppily plaited hair and combed through the tangles.

"Ow," Maewol hissed, raising the bronze hand mirror to glance at me. "That hurts."

Once the comb ran through smoothly with each brush, I took a hairpin and used the tip of it to part Maewol's hair sharply at the middle, then divided the thick cascade into three neat strands. Holding them tight, I braided her hair down along her back.

"It's already been several months since the inquest ended," Maewol said, her voice too light and apathetic, like she had practiced this tone of indifference many times before. "Do you still plan on returning to the peninsula?"

My hands paused, remembering the letter Aunt Min had sent me, ordering my return. I had no intention of obeying her, and I didn't care to leave Maewol. But a shyness crept into me and instead of the firm truth, I answered, "I haven't decided yet."

Maewol shrugged. "You can go if you prefer the civilized peninsula life, with all its rules. Not being able to freely leave your home. Not being able to manage your own inheritance. Aunt Min or your future husband would take over."

"But I don't prefer it," I said quietly.

She waved her hand. "Then why even think of returning?"

I continued to plait her hair until I reached the end, tying the braid with a red daenggi ribbon.

"I couldn't live like that, with all those rules." Maewol ran her thumb up and down the rim of the bronze mirror. "It's different here in Jeju."

It was true. Life in Jeju was indeed rough, rife with poverty and hardship, and perhaps because of this, the Jeju people did not bother being so rigid and strict. The women were freer. Many of them were haenyeos; they worked outside the house, earning money independently and sometimes traveling far from home. The boundaries of what I could and could not do would be less marked.

"It's not that I haven't considered staying in Jeju," I confessed at last. A glance at my sister's reflection showed her biting her lips with poorly restrained delight. "These days more villagers are coming to me with their mysteries, most of them trivial ones."

Maewol expelled an excitement-laced sigh. "The village still hasn't elected a new elder. They have no one to turn to but you."

That was what Inspector Yu had mentioned as well.

From the corner of my eye, I could see the shape of a book resting on my table. The inspector sometimes wrote to me with updates on the search for the other missing nine girls, likely hidden deep in the gilded cages of the Ming court. Only once in those notes did he ask me how I was faring, so I'd told him about the new cases I was solving in Nowon and how much I appreciated the distraction. In response, Inspector Yu had sent me *The Muwŏllok*, a forensic science handbook compiled by Wang Yü, to "aid me in future investigations."

I blinked, returning my attention to Maewol. "If I do stay, I could perhaps go live in our old home." Father's estate now belonged to me. "It's too small here for all three of us."

And too loud. In the middle of the night, I'd wake to the sound of Shaman Nokyung shaking her rattle and Maewol beating her drum while a villager moaned and wept.

"You should speak to Gahee and Bohui." Excitement bubbled in Maewol's voice. "You could hire them as helpers, if they wish it. And I'm sure they do. They're in need of work."

"And you?" I rose to my feet as I imagined this new life

here in Jeju, living in Nowon Village, Maewol not too far away. Crossing the room, I collected the wine bottle and bowl. "What will you do?"

"Continue to assist Shaman Nokyung."

"And one day become a shaman?"

"Eung," she answered.

"Do you truly wish to become one?"

Maewol joined me on the veranda. "A frog in the water sees only a portion of the sky and thinks it knows the universe." Crouching, she slipped her feet into her straw sandals. "Grief and darkness, sometimes that is all the villagers here can see . . ." She straightened and gazed out at the blue sky, the rolling field, the large black rocks stacked into fences that wound their way through the billowing grass. "But I am a different type of frog, and I realize that's why I was called to be a shaman. I see the portion and try to imagine the rest. That is why they come to this fortune-telling hut, the villagers; it's because they want to see more."

"And what more is there?" I asked quietly.

Maewol sighed. "I don't know for certain yet. All I hear are echoes from the other world; there is more than meets the eye."

We set out on horseback and arrived at the peak of a high hill where Father's burial mound was, protruding from the earth like a great tortoise shell, and surrounded by a double wall of stacked stones. Maewol filled the bowl with rice wine and passed it to me. Rolling back my long sleeve, I poured it over his grave.

Afterward, for a long time we sat leaning against the stone wall, watching the sun blend into the canola flowers and gleam against the swaying grass.

"Are there any cases you need help with?" Maewol asked.

"Hm." I took out my journal, which I always carried with me. I flipped through it, then stopped. "Here's one. Someone broke into Villager Seobi's house and broke all the jars."

Maewol tapped her lips. "Hm."

Our heads bowed together, we shared ideas of what could have happened and why. Then she smiled. "It's like when we were young . . . you always had a knack for finding answers, and I'd follow you everywhere as you solved cases. That's why Father called you daenggi mŏri tamjŏng."

"And Father called you musuri."

"A palace servant? I forgot about that. It's because you treated me like your slave."

A laugh escaped me. "That is not why Father gave you that nickname. He told me it was because you never refused any challenging or dangerous work and always maintained a positive attitude."

Maewol nodded, looking pleased and content, and in the ensuing silence, I gazed around. We had lost so much on this journey. Yet I noticed now how the sky seemed a pure, brilliant blue, the trees below the hill a deeper green. Grief had carved out a valley in us, allowing a warm breeze to pass through. A warmth that made the rustling grass and the twittering birds sound like music, and the land under my feet feel like fire.

A whisper like a gentle breeze passed by. *Hwani-yah. Maewol-ah.*

I jolted a glance around. There was no one except my sister, but she was frowning, as though she'd heard something too. The long grass danced. Birds chirped. It had been another trick of the mind; we had been imagining Father's voice everywhere these days.

Then I heard it again, the wind that sounded so familiar—Father's voice, deep and melodic.

Jal itgeola.

A farewell.

And a request that we be happy.

I raised my hand to shield my eyes as I squinted past the sun, at the shimmering blue water, the shadows of the lava rocks tracing into the sea. The white frothy ripples of the waves moved and crashed with a rush of life.

Father was gone—truly gone. He would not even linger on this earth as a chuksani, a spirit that wandered restlessly, unable to move on to the next life because of their unjust death. Maewol and I had solved the case that Father had begun. Together.

"Maewol-ah." I rose to my feet, dusting the grass off from my skirt. "Gaja."

"Go where?" she asked.

I took in a deep breath, then sighed as a lightness filled my chest. For whatever world Father had left for, I wondered if he could see us now, and if he felt at all surprised to witness, at last, his lifelong wish come true: his daughters, together at last.

"Let's go home."

historical note

I grew up hearing stories of Korean women and girls who were trafficked during World War II—commonly known as "comfort women"—but I never knew that Korean girls had been traded long before then. That is, until I stumbled across the term *kongnyŏ*, which refers to the "beautiful women" who were taken from their homes and given up as a human tribute.

I was haunted by the idea of kongnyŏs, and knew I wanted to write about them when I stumbled across this group of women again while reading a letter by Yi Kok (1298–1351) in *Epistolary Korea: Letters in the Communicative Space of the Chosŏn, 1392–1910*. In Yi Kok's letter, written in 1337, he addressed the Mongol emperor of Yuan China, requesting that the practice of seizing Korean girls be prohibited. The passage that caught my attention and sparked the heart of the mystery in *The Forest of Stolen Girls* was the following:

> "I am told that when people of Koryŏ (Korea)
> have a daughter, they immediately hide and
> guard her against being detected, so that even

close neighbors cannot see her. Whenever an emissary comes from China their faces turn pale with fear . . . Military clerks go from house to house in all areas searching for hidden daughters . . . When the seized maidens are gathered for selection, their numbers include both attractive and unattractive persons. But if a bribe is large enough to meet the emissary's greed, even a beautiful maiden will be set aside. Once a maiden is set aside, a search is conducted to replace her, so that several hundred houses are searched just to obtain one maiden."

Thirteenth-century Goryeo dynasty–era Korea was under Mongol rule during this time, and so Korean maidens were given as tribute, among other things like horses and fur. It is true that some women (like the teen who would become Empress Ki of Yuan China) were sent by Korean aristocratic families to try to build closer ties to Mongol elites, but in many cases, women were taken against their and their families' wills. It is estimated that over the span of eighty years, the number of Korean girls who were taken as official tribute, along with those taken privately, would total two thousand girls.

Unfortunately, the practice of human tribute giving continued into the Joseon dynasty era, because after the fall of the Mongol empire, the Ming dynasty was established in China, and Korea became a vassal state again in order to prevent war. A meticulous record was kept in the *Veritable Records of the Joseon Dynasty* of the number of women taken: 114 women were taken to Ming over seven tributary missions. However, it is said that a great number of girls were privately seized by envoys, nobles, and officials, and they were usually unmarried girls between the ages of eleven and eighteen.

It was only after 1435 that Korea finally ended this practice of sending human tributes.

acknowledgments

The second-book syndrome hit me hard. I was filled with so much doubt and fear, but I ended up with a book that I adore—largely in part due to the support I received.

To my agent extraordinaire, Amy Elizabeth Bishop, thank you for being in my corner. While drafting this book, I struggled with self-doubt and wanted to jump ship so many times. But each time you anchored me and gave me the courage to write on.

To my brilliant editor, Emily Settle, who recognized the gem buried in the messiest draft I'd ever written. Your enthusiasm for this book sparked my own, and your notes breathed life into my imagination. Also, you've really convinced me that you have some hidden superhero strength to be able to do all that you do.

Many thanks to my publishing team at Feiwel & Friends, including my fantastic publicist, Brittany Pearlman; my copy editor, Erica Ferguson; cover artist, Pedro Tapa; production editors Dawn Ryan and Kathy Wielgosz; my designers, Michelle Gengaro-Kokmen and Rich Deas; and production manager, Celeste Cass.

To Maria Dong, thank you for being my early reader and for saving my sanity. Writing under a tight deadline left me spiraling into panic, but you encouraged me to rethink my approach and helped me create a writing schedule that lifted the anxiety away. I also want to thank Kerrie Seljak-Byrne for checking in on me and supporting me through this entire journey of writing my second book.

I'm so grateful for my Toronto Writers Crew; thank you for cheering me on, and for being a group of writers whom I can turn to when I'm in need of advice. A special shout out to Kess C. for reading all my manuscripts and offering me a much-needed boost of confidence. I love your writing and am always here to cheer you on!

To Jamie, Eunice Kim, and the Mudang—thank you for assisting me with my research. To my dad (love you so much!), a native of Jeju, thank you for your stories about your life on the island. I'm also grateful to the following resources that I relied on the most heavily while writing: Yung-Chung Kim's *Women of Korea: A History from Ancient Times to 1945*, Linda Stratmann's *The Secret Poisoner: A Century of Murder*, Jinyoung Kim, Jaeyeong Lee, and Jongoh Lee's *Goryeoyang and Mongolpung in the 13th–14th Centuries*, Yuan-kang Wang's *Harmony and War: Confucian Culture and Chinese Power Politics*, Kyujanggak Institute for Korean Studies' 조선 사람의 세계 여행, Jahyun Kim Haboush's *Epistolary Korea: Letters in the Communicative Space of the Chosŏn, 1392–1910*, Peter H. Lee's *Sources of Korean Tradition, Vol. 2*, Han Hee-sook's *Women's*

Life during the Chosŏn Dynasty, Anne Hilty's *Jeju Island: Reaching to the Core of Beauty (Korea Essentials Book 5),* and the wonderful resources provided on www.jeju.go.kr.

I wrote the draft of *The Forest of Stolen Girls* while I was pregnant, rewrote it while caring for a newborn, and revised it during the COVID-19 pandemic. It was not the easiest time to write a second book, yet my family went above and beyond to help me find the time and the brain space to write.

Thank you to Sharon for taking the time off to babysit and to help me out with house chores, and to Charles for saving me time by always buying skin-care products for me. Endless thanks to my parents for their prayer and constant support, and to my in-laws, for babysitting whenever I was in need of time. And a special thank-you to my husband, Bosco: You're my greatest supporter, and I appreciate that you always make sure I don't skip meals while I'm on deadline. I'm also so glad that you nudged me to go on a research trip to Jeju Island. Also, many thanks to my daughter, Johanna, for training me to become a more productive writer.

And last: I thank Jesus, my Lord and Savior, for loving me despite my proneness to wander.

Thank you for reading this Feiwel & Friends book. The friends who made *The Forest of Stolen Girls* possible are:

Jean Feiwel, Publisher

Liz Szabla, Associate Publisher

Rich Deas, Senior Creative Director

Holly West, Senior Editor

Anna Roberto, Senior Editor

Kat Brzozowski, Senior Editor

Dawn Ryan, Senior Managing Editor

Celeste Cass, Assistant Production Manager

Emily Settle, Associate Editor

Erin Siu, Associate Editor

Rachel Diebel, Assistant Editor

Foyinsi Adegbonmire, Editorial Assistant

Kathy Wielgosz, Production Editor

Michelle Gengaro-Kokmen, Designer

Follow us on Facebook or visit us online at mackids.com.
Our books are friends for life.